THE GURU AND THE GOLF CLUB

The Guru and the Golf Club

BY

David Benedictus

ANTHONY BLOND

for Simon, with love

*First published in Great Britain in 1969 by Anthony Blond Ltd.,
56 Doughty Street, London, W.C.1.* © *Copyright 1969 by
David Benedictus. Printed in Great Britain by Tonbridge
Printers Ltd, Peach Hall Works, Tonbridge, Kent.*

218 51519 7

They all walk the Wibbly Wobbly Walk!
All talk the Wibbly Wobbly talk!
All wear Wibbly Wobbly ties,
And wink at all the pretty girls, with Wibbly
                                    Wobbly eyes!
Oh, they all smile the Wibbly Wobbly smile,
When the day is dawning;
And all through the Wibbly Wobbly walk
They get a Wibbly Wobbly feeling in the morning.

(Old song; written and composed by
J. P. Long and Paul Pelham)
(B. Feldman & Co. Ltd.)

PART ONE

PART ONE

CHAPTER ONE

The Arrival · *Friday Afternoon*

O noble man! O petty aspirations!

Slicing through the English countryside like a razor through the wrists of past eras, the Motorways carry their cargoes of metal and chrome. Caught up in the carnage of the mid-twentieth century, small flying creatures are dashed against radiators and windscreens to a blob of yellow pulp which is then washed away by relentless wipers. Badgers, foxes, rabbits pay the price of their tenderness and are savaged into their component parts. Dazzled by the lights, deafened by the noise, they are served right by the machines and end up winded by metal, flattened by rubber and finally dispersed by the wind across the fertile English countryside. Huntingdonshire is full of flying molecules of hedgehog. Dust to dust and Birmingham in a couple of hours.

It is not fashionable to walk along Motorways. Indeed one might almost suppose such behaviour to be discouraged by the authorities who provide none of the comforts that the pedestrian has a right to expect, such as benches, country stiles, friendly inns and the like, and by the arterial architects who turn a hard shoulder to the solitary stroller.

But late one afternoon in the autumn of the current year a pedestrian did walk along the M Something-Or-Other, arrogantly eschewing the grass verge and the central divide. Right up the middle of the Southbound carriageway he walked —in a Northerly direction (or maybe he walked Westward along the Eastbound track).

He was barefoot and distinctly brown. His eyes spun like catherine wheels. Pantechnicons chundered past brushing his shoulder and one of them, on one occasion, spun him round where he stood. White sports cars flashed towards him in the fast lane and blew his silky hair into his eyes. Apparently undiscouraged by such setbacks, he continued to walk, blind to the

11

danger, deaf to the curses, heedless and resolute, until he came
to an exit lane some several miles beyond such and such a place
and a few miles short of somewhere else. Then he turned right
and, neither quickening his pace nor pausing in his stride,
followed the signpost to Soft Meadows Cross, which he reached
just as the sun was about to dive over the edge of the world to
enlighten the ignorant Australians.

'I am Guru,' the brown man shouted to the unresponsive
village.

Soft Meadows Cross was once a coaching stop on the way
from London to ... some large centre of commerce. The Cross
(long since hauled down to be replaced by a memorial to some
war or other) would have indicated just this. As for the Soft
Meadows there were some, were still some, although not, surely,
the original soft meadows. The soft meadows that now survived
formed an open area of National Trust land where real cows
grazed and, at week-ends, real love was made—to judge by the
dead contraceptives on Monday mornings.

'Have you been down the meadows then?' was what many an
anxious mother waiting up until the small hours inquired of an
errant daughter.

And ... soft meadows ... were beautiful sometimes ... soft
times. When the light was amber after a day of storms, amber
at dusk, an amber dusk, the light low and slanting, deepening
the dimensions of a cow, a tree, a hedge, softening (Soft
Meadows) the edges of the estate where the poorer people lived.

When I was younger, thought the Vicar, who had a view
from the organ loft to these same soft meadows, I liked the
view when the day was clear, the horizon a good religious
distance away. And humming Brother James's Air he would
try not to see the housing estate, the gas holder, or the squalid,
spent snakes in the grass.

To all the inhabitants of the village the Soft Meadows meant
something, a reassurance, a symbol or an amenity; to the
Admiral, to the Vicar, to Cecil Sparks in his aesthetic world of
trembling sensitivity, to Jack Rubin, Bookmaker, no less than to
quivering malicious Mrs Connelly, to each and to all was
granted some privilege by the melting green of that lush
pastureland. To the Tomlinsons, rich from generations of
watering the workers' beer, to the ambitious Worsleys, to Vic-

toria Bushey, Doctor's daughter and schoolmistress and to Throggie, the golf professional, to these and others the Soft Meadows stood as a monument to ... something, a symbol of ... something, but to the three Angell sisters with their six, soft, grey eyes, who knows?

'I am Guru!' said the Brown Man from outside the Esso Service Station and a Vauxhall hooted unsympathetically. His eyes spun like wheel-caps. He walked towards the Vicarage and repeated his cry from the middle of the Main Street. He carried himself with quiet authority and a sparrow fluttered obsequiously above his head.

Up by the Royal Fairway Golf Club, showing no signs of fatigue, Guru turned his liquid brown eyes upon the Admiral, who was preparing to drive. How wide apart his legs are as he takes his stance; if a sudden squall blows up, if the earth takes a toss and a tumble, if the clouds take in a reef above his head, yet he will not bend his left arm, nor will he raise his head, nor fail to carry that hidden brook, scourge of the week-end golfer. But when Guru whispers his message to the fern and the bracken the Admiral hesitates in his swing, the ball sails off sliced like a sickle, way out of bounds. Guru turns his face up to where a couple of hundred yards away on a wooded hillock beyond the third fairway, there! there! stands the House. The House, wherein dwell the three beautiful Angell sisters; dwell and *dwell*. Never emerge. Never associate. Never trade nor toss back a sportive martini. The Angell sisters, Tessa, Abigail and Genevieve. Tattered lace curtains hanging awry, and a stack of milk bottles outside the peeling door, evidence that they do, or did, exist. Although the milkman denies that he ever delivers milk, and even the Macfisheries Man, who insists that he knows about grouse, admits that he is a babe-in-arms where the Angell sisters are concerned. 'They should hang a week before you—' 'No, no, not the grouse, the Angell sisters!' 'Aaah.'

Guru had other calls to pay. His shadow flitted outside the window of the Tomlinson's large house (each brick a lash on the bowed back of the proletariat), and Timothy, big and black and smelly, barked. His mistress ignored him. Celia Tomlinson was busy. The Scrabble sat before her on the patience table, the Thesaurus on her knee. Her docile face was amiable and amiably her index finger ran down the columns, as her lips mouthed the words. Guru peeked in, a little brown face above the window-sill, like a tiny commonwealth Bishop in a huge pulpit. Mrs Tomlinson never saw him. She picked up the telephone and dialled that amiable, familiar number :

'Colonel Tomlinson's office, please.'

'Tomlinson speaking.'

'Clay, wax, butter, dough,' with mounting affection, 'pudding, cushion, pillow, feather-bed, pad, down, padding, wadding.'

Her husband raised his eyebrows each of which had amputated the careers of a dozen young men, and wistfully glanced at the Pirelli Calendar.

'Attract, attach, endear, charm, fascinate,' she continued, 'captivate, bewitch, seduce, enamour, enrapture, turn the head.'

The Colonel hung up. Celia kissed the mouthpiece of the telephone.

And Guru moved on.

Guru called next on the Vicar but nobody answered the door. The Vicar was deaf to (in order of preference) the world, the flesh, and the devil.

He was trying to write a hell-fire sermon and couldn't. It is impossible to write a hell-fire sermon unless one believes in hell, and such a belief is reserved these days for atheists, who understand the true meaning of the word.

Poor Vicar !

There was no purpose in his life; and he had to appear purposeful. There was no love in his life; and he had to seem loving; there was no continuity in his life; and he had to preach eternity. There was nothing in his life, and he had to teach everything. How did the others manage? The Jews, for instance?

On a sudden impulse the Vicar picked up the telephone and dialled the number of the betting shop.

'Can I speak to Mr Rubin, please.'

'Why, Vicar, of course you can, Vicar.'

'Is that you, Mr Rubin?'

'Who else?'

'Eternity, Rubin. What about eternity?'

'For you, Vicar, five to one, win only. Are you on?'

Sadly the Vicar put down the phone, and, sighing, sat down at his desk and revamped an old sermon on Doubting Thomas.

Soft Meadows Cross was suddenly full of sighing. The wind sighed, and the water sighed, and the Macfisheries Man sighed as he put away the haddock for the night.

'Sleep well haddock, in your paddock,' he murmured.

Guru popped his visiting card through the letter-box of the vicarage, and moved on.

Dick Worsley, home from Tesco's, where he was Area Manager, sighed heavily as soon as he saw the discouraged expression on the stained-glass face of his well-meaning but ungainly wife. Bravely she tried to act as though everything was as it should be. 'Have a good day at the Supermarket, darling?'

'Yes, thank you, Thelma, apart from a sub-standard consignment of Cape Grapes.'

Thelma sat mournfully on a pouffe, while Dick opened the cocktail cabinet to pour himself a Cinzano Bianco. An electronic organ played 'Sophisticated Lady'.

'Is anything the matter, dear?'

Thelma nodded. Now that Dick had been promoted from Services Manager to Area Manager of Tesco's, it didn't seem unreasonable to her to hope that they might rise a little higher —socially not genetically—in the scheme of things. Accordingly she had set her heart on giving a cocktail party for the élite of Soft Meadows Cross that Saturday, the very next evening. But of the forty-six humorous We-Are-Giving-A-Party cards which she had laboriously despatched, only four had produced replies and only one an acceptance, that of the Vicar.

'I did a rash thing,' she admitted to Dick taking his hand in hers; his were dry as dust, hers damp and cold from the confluence of fresh frozen prawn cocktail. 'I hope you'll forgive me?'

'Do not ask for credit, since a refusal might offend,' joked her husband.

'The Macfisheries man came round—'

'Oho! Do I smell lechery?'

'No dear, prawn cocktail.'

'What did he want?'

'Well, he wanted you, really. He said they were all out of tomatoes and would I ask you—for tomorrow I suppose—could Tesco's let him have some to bide him over. I said I would.'

'But that wasn't rash, dear, that was perfectly correct.'

'I know, but then . . . well I asked him, that is, I invited him for tomorrow. And he accepted.'

'Thelma!'

Dick sat down heavily and sadly. 'Trade! Not even *upper*-middle class,' he said. 'We shall never improve our station. We shall not pass on to our offspring the birthright of social privilege, Ascot and Agatha Christie, and why not? For one thing because we have no offspring. But far more important than that—'

'Dick!'

'What?'

'That's another thing. I wasn't going to tell you till I was sure. I think I'm pregnant.'

Dick Worsley stopped whatever he was doing. Kissed his wife with gratitude. But his mind was full of the Indian holy man who had come into Tesco's late that afternoon to buy joss-sticks. What a strange chain of thought!

And joss-sticks! Tesco's had no joss-sticks. He would have to speak to head office about that. He liked speaking to head office. They must get him joss-sticks. An Area Manager, why he could ask for joss-sticks, and they would come. That was the function of an Area Manager. Must be.

But the Indian's eyes had whirled like peacocks' tails.

In 'Elsinore', a small house just out of bounds beyond the fourteenth fairway of the golf club, a house built to represent a modest Queen Anne edifice but with touches of Tudor round the edges lived Cecil Sparks succoured and spoiled by his house-keeper Wendy Pakenham, a genteel lady sinking into unselfishness. Cecil was the Soft Meadows Cross intellectual and lived on a private income which he wisely kept private. In the cold autumn evenings his pretensions kept him warm.

'It's the callousness of modern art I so much abhor,' he remarked to Wendy Pakenham, 'so much feeling for style, so little for content. One can only deplore the passing of the Dashiell Hammett syndrome, can't one?'

(He went on, like this, by the hour, dropping names as copiously as Onan did his seed, and with apparently as little shame and as little effect.)

'Take Jean-Luc Godard, for instance, what would you say he offers as his message?'

'You're the clever one. You tell me.'

The aesthete sighed. He had to work hard on behalf of his pretensions.

'Live. That's his message. Live and die. Life is death. What's the difference? What's it matter? Now, I appeal to you, duckie, what kind of a message is that?'

'A very clear one I should have thought, dear.'

'Not clear at all. (What a silly old crow you are.) Not even much of a message. And then there's Proust. What have you to say to him?'

'Nothing just at the moment. But there was an Indian gentleman came to call on you while you were out walking the dogs.'

'You can't walk with them any more than you can walk with God. Tugs-of-war both. What Indian gentleman?'

'He left his card.'

'Guru, eh? Well, well, well.'

'Will you be going to the council meeting this evening and shall I keep supper for you?'

'Yes, and yes, duckie. Was there a message with the card?'

'Just the card dear. Will Mr Proust want supper?'

'Everything contrives against me.'

'I'm sure you'll win through in spite of it all.'

'Don't patronise me.'

'No dear!'

'How can one write a Great Novel under such circumstances?'

'If anyone can, I'm sure you can.'

'My point exactly. I don't want to see any bloody Gurus.'

The struggle for power at the Royal Fairway Golf Club was not unlike the struggle for power in the field of international politics, but fought with less hypocrisy and more intensity. There were four relevant factions, parallel if you like, to America, Europe, the Commonwealth and the Communist blocs. America, brash, rich and vulgar could best be represented by Solly Schneider and Sammy Green and kindly little Jack Rubin himself, who ran the local betting shop. They were a formidable threesome, circumcised and -spect. Their golf was all low trajectory and high stakes. Solly was a director of Yom Tov Properties Ltd., which owned the land upon which the golf course had been, in the 1930s, constructed. He was therefore on the Committee and threatened, when angry, to start building semis on the fairways. Sammy was fat and bristly and knew about jewels. Jack *was* a jewel, a dear rotund little man stuck on the end of a long cigar like a toffee-apple on a stick. After his cigar and his golf he loved his Mendlessohn record collection and his debenture stock, and should have loved his wife Miriam and his six children; somehow was unable to.

The second faction, the Europeans, consisted of Cecil Sparks and his three long-haired miniature dachshunds, Garrick, Irving and Gielgud, who—living just out of bounds alongside the fourteenth fairway—used to dash on to the course and appropriate many of the balls struck from the third tee. Far from dicouraging them, unsporting Cecil Sparks would reward them with biscuits and display the spoils in an ever-growing modernistic display which he wittily entitled 'Balls'. The European faction, underhand in its methods, was none the less powerful for all that.

The third and Commonwealth faction was headed by the Admiral, Captain of the Club, and included most of the uncircumcised, ex-public-school and bald members of the Royal Fairway. They wore check jackets and were unfaithful to their wives, but never to their Bentleys. They gardened and they stood still for 'God Save The Queen', and they believed that the unions were ruining the country. They couldn't believe in hell (not that they thought about it much) but were kind to animals and only very rarely killed themselves. As a faction they were not too well organised, which explains their continuing failure to show the Americans, Europeans and Communists the door.

The Communist bloc, of course, was represented by the

artisan members of the club – and the less said about them the better.

Guru stood on the third green as dusk washed over the golf course and stared in the direction of the House, where the Angell sisters lived. There are shutters on the windows; behind them in that strange dusty world, a little like the inside of a mouldy chestnut, stands a full-length mirror. The glass is not cracked, although the gilded frame is almost black with grime; it still reflects. Reflects in fact the three opalescent figures of the Angell sisters as they glide to and fro behind their flowing veils and . . .

Guru could not see through the shutters, but his eyes were like fireflies hovering in the twilight. He lit a match and consulted a notebook in which he made a series of tiny, resolute jottings. A fox pattered up on emery pads and nosed his knee. Guru sighed. There would be time enough for the Angell sisters. He turned back to the village.

Dr Bushey, who had not left his house for ever so long, was in conversation with his burr-headed daughter, Victoria, the schoolmistress. She was very persuasive, he very obstinate.

'Papa, you *must* go and visit him. He's over eighty.'

'Nothing to be done about that. Are there pills for putting a man's life into reverse? If so, they haven't told me. *The Lancet* hasn't mentioned it.'

'But Albert Skullham's an old friend. You always go and see him when he has one of his turns. You play cribbage together.'

'One for his nob.'

'Papa!'

'Well, there are too many old people altogether. Too many people. Too many doctors.'

'Honestly that's a very negative attitude.'

'Do I need a daughter to tell me so?'

And the doctor relapsed into a reverie. He was thinking about the Americans and the Viet Cong. They filled his thoughts obsessively these days. A knock at the door disturbed him.

'Who is it?'

'An Indian, papa.'

'Is he from Oxfam?'

'I don't think so.'

'Oh.'

'Shall I invite him in?'

'Please yourself.'

Guru padded into the lounge and bowed.

'I'm Guru.'

Doctor Bushey made an effort to be civil.

'How de do.'

Victoria, who did part-time work for Anti-Apartheid, smiled a good hostess's smile at the little Indian chap.

'Have you been over here long?'

'Ugly girl,' said Guru, pinching her arm, 'overweight.'

'Don't do that!'

'Advice for ugly girl. "Work out your own salvation." My card. Good-bye.'

Thrusting a visiting card upon Doctor Bushey, Guru turned and left. Victoria pursed her fretful lips.

'Insufferable creature! Sometimes I feel like joining Enoch Powell and his gang.'

'Charming fellow.'

'Powell? Or the Indian?'

'Wouldn't he stay for a cup of tea?'

'Certainly not, papa!'

'If only they'd stop fighting each other. That's all I ask.'

'The Indians?'

'No. The others.'

'Oh.'

It's tea-time and Soft Meadows Cross sips its communal cup. Tannin dyes the stomachs of the citizens and Typhoo sweeps them away on magic carpet rides of hallucination. They munch peppery tomato sandwiches and Fullers Walnut Cake—not what it used to be.

Throggie, the Royal Fairway Professional in his shop, plays host to Old Porson, the senior caddy, amongst the wristlets, the repaints and the metal shafts which border his demesne.

At the Burnt Scone, Mrs Connelly chews home-made chocolate cake, which Candida, the beautiful waitress, offers her on a plate ungraciously devoid of doilies. Mrs Connolly complains, but there, she complains every day, and no one cares. Candida doesn't, for she is Princess of Indifference.

Miss Skullham, waiting for the return of her lodger, the Macfisheries Man, takes a tray up to her father, old Albert Skullham, where he sits in front of the television. There is skin on his Horlicks. ('Does she think I don't notice? Or don't care?')

'What are you watching? Crackerjack? How nice! And do you feel better? Doctor Bushey will be here soon.'

The Village lies in the shape of a double-ended T, or, more picturesquely, a lady lying on her back, where her head is the War Memorial and her arms are extended above her head. Thus her left arm is the London Motorway escape road, and that naturally is where the service stations have their piles. They compete savagely and would be sure to run into the road and pressgang motorists into their forecourts were it not that that is not the way business is conducted in such places as Soft Meadows Cross. Instead they pass on the tartan stamps and tiger's tails and coupons with which the big companies supply them. But we are not concerned with garage men. They are beyond the pail.

The lady's right arm is the minor road to Gruntham, which runs through the Soft Meadows themselves and passes, sheltering its pained eyes behind a straggly copse of silver birches, the housing estate which the Vicar hopes not to see from the organ loft on foggy mornings.

If Gruntham itself is the lady's spread fingers, then she has long arms, that lady, for Gruntham is a brisk five miles away.

Should we return to the War Memorial (a beautiful marble widow commissioned of a local sculptor) and look along the High Street, we would find the left bosom to be the infants' school and the right bosom (a rather more impressive bosom) the 14th Century church, behind which, screened by myrtle, cypress and the mysterious mist of dead but resurrected Christians, stands the Georgian Vicarage. This was once magnificent in its country way and still looks good in snowdrop, crocus and daffodil-time, but could do with a lick of paint.

As a lady (even one prone on her back with her limbs outspread) tapers to the waist, so does the Main Street of Soft Meadows Cross, the Midland Bank on the left being in a ticklish place under the ribs and the Tesco Supermarket opposite overshadowing the modest proportions of the Burnt Scone and outfacing Macfisheries, a few yards down the road. The lady has poor hips, and a funnel pelvis. Between her legs, however, behind a rock garden of mosses and shrubs, anemones and asters (a very beautiful garden, much admired by visitors and with an almost sacred air to it) live, most inappropriately, Colonel Gilbert Tomlinson with Celia and their two children Caedmon and Ethel. The Tomlinsons are very rich, and the more they brew, the richer they become. Their house is called Gin House. People respect them. Dick and Thelma Worsley take them as their model of respectability and success, but as Area Manager for Tesco's, Dick has still some little way to travel. (Moreover he can't play bridge.)

If you continue down the left leg, which is the Boggley Road, you leave the Raven on your left, also the lane to the golf club and its estate. Mon Chalet, the Admiral's seat, borders this road and lies adjacent to the club-house. The Boggley Road itself is an intimate but thrilling drive with sudden sharp gradients, unexpected bends and vistas which come and go. In places the road is overhung by elms and in places it seems to tunnel through the undergrowth. The more imaginative and morbid young lovers of the district use the interstices of the Boggley Road in preference to the more open and healthy romanticism of the soft meadows.

The lady's right leg is a very different matter. Broad and well-maintained it crosses the main railway line at Soft Meadows Halt and then nudges the new shopping area, amongst whose neon and formica delights stands Jack Rubin's emporium, a picture of a horse at the front, and a picture of dejection at the back.

Beyond the new shopping area, the lady's right leg leads to the Cauliflower Arms, a small and much too clean Trust House, catering for the occasional business visit and only really busy during the Gruntham Agricultural and Flower Show. Opposite the Cauliflower Arms some little houses are sited, certainly too little for Jack and Miriam Rubin and their six children who inhabit one of them. See how the walls bulge! Oh, it *is* crowded.

But beneath the knee what a wasting away! Thereafter shiny tarmacadam loses its gloss and grass grows along the shin-bone. An inelegant leg and it only leads to a deserted gipsy caravan encampment. Stay away!

That is the anatomy of Soft Meadows Cross.

Guru had studied it; was to study the inhabitants. He came as a prophet, but his eyes were like knitting needles. Those villagers who were exposed to him looked at him curiously and nudged each other. Who were they to make the first move? Anyway he wore no shoes, and even if India was a part of the Commonwealth (*was* it? nobody was sure), there were limits to hospitality.

And Guru was capable of looking after himself. There's no need to shed tears for him.

And in their heavily curtained parlour the three Angell sisters sat embroidering samplers. Their dresses were long, their faces pale, their tresses fell like cobwebs about their mysterious shoulders. They spoke seldom and low:

'Abigail,' said Tessa occasionally, 'you look pale.'

'My mortality lies heavily upon me these autumn evenings.'

'We all pray for a merciful release,' whispered Genevieve. A tear trembled in the net of her eye. Abigail's fingers fluttered about her embroidery, whose bosky shades and historical patterns were suddenly stained by a drop of blood from her left thumb where the needle had penetrated the skin. Abby thrust the largesse of her long hair back over her delicate shoulder and let out an involuntary cry.

Genevieve quoted:

> 'Some men dream bright
> Stains on ancient tapestry
> With heraldic horse and dog
> Forever rampant in the ancestral fog.'

The Macfisheries Man remained kneeling in great discomfort outside the window. A snail crawled for sanctuary between his fingers. His nose went white, flattened by the intensity of his surveillance. He should have gone home for tea.

CHAPTER TWO

The Council · *Friday Evening*

Dick Worsley, as Chairman of the Parish Council, called the meeting to order at eight-fifteen. Secretary of the Council, Mrs Connolly, clutched the minutes of the last meeting to her ungenerous bosom, and they ticked by.

The meeting was held in the School Hall. Besides the Chairman and the Secretary, Thelma Worsley, Cecil Sparks, the Vicar, the Admiral and his wife, and Jack Rubin were present. The Art work of the local children looked down from the walls, huge round blobs of paint representing 'My Mother', a green rectangle for 'Aunt Harriet', a black toad-like object for 'Dad'.

Mrs Connolly concluded her report and Dick Worsley announced, 'matters arising out of the minutes'.

This was the moment for the Admiral's wife's traditional first assault on the electricity board and the pylon they had erected.

'What do you think it's like waking up every morning and finding that . . . that *thing* outside the window?'

'You poor creature!' murmured the Vicar without irony.

'I mean I'm not unreasonable—I believe in give and take as much as the next man—but when the electricity people without so much as a by your leave—' her voice faltered and died away. Her knuckles were white like babies faces as she grasped the twelve inch ruler which she had taken to carrying around with her everywhere. The Chairman asserted himself.

'I would question whether this particular matter arises out of the minutes of the last meeting . . .'

'It arises out of my back garden!' cried the Admiral's wife passionately.

Every council meeting it was the same, thought Thelma Worsley. There is real work to be done, there are real decisions to be made, and all we ever get to is Jessica's pylon. But her mind was on other things too. The life stirring inside her. She

24

imagined herself to be a ship at sea, a galleon with a casket of precious jewels in the hold, a country-house with a martyr hiding away from the wicked Cromwellian soldiers in the warm, dark priest-hole, a mountain with deep inside it a concert hall where they played sweet music like Mantovani and that lovely young man with the funny German name. The poor Lady Admiral, her ship had been scuttled some months ago, her house had been razed, her cavernous concert-hall for ever silenced.

Jessica herself fell silent. And, as Thelma's dear Dick rose (so fine he looked, so fine and round and whiskery) to thank the Admiral's wife and hurry on to the next item on the agenda, she caught his eye and he smiled.

'The floor is Thelma's.'

'Out of order,' cried Mrs Connolly, and of course she was quite right. However :

'Well one might call it a matter arising out of the minutes, if one had to. I just wanted to remind all our dear friends here assembled, ha ha, that, well, my husband and I are having this little get together or omnium gatherum at our home, tomorrow night as ever is, and we'd be so glad if you'd all come.'

'That's very kind of you, I'm sure,' said Jack Rubin.

'Now, about our Arts Festival . . .' began Cecil Sparks.

But Thelma bit her lip. First the Macfisheries Man and now Jack Rubin. Tradesmen and Jews. That was *not* what she had intended. Oh, and the Vicar of course but he didn't really count. Such *shabby* gentility. It was too bad. All her life she had dreamed of recapturing those golden days meeting wonderful people like those wonderful people in those books by wonderful people like Vicki Baum, Georgette Heyer and Angela Brazil. She had sat in her bath while the red dye from the covers of the old volumes had stained first her fingers, then the bath water itself, dreaming of the International Set, and her role at the head of it. With the passing of the years her ambitions had become more modest, yet still she hoped that . . . some day . . . in some way . . . She looked at her big, strong husband and remembered how he used to roar over from Bromley in his little Singer, all mouth-wash and after-shave, hair slicked down with Brilliantine—*lovely*—and take her first

to the pictures and then to the Chinese Restaurant, between
Macfish and the Midland Bank.

'My little fried noodle!'

And their toes would touch under the table. And after dinner
they would waft to the Soft Meadows, and he would confide
his ambitions to her, and go so far as to slip a tremulous hand
inside her dress. Then while her little tit throbbed and twitched
like a spaniel's eager, brown nose under his horny thumb he
would talk to her of 'sales promotion techniques', of 'loss-
leaders' and 'taste panels' and 'profit-margins'. Could he know
at such times of her tremulous thighs, that struggled to open
of their own accord like the doors of the Tesco Supermarket?
Could he know of the quiverings and scuttlings and comings
and goings in her secret corridors of power? A fearful frustration to her then, the memory of such moments had become a
consolation to her now, in her disheartening sexual life as a
married woman.

Another consolation to her would be (shamefully she
thought) the image of a vast black acrobat she had seen at a
circus once in childhood; how he gleamed and shone and
glistened under the arc-lights of that shabby little tent—not
at all like her beautiful, paunchy Dick, whiffling and grunting,
half in and half out of his navy blue serge.

And five caustic years later, she clears her mind, sets herself
down cautiously on her back on the hearthrug and kisses her
husband provocatively on the chin, shutting her eyes, rather
in the manner of a child trying to be invisible . . .

And he, prodigal as always, flings his seed around, as if it
were packets of chewing gum, and she a hungry little French
girl in front of her ruined home, and he in a Centurion tank,
and she cheering . . . cheering . . . and (change of scene) *she*
Lady Mayoress, and he hung around with chains of office and
them cheering and . . . time for bed.

'I thought that *Hamlet* would do for the major production of
our little festival . . .'

'You mean *Shakespeare*'s *Hamlet*?' inquired Jessica, the
Admiral's wife, and everyone wondered to what other Hamlet
she could possibly refer.

Cecil Sparks rubbed a sensitive neck with an aesthetic hand.

'You see, my loves, there's a wealth of talent in the village, and an ambitious choice like *Hamlet* wouldn't limit us, so much as extend us. Always extend.'

'I do so agree,' remarked Jessica.

'The bigger the field, the bigger the certainty,' Jack Rubin offered irrelevantly. He, as well as other members of the council, was apt to question Cecil Spark's motives. At the moment it was hard to see where he was leading them by the nose, but they felt instinctively that their noses were involved somehow.

'We can take the School Hall for a few nights, give a performance over in Boggley and I'm sure we could fill the Corn Exchange in Gruntham if we were well organised. And we shall have tours of the local monuments—'

('There aren't any.')

'—and a concert . . .'

'And flower-arrangements,' suggested Mrs Worsley shyly, her eyes blue as forget-me-nots.

'And bell-ringing,' added the Vicar, 'for the children.'

The Admiral rose to his feet and took up his stance as if for a long three wood.

'Yes Admiral?' the Chairman inquired, pleased and surprised that the elderly sea-dog should volunteer his opinion. 'You have a suggestion, no doubt, for our festival.'

'Yes,' grunted the Admiral, his mind in the China seas, the rumble of surf in his ears.

'Well . . . em . . . ?'

'Sea-shanty.'

'Oh yes?'

'A sea-shanty, fancy that,' murmured the Vicar.

The Admiral glared at the Vicar: 'Speak up, speak up, no wonder yr. church is empty.'

An attack on his administration the Vicar could not stomach. He shifted the responsibility. 'It's not only my Church, you know, but Christ's.'

'Tell him to speak up then. Too much mumbling all round.' The Admiral cleared his throat. Jessica feared the worst.

And sing he did:

'Oh, I have sailed the Seven Seas from Bot'ny Bay to Maine,
And if I were a young man now, I'd go to sea again

For the white waves are my pillow and the salty foam my bed
But there'll be no girls like the girls I've kissed when I lie
    cold and dead.'

Thelma sighed with relief—'What a nice sea-shanty. A nice
sentiment to it too.'

But the Admiral continued singing:
'Oh Susie of the dark eyes was fair as she was bold
I left a precious treasure in her capacious hold
    But the ocean is my pillow
    And the Seven Seas my bed—
Oh Susie darling, hold me tight, when I lie cold and dead.

Oh batten down the hatches, for Susie's come astern
As neat a little frigate as ever I did burn
    For her white breasts were my pillow
    And her soft, warm thighs my bed—
Oh Susie darling, stay on board when I lie cold and dead.

Oh I have sailed the Seven Seas from Maine to Bot'ny Bay
My main tops'l is lowered, my rigging blown away
    And the cold grey earth's my pillow
    Six feet deep lies my bed
No seas, no foam, no Susie, when I am cold and dead.'

While the Admiral ululated, Jack Rubin sat thinking of
Miriam, whom he had left with the children after an early
supper. As it was Friday Jack had lit the candles ('We praise
You, O Lord our God, King of the universe, Creator of Light')
and five of the six little Rubins sat variously around in pyjamas
and nightdresses.
    Miriam had been thinking: 'How like striped candles they
are, which have all been left burning, the youngest the longest,
but how can that be? Yet I am proud of my menorah!'
Little Joe's hair stood straight up on top of his head like a
wick. Jack, who was twelve, was away at school, but there was
Ruthie, ten, and David, a big-bellied seven and Little Jo, four,
and Rachel, only two. Miriam intended to have no more
children, but then she never did intend.

Jack's cigar had lain by his plate, one end black, one end damp, and he had wondered, as so often, why he felt no more for them than for any other children (in theory he liked all children well enough) and why he felt only distaste for Miriam. ('Blessed is the home in which the hearts of the parents are turned to the children, and the hearts of the children to the parents, and all are bound together in devotion to you.')

Miriam had smiled, amiably and proudly at him, and he had managed to squeeze out some kind of a smile in return.

And Guru had walked in, eyes veiled like cobwebs.

As Jack led the prayer for that nice Jewish family, Liz and Philip and the kids, the door-bell rang, and since the door was always left open on Friday nights, Guru had walked in.

The children had been variously frightened and intrigued.

'Hello, funny red man.' Rachel the littlest, had not quite learnt her colours.

'Shalom,' Miriam had said.

'I am Guru.' Guru's brown eyes roamed from tousled head to tousled head, but his face remained expressionless.

'Friday night,' said Miriam, 'you are welcome to join us.'

Guru had shaken his head slowly. 'Not here, not here,' he said, 'I am Guru; not here.'

He left the dining-room and the small house on his silent, soft paddy-pads and never once touched any part of the building. And Jack chewed on his nervous cigar, still not alight, for reassurance, while Miriam went through to the kitchen to fetch the fried fish.

Plans for the Arts Festival were proposed, seconded, ratified and amended with unnerving rapidity now. Cecil Sparks's athletic little uvula was leaping up and down like a trampoline dancer as he outlined more and more ambitious plans for the (as he secretly thought of it) Cecil Sparks Festival of Music and the Arts. Mrs Connolly's pencil darted across the page as she tried vainly to get the notes for the minutes accurate and up to date. 'Just a minute, just a minute,' she would occasionally moan, taking down several, her lips stained indelibly, the flavour of pencil lead tangy on her tongue. It was as if the Admiral's sea-shanty had put fresh heart into all of them. Jack Rubin volunteered to produce a music-hall programme—(Cecil Sparks wasn't too keen on the idea of *being produced*, but was pacified by the promise that he should do his Vesta Tilley impersonation) and gave them a foretaste of things to come with a snatch of the ever-popular 'Vot a game it is! Oi! Oi!'

Jessica took it into her head to offer to run an art exhibition exclusively for the works of local artists. Cecil, approving the idea, hoisted the troublesome work of the hanging committee on to his own sloping shoulders.

So, add to all this the tours of local monuments—Thelma's flower arrangements, the Vicar's bell-ringing and whatever bacchanalia the Women's Institute chose to provide, and, in the stirring words of Cecil Sparks, 'you have a festival'.

After Cecil Sparks left the house, Wendy Pakenham had laid her distinguished grey noddle on his pillow. She frequently did this when he was out and she alone. She could smell the faint odour of him (or his after-shave or his shampoo or some unguent or medicament associated with him); she breathed it in adoringly. Oh she knew he lived a life of pretence; that he spoke to hide rather than to display his feelings; but she didn't mind. She didn't even mind that he ignored her, for she had love enough for two. And if he wished to think only of himself, then she would think only of him too.

But in spite of this new resolve she found herself pondering on the Indian Gentleman, not so much on his smooth brown skin and dusty clothes, but on something in his eyes. He had stood close up to her, and his gaze had never wavered (his eyes had been like planets) but had searched out not only her undisclosed passion and the limits of her social personality, but the core of her, the . . . fear that lurked like a snake in a pit, the fear that gnawed at her self-confidence, that chewed on her comfort and routine, the fear that maybe, in spite of everything . . . the fear that it was not all over, the anguish, the fear that . . . the pain . . . the . . .

Well, never mind about that now! Her head went back to the pillow. 'Master,' she murmured, 'my friend, my darling, my own . . . Guru!'

It couldn't bode well. A middle-aged spinster of county origins, set in her ways, doubly in love. Well, could it?

And Guru set out across the Golf Course. He was everywhere.

CHAPTER THREE

The Settling in · *Friday Night*

As the night closed in on Soft Meadows Cross, there were those whom it found sad and uneasy. There was the Mac-fisheries Man, cold and stiff, smelling faintly of haddock, loyally at his watching post, watching for he knew not precisely what, he knew not precisely why. But the same compulsion drove him each evening from the comfort of his lodgings with old Albert and Doris Skullham on the Gruntham estate through the Soft Meadows on his rusty red bike and across the golf course to The House. What kind of compulsion? A jealous one. But his jealousy of the three Angell sisters was protective in its motive. No one should hurt or offend Tessa or Abigail or Genevieve.

They were too soft and warm and beautiful to be expected to secure themselves from the hard men with implacable desires, and so he had taken it upon himself to do all he could to make their existence softer and safer and more comfortable. An important charge. A great privilege.

An anonymous grouse left by the back door, a rare gift of oysters in season, such things were but petty symbols of the depth of his devotion, and the criticism that, had he wished to guard them most efficiently, he should look out not in, prowl round not crouch down, credited him with too much of sense and too little of sensitivity. He was sad in a way that the Angell sisters must remain ignorant of his vigil, but knew that that was the price he must pay if he were to do his duty by them. Had they known, they must have invited him into the warmth and cosiness of their little circle (triangle rather) and what kind of warder would he be then? And they might—but please, no, surely they wouldn't—have turned him away. Some day, per-haps, when the wind was in the South . . .

A gentle tap-tapping at the front door roused the Macfisheries Man from a reverie and caused him to leap to his feet and plunge into some nearby honeysuckle, whence he could most safely observe the intruder, who turned out to be an Indian.

31

This double blow, that there was an intruder at all, and that the intruder was an Indian, stepping where he was not wanted, caused him almost to spring at the dusky stranger's throat, but it was more cunning to do nothing ... for the moment. The Indian was admitted the nose was flattened once more against the window. An angry, frustrated, jealous nose. They had admitted him and not *him*. He was inside, flattered by triple glances, caressed by triple tongues; *he* was outside, unflattered, uncaressed and bloody cold.

Why should Indians have all the fun?

All over Soft Meadows Cross this cold Friday evening, dogs are let, shown, pushed out to snout around in the damp, rich earth, to feel the green grass under their paws, to howl unaccountably out of a sudden irruption of melancholy at the dog-faced moon, to deposit their little packages in the dahlia beds or at the foot of the wistaria or in that lovely, secret, smelly spot where nothing ever grows.

'Has he done it yet, dear?'

'He's done the little, not the big.'

Cats, disguised as shadows, slide, whiskers foremost through a hole in the darkness, and disappear into an invisible world of lechery and rats.

All over the village hot water bottles are being filled. The Vicar's is shaped like a bunny with a fluffy little scud; Doctor Bushey hurls his from the bed to the corner of the room, and waits for the explosion, thumbs to ears. Old Albert Skullham gets a heavy, porcelain one with a sort of a tap to it, much too hot to cuddle (Doris has made sure of that), so the old boy cuddles his past; Primo Carnera spars with Jersey Joe Walcott at the bottom of his bed, while Elsie Carlyle sings soothingly, sentimentally from the firescreen. Ah! A shaft of moonlight patterned with moon-dust fragments upon his china chamber-pot and gradually the whole familiar world is contained within this shining bowl. What then is the handle? Soon enough (as the light dies) all will be made known.

Does your pot have a handle too?

Dick and Thelma Worsley sit up in front of the fire. The gas fails to consume the artificial fuel. A reassuring clergyman in an open-necked shirt mouths generalities from the silent, blue television screen. His presence offers a comfort which his words might dispute.

'Would you like a boy or a girl best?'

'Oh yes, please,' says Dick, giggling.

'This time tomorrow . . . our party . . . just think.'

'Will they still be here?'

'Oh dear me no. That's not the way of cocktail parties.'

'Honest? You're not having me on?'

'Did I ever?'

'Once.' And Thelma simpers. She is very proud of herself. It's lovely to be 'with child'. But what will the black acrobat say?

Nor has Cecil Sparks retired yet for the night. Already he is rehearsing his Hamlet. He has changed into black tights and a black polo-neck sweater and has cleared the living-room of furniture. Garrick and Irving snap around his ankles in passable imitation of Rosencrantz and Guildenstern, while Gielgud is hiding behind the fire-irons like Polonius behind the arras. Cecil's reading of the part is unusual. He sees Hamlet as an artist in a world of Philistines, a student, a poet in a world of plutocrats and technocrats. Nothing eccentric there. But he fancies Hamlet to be in love with Laertes; ah! Thus Hamlet's distaste for Ophelia is plain jealousy, his mockery of Polonius an unavailing effort to work out his hidden guilts regarding his seduction of the old man's son. Cecil Sparks has it in mind (if he can arrange it) to cast as Laertes, young Caedmon Tomlinson, heir to the Tomlinson fortune.

During the course of the impromptu rehearsal Irving got himself kicked on the snout. While administering a salve to the yelping little animal Cecil Sparks was suddenly blessed with a really *great* idea for Claudius (always a difficult part to cast within the confines of a small community). That arriviste Dick Worsley could play it, in an accent just a little bit *off*, Duckie; oh, the implications were endless! Of course that Thelma creature would certainly not do for Gertrude but . . . Perhaps his Auntie!!! How audacious! There would be little sleep for him that night. Passionately he strode up and down the stairs for hours on end striking his head occasionally against the newel post as another and yet another thunderbolt of inspira-

C

tion left him shaking and gasping at his amazing inventiveness.

'I am Guru,' said Guru.

'May I fetch you a cup of tea?' Tessa's serious face was like the face of an old grandfather clock.

And she had something of the tranquillity of such a piece of furniture. Just now her beautiful eyes were filmed over with anxiety, but not for her guest, who seemed quite at ease, cross-legged on the floor, arms folded on his chest, subjecting Abigail to an unblinking and unnerving stare. Poor Abby, so frail and unsettled, might easily be frightened by such rough treatment. Genevieve had her arm about her sister's shoulders and such protectiveness *would* help Abby, if Abby would let it.

'A cup of tea?' Genevieve's soft, low voice was earnest and kind and it achieved the required result, for Guru turned his attention from Abigail to Genevieve.

'Yes. Cup of tea.'

Abigail started to rise, but: 'I'll go,' said Tessa, 'it will be better.'

'You are a darling,' said Genevieve. Although Abigail made no sound, a tear trembled on her eye-lash, which her sister was pleased to remark, since with Abigail tears were the aftermath and not the forerunner of the storm. Not so Genevieve herself. But now she was perfectly calm.

'Are you familiar with the poems of Rabrindranath Tagore?' —in that household this was small talk.

'No.'

'Oh, he is a fine poet, a star above Matthew Arnold's head.'

'A philosopher too,' added Abigail, the first time she had spoken in Guru's company. 'He has written much philosophy and some of it is very true.'

'Oh, Abby, you know that it's all true. That's why he may be termed a philosopher. If he were to say things occasionally which were of doubtful veracity, he would be a charlatan and not a philosopher at all.'

'It's easy for you to talk, you to whom truth and falsehood are as clear as day and night.' Abigail's voice trembled on the edge of hysteria; a mouse approaching cheese.

'Now Abby . . .'

Snap! The cheese was gone. Poor mouse! Abby's head

twisted and turned within its wind-funnel of hair. Strange, soft, grunting noises. Guru lifted a bony brown finger. The third of his left hand. His eyes became steady as buttons. They held Abby briefly. And he crooned to her gently. At once she was still and placid. She even smiled. Tessa returned with tea in a fine yellow cup; she knew nothing of the little drama enacted in her absence. How could she?

But Guru hurled the cup to the floor. It splintered into many yellow pieces, and a spot or two of tea stained Genevieve's long silk dress, temporarily only because :

'Tea doesn't stain,' hurriedly remarked Tessa.

'Tea!' cried Guru, 'bloody Chinese muck!'

Ethel and Caedmon Tomlinson were giving a party in the barn at Gin House. A November 5th party. But the Angell sisters were not there.

'It's not that I mind them being, well, like they are,' reasoned Ethie to an admiring group of disciples, 'but the least they could have done would have been to answer.'

'You're wrong there,' a pale young man said, 'that would have been the most they could have done.'

Anyway the party was a success without them. The evening had been fine, though cold. The buffet, chicken and ham and salmon and tongue and rice and fruit salad and cream, had been eaten voraciously up and the local beat group, The Loins, had been playing on as if music were the food of love. Everyone had been obliged to come as 'Something beginning with "G" ', and, now the smooching stage had been reached and the Lady Godivas were beginning to have trouble with their flowing locks which made kissing ticklish and also with their body stockings, which had proved to have one other disadvantage. There was an objective observer in Rose-Marie Farquhar, invalided since babyhood by polio, to whom the pairings of a General Gordon with a Lady Ghost, a Guy Fawkes with a Guinevere, seemed grotesque.

Rose-Marie was indispensable at any party; knew it; but the knowledge was painful to her. She would rather have been dispensable and unparalysed. Still, as her mother, a great beauty and a homespun philosopher, had once said (spinning her pearls around her swan-like neck) : 'We all have our crosses to bear.'

It was not that nobody talked to her that grieved Rose-Marie. It was that everybody *talked* to her. She felt as if she were a master of ceremonies; the guests were not allowed to join in until they had given their details to her. And they talked to her so seriously. There was none of the casual flirting with which young men spice their conversation to strange and attractive girls, and, from the girls themselves, none of the barely concealed hostility which is the most patent sign of sexual jealousy amongst the young. Which is not to say that Rose-Marie was without her own attractions. It was partly that people were put off by the bloody surgical-looking thing she sat in and partly that they didn't know—and certainly were not likely to investigate—whether she *could*.

So that at about this stage of the evening Rose-Marie would be driven home by DuPont, her chauffeur, to her cold bed full of hot fantasies, and the atmosphere of the party would undergo a considerable lightening; which is why Rose-Marie Farquhar was regarded as indispensable at parties.

On this occasion Rose-Marie, dressed as Gigi, stayed rather longer than usual, since she had quite enjoyed talking to a clever friend of Caedmon's from Oxford, Rusty Motorcade, who was studying at Keble to become a saint and didn't mind spending this evening getting in a bit of practise on the sly. He was quite amusing too, in his way, although he would have no truck with fancy dress. 'I am that I am,' he remarked wittily to anyone interested. But he proposed nothing which might have encouraged Rose-Marie to stay, so Rose-Marie went home.

The Colonel and Celia retired to their bedroom to play Scrabble and listen to the distant, plaintive cries of hide and seek from the herbacious border and beyond.

It was rather cold for Lady Godivas and Nell Gwynnes but some had brought polo-neck sweaters and these, with the coats which they had arrived in, enabled them to go out of doors and be undressed again by comparative strangers.

Meanwhile Caedmon was in the billiards room with those of his guests who had not yet set anything up for themselves and were unlikely to do so now.

Rusty Motorcade had joined this group and was sitting on Caedmon's left, too close for comfort. The talk was of a civilised sort. Superficial but not frivolous, and generally political in character. Socialist ministers had been excoriated.

But Rusty Motorcade, who had an altogether higher, more saintly view of politics, remarked :

'Politics is about moles, socialism is about proles.' This seemed to go over quite well considering the lateness of the hour, etc. etc. (as Ethel liked to say, and Ethel who was in the greenhouse with a youthful General Gordon whose hand had just returned unopposed, like an Ulster Unionist, into her bloomers, was wondering about Politics herself, wondering in fact how best she could be politic in such a situation) and Rusty continued to astound them all with ideology :

'The thing you must remember about the workers,' he said earnestly, 'is that they're not at all like us. That is to say they enjoy different things, say different things, eat different things.'

'Chips with everything,' interrupted a red-cheeked girl called Pamela, after which she subsided into a friendly lap.

'So, is it sense or is it not sense to treat them as we ourselves would like to be treated? Pamela here is quite right in what she says. They don't need the money we need. Chips are cheaper than caviare.'

A male voice : 'Absolutely true. Abs-O-*Lutely* true.'

'So when we use phrases like "equality of opportunity" we must realise that the workers don't want the same opportunities as we do. A small down payment on the semi, enough for the weekly flutter on the pools or at the Bingo parlour, the odd pair of shoes, the holiday at Bognor—'

'Capri more like,' said someone bitterly and there were murmurs of, 'Quite' 'Exactly' and, 'If it stopped at Capri . . .'

'—the pint at the local—'

'—the telly—'

'—yes, mustn't forget the telly, the down payments on the packet of Woodbines, all of these things add up to . . . anyone know? Just about the average weekly wage over the whole country. Give them more money and what do they do with it, eh?'

'Throw it away.'

'Betting shops.'

'Talk of the Town.'

'Exactly.'

'Have you *been* there?'

'No but have you?'

'No but does one need to?'

'But if H. Wilson were to tax people like yourselves a little less heavily, what would you spend the extra money on?'

'That's quite a question.'

'Well . . .'

'There's this *fantastic* dress at that little place in the Brompton Road, *you* know, it's all sort of, you know!'

'Exactly. Quality goods. Well, think what the effect of this would be. A boost for the home market, more productivity, higher dividends for the shareholders and—' (A tense moment) —'because of the greater profits higher wages for the workers. There, see what I mean?'

There was an universal exhalation of admiration at this superlative logic. Caedmon looked up at Rusty Motorcade with a new respect.

'You should be in politics,' he said admiringly.

Rusty snorted: 'Politics? Not me! Wouldn't dirty my hands.'

One by one the lovers trooped in from the Tonks garden, blinking in the light with mothy eyelids. Their clothes were dishevelled, and they carried back with them from their escapades a strange, shocked look as if the forces to which they had been exposed had been too strong for them, too elemental altogether. There had been during the course of the evening several cases of premature ejaculation (inclined to be something of a dampener) and pretty well universal frustration. Almost all of them bore the dazed look of those who have been wheeled to the limit of sexual restraint. The girl who was pushed over Niagara in a wheelbarrow had something of that look. Ethel was actually quivering.

And from every other part of Soft Meadows Cross . . . snores. And on every part of Soft Meadows Cross . . . stars. And in the Churchyard the newly dead fidget, trying to get comfortable for the aeons ahead. The Macfisheries Man, taking a short cut through the Churchyard to the Gruntham housing estate, is startled to see one of the gravestones rising in front of him. He stops in his tracks but it's only an owl flapping its cumbersome, amber wings. 'Birds!' he says aloud in disgust to reassure himself. The Church clock strikes midnight in reply. 'I'm not arguing with a bloody clock!' But his mind is full of those clock-faced girls and that dapper India-rubber man. 'I'll get him!' But in the meantime he walks on, treading quite lightly over the dead who croon their chorus to him :

'One of us . . . one of . . . one of us . . .'

He shivers, but stays alive; they draw him sure as gravity to them, they heave slowly. 'One of us . . . one of us . . . one of us . . .' and in time to this dirge the whole village, from the Boggley boundary to the Gruntham estate, from Jack Rubin's betting shop to the whining motorway, rises and falls, rises and falls. A distant train, the night sleeper from London, roars by in a brash affirmation of the life force, but the throbbing after its passing is all the more sombre; it was a ghost train. Clay and dust winnow along the deserted streets, hop onto door-steps, insinuate into crevices. Ash blows silently on the breeze, the stagnant pond on the Boggley Road bubbles and hisses, a silver birch bursts into flame, the flame becomes leaves, the leaves fall. Smoke permeates the copses.

In the big house under the motorway Dr Bushey dreams of the Vietnam war, and mutilated bodies piling up. He is operating, amputating, but for each gangrenous limb which he excises, three grow. Victoria, his daughter, in the next room, draws her knees up to her chin and clasps her hand in that warm, secret nest. She sleeps cosy, unbothered by politics. A pile of exercise books lie corrected on a desk under the window. Twenty-eight different versions of : 'What I like about my Mummy.' Little Jason Fishbound, who learnt only the other day that he was adopted, had left the page blank.

Wendy Pakenham sleeps like a fish, breathing stertoriously through her gills. The Tomlinsons in their twin beds are just heaps under the quilts. But the Admiral dreams of hot sweaty nights in Port Said. Maryka, they called her, and when she spread her legs a sunflower appeared . . . And his wife's dreams are full of guns and turrets and coils of heavy, oiled rope. She squeals in her sleep. But Cecil Sparks is not asleep. *Hamlet* is laid aside. 'Leaves of Grass' taken up. He cries aloud :

'You sea! I resign myself to you also . . . I guess what you mean,
I behold from the beach your crooked inviting fingers,

I believe you refuse to go back without feeling of me;
We must have a turn together . . . I undress . . . hurry out
of sight of the land,
Cushion me soft . . . rock me in billowy drowse,
Dash me with amorous wet . . . I can repay you.'

Jack and Miriam Rubin are like two porpoises—their school
thresh about in sleep the other side of the peppermint door;
Jack dreams of a wondrous handicap, farmyard animals in reins
and bridles bowling along an air-strip somewhere. 'Ten to one
the porker!' he cries, and there are many takers. Asleep, Mrs
Connolly is a crab and, as the night splashes on, she shuffles
sideways across the mattress, ending on the floor. Her husband
died in a road accident twelve years ago. She misses him.

Whereas Thelma and Dick Worsley, the sheet cast shockingly
back, reveal themselves intertwined about each other for all the
world like one vast pink octopus. The Vicar dreams of eternity
which in his vision is a sort of marble palace, very cold and
bare, with railway time-tables on the wall. 'Up this for a lark!'
he hears himself shouting, 'If this is heaven I'm turning
Catholic.' 'Too late, too late,' mutters an old porter with Judas
braided on his cap and a massed choir start chanting the cold
100th. 'Silence in court!' cries the Vicar, and wakes himself up.

And in The House in a big, brass bed lie the three lovely
Angell sisters on their backs, wearing long, white nightgowns,
with a Guru between Tessa and Abigail. Genevieve is quietly
crying. Tess and Abby are asleep. They smell of apples.

'There is no life without death,' mutters Guru; Genevieve
tries all night to work this out, but by dawn is a great deal
tireder, and no wiser.

Heigh-ho.

CHAPTER FOUR

The Cure · *Saturday Morning*

It being Shabbat, what more natural than that nine forty-five should find Jack Rubin with his two friends, Sammy and Solly, on the first tee of the Royal Fairway. He blows on his hands. It's a beautiful morning, with wisps of fog like tulle skirting the silver birches.

'The usual?' asks Solly, meaning ten pounds.

'Of course,' says Sammy.

'Well . . .' murmurs Jack.

It was a regular three-cornered contest each Saturday and Sunday morning. Jack very seldom won. He would lose £10 on the match and £1 in the fruit machine and could not afford the regular drain on his resources. Perhaps if he took an iron from the tee, and swung very slowly.

'I think you can go now, sir,' says old Porson, Solly's caddie, respectful, rubbing the face of the driver up and down his sleeve.

'Committee members' privilege'—and he addresses the ball. Solly Schneider wears check trousers and a natty red woollen shirt with a Rex Harrison pullover which completes the ensemble of an almost country almost gentleman, were it not for the ebullient wristlet watch, the big ruby on his little finger and the peaked cap which doesn't work at all. His swing is long, low and inelegant and the parabola of his ball equally business-like, straight down the middle, 220 or thereabouts, nothing wrong with that one.

Sammy's drive is a high, high one.

'Good morning, God!' he calls, but, though straight, the shot is considerably less effective than Solly's.

As Jack prepares to drive the ball, his short chubby arms and wrists waggling busily, his little round rump thrust aggressively out, Solly asks Jack, has he any good things for Newbury.

'Sssh,' says Jack, but his drive is sliced into the trees.

41

'Bacon,' shouts Solly, and 'Bad luck, sir,' from little Jasper who is Jack's regular caddie, and out at knees, the sort of caddie who always lands golfers like Jack, the sort of evil genius (although a very little one) who always infects his employer's ball with a built in curve and slide and dip.

He and Jack vanish into the trees to emerge some five minutes later without the ball. Little Jasper's hands bear the stains of a few late blackberries. Solly and Sammy are already on the green. 'Come on Jack!' they shout, 'we've not got all day.'

The Macfisheries Man came down to a Skullham breakfast half an hour earlier than usual for a Saturday.

Mrs Skullham was not yet about and he tramped up and down the living-room on cold, flat, bare feet. He had worried all night about those girls, his face a nasty mottled colour and his eyes sullen scarlet in their black sockets. 'Where's my bloody breakfast?' he whispered so as not to upset Mrs S, who was quite capable of serving him none at all. And then to himself muttered many times over the word 'Bitter'. He found that he could slap his tootsies on the floorboards in time to his Bitters, so that after a while it was only natural for him to change them to Pitters and add the occasional Pat.

'Pitter Pitter Pitter Pitter Pitter Pitter Pat,' said the Macfisheries Man in time with his feet. He felt less bitter already. He felt more better. He did a soft shoe shuffle.

'And what may I ask are *you* doing?' inquired Mrs Skullham, gaping like a crevasse in the doorway.

Jessica sat staring fixedly at the two toothbrushes, the pink and the blue, in the mug in front of the mirror in the bathroom at Mon Chalet. The suggestive manner in which they leant against each other was too much for her so early on a Saturday and she subsided onto the bathmat, a pathetic heap of jumbled nerves like Pik-a-Sticks. The telephone rang. She knew that her husband, asleep in the next room, would never bestir himself and dragged herself upward by the cord of the Venetian blind —which opened as she did so to reveal the pylon, as stark as you please—'Ooh'—and she pressed her anguished temples against the glass, and then felt her way in braille through to the bedroom and the telephone. It was Mrs Connolly, agog with gossip.

'She had it from the landlord of the Raven that the Macfisheries Man ... and we all know what that ... not buy *my* turbot from him again ... *not only that* ... and as for that Guru—'

'Guru?' Jessica found it very restful to be telephoned by Mrs Connolly. She could just sit and think and let the words soothe her like steam from a Turkish bath. Sometimes indeed she would let the mouthpiece lie in her lap while she read a book or applied nail varnish or composed a letter to the Electricity Board, occasionally lifting it to murmur, 'Just what I've always said' or 'Fancy'.

'Yes and it seems that this Guru—well, I mean to say ... not that we can rely upon ... *but* ... well, my dear at the Worsleys this very night ... Imagine it!'

The Admiral's lady was still sitting on the bed, cord dangling (the telephone cord, that is) when in surged the Admiral, plunging about in the rough seas of the just awakened.

'Give me that thing,' he croaked. Could this be a demand for his marital rights? It wasn't a bit like him, let alone on a Saturday morning. But no, it seemed that all he wanted was the telephone.

'Supposed to be golfing with the Vicar. Bloody nuisance. Forgot all about it.' And he dialled a number.

'You'll not be late for lunch, I trust?'

'Don't nag, woman.'

When Throggie, the pro at the Royal Fairway, brought the Admiral's apologies to the Vicar, the latter was waiting on the first tee, crying with the cold, and repeating under his breath the verses from Ecclesiastes about charity suffering long and so forth. There were times when the Holy Scriptures seemed to him quite inadequate. However Throggie's words cheered him up a little; he was not utterly abandoned. If the Vicar had realised his pristine ambitions he would have become a golf professional. His uncle, the great 'Bogey' Bellingham, had remarked once that he had the wrists for it. Thereafter he had looked at his wrists with a new respect. But, alas, wrists are not everything in life (as in golf) and he had entered the church, in which profession lack of money is the most potent handicap, but loose wrists no bar. It sometimes bothered him that the Church had been his second choice. Surely if religion meant anything to him, it should mean everything, and yet here he was playing golf when he might have been snugly smug in front of a blazing fire, composing sermons to spin like catherine wheels through the force of their unanswerable logic. Nor was there in a religious career (which was what made such a career so lonely) any kind of interim report. How were profits? And turnover? Was the boss pleased? He needed a sign. He would help God prepare a sign for him. He would chip a ball in the direction of the trolley hut and the nearer the ball ended to that rusty green trolley, the better God would be pleased. Should it strike it, why then . . . He struck an old Dunlop '65, lofting it over the putting green. It landed on the head of Cecil Sparks, cutting across the golf course on his early morning walk.

'Ow!' said Cecil Sparks, and then recovered himself and hurled the ball way down, down, down into the miniature lake behind the club-house. His three stupid dachshunds leapt into the air excitedly like grasshoppers.

'What did you do that for?' cried the Vicar.

Cecil tossed his head in the air.

And there and then the Vicar went down on his knees to plead for an increase of faith and greater inspiration in his struggling ministry.

The Admiral, shaving, looked out of the back window and noticed the Vicar in this unexpected attitude. 'I can't see what good all that'll do him,' he snorted. 'It's his left arm on the down-swing he should be worrying about.'

The Worsleys lay in on a Saturday morning to celebrate their emancipation from the underprivileged masses. For them now the sensual, degraded pleasures of the upper-middle class, and on a Saturday morning too! But Thelma rolled away with a shake of her head.

'I am in an interesting condition now,' she explained. Shining with exertion, soft and pink as a skinned sausage and healthier in these early months than ever before, she elaborated:

'There's my soirée to think of. I've got all the catering

arrangements to see to, and there's all the furniture to move
and the rubber plants to dust and I shall have to get the
Art Books out and arrange *them,* and fry some scampi,
and—'

'But are you expecting an army, my love? After all we've
only had three acceptances.'

'I'll go and see if the postman's come.'

The Macfisheries Man and Jack Rubin and the Vicar,
thought Dick with distaste, that's absolutely no way to entertain; and all the fuss!

'Any letters?'

A downcast Thelma held up a bill from the TV rentals and
a catalogue for the white sale to be held locally at Tuffin's.

'Pillowcases are down.'

'It doesn't matter, you know.'

'It does though. For you.'

'For me it doesn't matter.'

'For you it does *for me*'—and she reached for the telephone.
But as soon as she picked up the receiver she was startled to
hear two not unfamiliar voices already in conversation.

'I hope I didn't wake you up, Duckie. Procrastination as the
bard says, is the thief of . . .' Though it was distorted (by the
telephone), Thelma could recognise the prissy alto of Cecil
Sparks. And the other voice, heavily drugged with sleep belonged to Caedmon Tomlinson.

'Whozzit?'

'Cecil speaking, none other. None, none other but me.'

'Cecil who?'

'Sparks, dear boy, Sparks. You remember me, old sparking
plug?'

'Christ!' said Caedmon, not yet conscious enough to put a
hand in front of the mouthpiece.

'What?'

'Whazzit you want?'

'What?'

'Whazzit? Whazzit?'

'Just a cosy little chat; about this and that.'

'Whaz?'

'Caedmon, my dear child, have you ever considered an acting

career? Join the profession. Tread the boards. The smell of the greasepaint, late night coffee parties in Barnsley, Yorks, breaking hearts under a painted mask . . .'

'What *are* you on about? Honestly, if—'

'Now no ifs. You, my little Caedmon, are, *thou art*—the perfect Laertes.'

'Whazzit?'

'Look, I'm awfully sorry and all that, but I'm afraid you're on my line—'

'Whazzit? Whozzis?' One could almost hear the bewildered shake of Caedmon's finely sculpted head.

'Your line? Who is that?'

'Does that matter who it is?'

'Why isn't that . . . ?'

'Why isn't it . . . ?'

With a groan Caedmon left them to it, put the telephone down and went back to bed.

In his red house, overlooked by the Motorway, Doctor Bushey, who never went out any more, opened his copy of *The Times*. His anxious old eyes scanned it until they lit on the latest report from Saigon. Atrocities; more atrocities. He sighed deeply and cried a little. He would not go out today. Victoria, his only child, had left him some liver-sausage and a half a tomato on a plate. Neither appealed to him. The telephone rang. He didn't answer it. He pushed the plate away from him. He didn't go out.

It was Rose-Marie Farquhar who had been endeavouring to ring Dr Bushey, since her legs were paining her again, and she needed a prescription for a further ration of the drug. She could have sent Dupont, the Chauffeur, down to the Doctor's and then to the apothecary's, but it was Dupont's day off. It was too bad for Dr Bushey not to answer the telephone. It *was* too bad. It was too bad.

Perhaps if she rang those nice Tomlinsons . . . yes, that was it. She could thank them for the party and, at the same time, explain her troubles. Most likely they'd offer to run the errand for her. She dialled the number. It rang; several times. Caedmon groaned and took the beastly thing off its rest. He had been dreaming of a fire escape at St Hilda's. He doubted that he would recapture the dream. He turned over and went back to sleep.

'Is there anybody there?' asked the telephone.

In the big brass bed in The Big House Guru woke up suddenly and sat straight up. Skin was stretched tight over his chest as over a drum and was of a beautiful light sand colour. Genevieve, eyes red with weeping, watched him intently. Without warning he struck Tessa on the head, contracting the fingers of his hand and making the sound 'Phat'. Tessa opened her eyes. Guru then struck Abby similarly making the sound 'Phut'.

'Oh,' said Abby.

Genevieve murmured: 'Where did you come from out of the sun, Guru?'

Guru smiled. He put the tip of his tongue against his teeth, started hissing, and indicated to the girls that they should hiss likewise. Tessa hissed at once, but Abigail who was still half asleep seemed slow to understand. Once again Guru struck her and made the sound 'Phut'.

'Don't hurt her,' said Genevieve wistfully, hugging her knees. 'Phat!' 'Phut!' 'Hiss.'

The telephone rang. Guru nodded his head at Genevieve who lifted the receiver:

'Yes?' It was Rose-Marie.

'Who is that? Genevieve? Look I'm awfully sorry to bother you, but—what is that extraordinary noise?' At a nod from Guru, Genevieve put the phone down and, coming to the foot of the bed, lifted her nightdress. Naturally a shy and sensitive girl, it was a little while before her hisses too joined those of her sisters in a charming continuum to Guru's 'Phats' and 'Phuts'—amongst which could now be heard the occasional 'Hin'.

But poor Rose-Marie didn't know where to turn.

Cecil Sparks took out a big, red notebook and sat at his window pretending to write, but merely admiring the sun. He found that if he looked at it and then closed his eyes extremely tight, brilliantly coloured submarines floated and sailed across the velvet darkness of his unexposed retina.

After a while the sun began to bore him rather and he held up his left hand between him and it.

The dogs were asleep on the floor. Wendy was cooking a veal dish with pimentoes in it to prove her love.

The light shone through the hand which became almost translucent, the veins spreading out like the Nile Delta from his wrist. The nails were in mourning; the skin over the knuckles pinched into little puckers of flesh. The hands were quite hairless but from the wrists up all was hirsute, all was devil's country.

'But this'll butter no parsnips,' muttered Cecil, and Gielgud grunted in his sleep, chasing a myriad of conies, no doubt, over unending moors by the light of a dog-faced moon.

Cecil wrote in the margin of his manuscript the date and the time and at the top the number of the page (Page One actually), then he paused for inspiration and fell to studying his right hand, which was, there's no denying, remarkably similar to the left. Except that the thumb was on the left of the right hand, whereas it was on the right of the left hand; unless he turned it over in which case . . .

Coffee time at the Burnt Scone. Under the hat stand the Tesco's bags and the Macfisheries' bags slump one against another in uneasy alliance like France and Germany. At any moment one could expect local but total war to be declared. Potatoes pop out their eyes, baked beans lift the lids of their tins to reconnoitre, sugar puffs are shot from guns, Danish butter is interned by home-cured ham. Six principles . . . unconditional surrender . . . the Macfisheries bag crashes to the ground. At once Mrs Connolly gets up and goes over to it to check that none of the eggs has suffered, then rights it and puts it ever more firmly up against its victorious enemy. Alsace Lorraine. As she returns to her table Mrs Skullham politely inquires was any damage done.

'No thank you. All is well.'

'May I join you?'

'Please do.'

'How are you, my dear?'

'Mustn't grumble. And Albert?'

'Mustn't complain, I suppose; *he* doesn't'—Mrs Skullham's father, a martyr to arthritis, is 82, doesn't go about much, and in the winter months . . . 'he'll be better in the Spring. Anyway, he's got his telly.'

A mini-skirted waitress comes to take the order.

'Good morning, Candida,' says Mrs Connolly politely, her eyes however jealously thigh-high. Candida, a moody girl, suffering from an adolescence full of torturing anticipation and enforced abstinence—but she has *splendid* legs—doesn't answer.

'Coffee please.'

'And for me, too, dear.'

'Tea cakes? Toast? Biscuits?'

A young American couple from the USAF base at Latchvine come in, trailing a sulky, crew-cut child. And get served first! Get biscuits without even ordering them. Well! And the Lieutenant, whose forearms are like giant's clubs and whose biceps are like bubble-gum, dunks his Maryland Cookie in his Maxwell House.

'These Americans,' says Mrs Connolly, loud enough—*almost* —to be overheard, 'think they own the country.'

'They do, dear, they do.' Mrs Skullham was ambiguous. Did they own it or did they think they owned it? Or, horrible to contemplate, both? The Lieutenant's wife is pregnant.

'I think it's disgusting,' says Mrs Connolly, 'no control. No control at all.'

'All these riots and things in the South, well, I mean, can you wonder?'

'No background.'

'The national disease.'

'Like the Jews.'

'What? No of course I don't.'

The child started crying. He was frightened by a pattern on the wallpaper that looked like a fierce, fierce, *fierce* dragon —only no one could be expected to understand that. The Lieutenant picked him up and cradled him. After a while his sobbing lost its seriousness of purpose, became a self-indulgence, became a gurgle.

'Did you see that?' hissed Mrs Connolly.

'What, dear?'

'The way he's spoiling that unfortunate child.'

'Scandalous!'

'Needs a good slap on his bottie, if you ask me. And, by the

D

way, did you hear about this Indian whatever-he-is and those Angell girls? I had it from Jessica, and she says that . . .'

Oh the vicious imagination of frustrated middle-class widows! And how far short it falls of the truth!

And how far Jack Rubin's golf fell short of perfection! Five down to both opponents by the time he reached the fourteenth tee, Jack was puffing on his third cigar as if cigars were the new religion and puffing the only way to heaven.

'Come along, Jack, get a move on,' cries Solly, 'you're not in schul now, you know.'

And, sure enough, the Vicar and the Admiral can be seen charging down the thirteenth fairway with their trolleys.

'God and the Navy!' exclaims Solly, 'that we should live so long!'

'Wheewhoosh!' Little Jasper, Jack's caddie, explodes with hay fever.

'Thwump! Crack!'

'A bad place that, sir,' says old Porson to Jack shaking his venerable head, fifty years of secretly pocketing members' balls and selling them on the sly behind him.

'Wheewhoosh!' says little Jasper.

'I'll 'old 'is nose while yer drive another,' says old Porson, and does, placing the boy firmly between his knees, so he shan't squirm.

Then Solly drives with an iron just to be safe and there's nothing wrong with it at all, that one, nor with Sammy's, and off they trot down the lush green fairway, descendants of Moses who owe their allegiance to a German royal family, and play golf every Saturday.

'Wheewhoosh!'

'What an extraordinary noise,' exclaims the Vicar, breasting the rise, 'I wonder if it could possibly be a bittern?' The Vicar, two up, can afford to be garrulous. The Admiral is grumpier than ever :

'I'm not going to wait any longer, that's what.'

With which the Admiral tees up his battered, weather-beaten, spume-flecked, Cape-Horn-stained, force-twelve-tumbled ball (the exertion of bending incarnadines his face and presents to the Vicar an expanse of tweed buttock not unlike an old sea map of eddies and currents and sandbanks and shallows with the straights of Panama right down the middle—oh, Vicar, could you be a Panamanian?)—and takes up his nautical stance and swings at the ball with all the violence of his corpulent figure behind it. Such a smack! The ball sails sweet and true. Jack sees it coming and scampers towards the green. Little Jasper, wheewhooshing, crouches to the ground and covers his head, but is safely out of range. Cecil Sparks from his shrubbery to the left of the fairway, unleashes his three hounds and, encouraging them with random blows on their hind quarters, whispers urgently: 'Fetch it, boys, fetch it!'

Irving, Garrick and Gielgud, whining and whimpering with excitement, squeeze through a hole in the fence and, after a brief tussle for possession race back to heel like the well-trained dachshunds they are.

A tremendous cry shatters the calm Home Counties air, even stops little Jasper in full sneeze.

'Bugger you, Sparks, you bloody little nancy boy, I'll get you for this!'

'Lies! Lies! Why does everyone tell lies all the time? Why are their mouths always open and their minds always closed? What's the point of it? Don't they want to communicate etc. etc.?'

Thus Ethel Tomlinson to the world as she sips her espresso and froth in the Café Cappriccio, a rather squalid shed on the London Road got up to look like a Neapolitan fisherman's nook. Not a vicious place, but a home from home for the village kids.

They were well looked after, and elegantly clad, these young Gods and Goddesses of the Welfare State; their mattresses were sprung internally and their convertibles were fast; yet blood streamed through their arteries and fluids of ripeness and sensuality informed each pore and vent ... Was this why (or was it boredom?) they walked around with mouths half open, gasping for air? Some of them panted to the Big City, where they Met People, Slept Around, Lived it Up. A few of them vanished utterly, and the ghosts of those heroes and heroines haunted the Café.

Under the fishing nets and lobster pots was a tawdry juke box, a 'free expression' wall, and other poignant visual aids to sophistication.

L.S.D. was not unknown there, but uncommon, and the fairly harmless 'blues' offered an escape from responsibility, a substitute for those old visions of peace and brotherhood, so well worked over by Bertrand Russell, Pete Seeger, and other old men.

Those who would have closed the place down would never have understood how harmless, how shabby, it all was. 'All that good money,' thought their fathers, 'and not a thing to show for it. Why can't they grow up?' 'Why *must* they grow up?' thought their mothers.

'No but it's true,' Ethie insisted, 'isn't it? Lies all the time. I mean, even the B.B.C.'

'Cool it, babe,' said The Loins, 'actually.' After playing at the Tomlinsons the previous night they had reverted to type and without their gold lamé waistcoats and low-slung hipster pants looked just what they were – bored and middle-class school-leavers with a desperate whim to be accepted by their own generation, who reject so many, and long, straggly hair. They were certainly not rejected by Ethie, who, in spite of her tirade, was quite happy in their company.

'Death!' cried the juke box, 'long live Death!'

'What a modulation!' cried the ecstatic Loins, who had just learned the word and were grateful for the opportunity to try it out, 'isn't it too much?'

'A rave!' affirmed Ethie.

'Where's the coffee?' they bellowed, and their fan club trotted off to fetch it. As soon as she was out of earshot, the Loins, fingers twitching, began to speak of her :

'Isn't it a groove?'

'What a sample!'

'Fab!'

'A gas!'

They knew that their language was already old-fashioned, but tried very hard to keep up to date. From time to time they spoke of going to San Francisco, but knew their mothers wouldn't let them.

—'Oh baby green and baby blue

—And baby bright vermilion' (sang the juke box)
—My india-rubber eyes anatomise, antagonise a million.'
'Wild!' cried a Loin.
'Something else,' cried another.
'Sock it to me!' cried a third.
'Don't be late for lunch, boys,' cried the mother of the third through the window of the coffee bar.
And: 'There's Caedmon,' cried Ethie, as her brother made his entrance with Rusty Motorcade's arm in the small of his reluctant but sweetly curving back.
'Honestly, Rusty, you're not like this at Oxford. What's got into you?' Caedmon, unaccustomed to flirtation, responded very prettily to it. Rusty was delighted.
The Loins started shrieking and clicking and working out a new number chock-full of modulations. They had none of them taken drugs but Hoots had had gas when his wisdom teeth were impacted and claimed to have 'seen visions of the universal soul'.
'Oh *honestly*, Rusty.'
'It's the Thames Valley air,' explained Rusty. 'They always build schools and universities on rivers and estuaries and in low-lying places. It's very enervating. It's called the Po Valley Syndrome.'
Caedmon wriggled in embarrassment. 'I just wish you'd keep your hands to yourself.'
'It seems so ungrateful somehow.'
Cecil Sparks, peeking through the window, snorted with jealous distaste. His dachshunds, snorted too. Then started bouncing impatiently and set off, pricking their six ears to empty their three bladders on the hub-cap of a Mini-Cooper.

'Oh, what shall I do? What *shall* I do?' Poor Rose-Marie had exhausted her supply of friends. Her legs hurt. They really did. She thought of Rusty Motorcade who had been so civil at the party, but he was staying at the Tomlinsons and no one there answered the phone. Then she thought of Cecil Sparks, sitting all alone in his den at Elsinore, writing the Great Novel, which only she believed in. She dialled Sparks's number. As she dialled, murmured:
'Poor, poor Rose-Marie, all alone and up a tree.'

Wendy Pakenham was angry to be called away from her veal just when it mattered most.

'Can I speak to—'

'Who is it please?'

'Mr Sparks.'

'It can't be Mr Sparks.'

'You misunderstand me.'

'Anyway that's a lady's voice unless I'm much mistaken.'

'No, you've got me wrong—'

'Oh come now, you are *not* Cecil.'

'I never said I was.'

'Pardon me.'

'Granted.'

'What?'

'I said "Granted".'

'Oh well, I'm afraid I have to get back to the kitchen now. It's been nice talking.'

'No. Wait. Listen. This is Rose-Marie speaking.'

'Oh. Why didn't you say so at once? 'It's not difficult.'

'I'm sorry,' Rose-Marie drew breath, I'd like to speak to Mr Sparks, please.'

'Not possible.'

'Why not?'

'He's out.'

'Oh. It's rather an emergency. I need a prescription made up.'

'Never mind, I'm sure it'll work out all right. Anyway you can always try Dr Bushey. Good-bye.' And rang off.

'Oh.' Tears of frustration filled Rose-Marie's beautiful eyes, which sparkled like Cleopatra's jewels; the tears themselves were translucent and wonderfully pearl-shaped. Rose-Marie wiped one from her nose with the tip of her finger and examined it. Tasted it. So pathetic seemed the taste of the salt on her tongue that a whole new platoon of tears (held in reserve behind the front lines) surged onto the ravaged battlefield of her face.

Timothy no longer took walks. Timothy was the Tomlinson's old, fat, black labrador. He was too heavy and his only exercise was his twitching as he lay, loose-limbed, like a wheel, dreaming of a million squirrels darting up five hundred trunks of five hundred trees. He whimpered with the excitement of the chase. Colonel Gilbert Tomlinson's slippered toe in his underbelly became a monstrous mole gnawing at his organs; convulsively he sank his teeth into it. Gilbert leapt to his feet, upsetting the Scrabble board.

Cecil Sparks's dachshunds were outside the window, whining and bouncing. It was just possible to see the tips of their long ears flapping.

'Timothy must be got rid of!' cried Gilbert in considerable pain.

'No darling, never,' said his wife. She tried to replace the Scrabble letters as they had been on the board, and, cheating a little, to reinforce her case by magic. 'Look, see what the Scrabble says.'

'LETIMLIVE? Nonsense, you just put them down like that.'

'That's how they fell. I *tidied* them only.'

'Anyway he smells.'

'We all smell, dear.'

'You may. I most certainly don't.'

'Darling, it's healthy to smell just a wee, tiny bit.'

'I can bloody well smell that dog!'

Timothy undoubtedly did smell. A long, luxuriant, canine whiff. Like an ostrich feather. After which he curled up in front of the artificial logs and nosed his way back into the grey squirrel-land of his dreams.

'Well, are we going to play, or aren't we?'

The game started sensationally when Celia, casual as you please, put down *Epaulet*, using all her seven letters and gaining a bonus of fifty. Her husband snorted. With his excess of consonants *Gnat* (or *Tang*) was the most he could hope for.

'*Hauberk*,' said his wife, making it.

'Challenge!'

'Oh Gilbert, you know it's a perfectly good word. It's just silly to challenge it.'

'I know my rights.'

'Yes, darling, but you're not right. There—' and she pointed to the word in the dictionary—'medieval coat of mail.'

By now Gilbert was in a thoroughly bad mood. He could

only manage *Cat* or *Cut* and if he put either of them on Hauberk good-bye to his chance of getting rid of his Q. 'Put that damn' dictionary down. You know you're not allowed to look through it.' And he snatched it from her, taking his opportunity to see if there was anything beginning TC. Tchaikovsky and Tchekov and nothing more. Typical! Or rather Tcypical! He put down *Cat*.

'Oh cat, that's nice!' When you're eighty points up, it's easy to be conciliatory.

'It's not nice. It's a bloody horrible word anyway. And I don't like cats.' Saying which he kicked Timothy awake again.

Although Celia was tempted to make *Knickers*, adding her seven letters to the K of *Hauberk*, and thus considerably augmenting her total, she contented herself with *Kink*, and enjoyed an ironical stab of pleasure as her husband triumphantly crowed:

'This'll show you,' and (dropping the 'Q' into his turn-up) flung down seven letters which, with the N for *Kink* rearranged themselves into *Numbness*! 'He's not such a mutt, your husband, is he?'

'Not a mutt at all,' and she kissed his forehead. He was still grainy with suspicion though and covered with an arm his new set of letters.

'You only come and kiss me to see what I've got,' he grunted.

'Ah, darling, how can you say that? It's because of what you've got that I still like to kiss you.'

Celia returned to her chair and picked up another three letters, a 'G' and two 'U's. Slotting them into her plastic rack with the 'C', 'E', 'R' and 'S' which were all that remained of her *knickers*, her forehead creased like a boxer dog's.

She could make *Curse* of course—but that was not very nice —and *Rugs*, but that was not very adventurous. Or, alternatively ... her fingers diddled the letters ... Guru! She shut her eyes and again stirred the letters, but ... Guru! She tried to make *Ruse,* but it came out ... Guru! '*Scurge*!' she cried, but she put down ... Guru!

'Ug!'—and she heaved the Scrabble board to the floor.

'What did you do that for?' Gilbert complained, 'I was winning.'

But four letters winked up at her from the astrakhan rug ...

G...U...R...U...and she shut her eyes and swayed gently to and fro.

'Bad luck, sir,' says Old Porson informally to Jack Rubin as they walk from the 18th green, 'it's only a game.'

Jack makes a bitter noise, blowing through his teeth. Little Jasper is cheerful at the prospect of his lunch and says to Jack:

'See, sir? I've stopped sneezing.'

In spite of everything, and with a heavy heart, Jack pats him on the head, leaving in his hair three half-crowns upon which the sun glints mischievously.

'Don't spend it all at once, little schnorrer.'—and he turns into the dressing-room, the reek of which is so strong that he makes a gesture as if to part the air with his hands. The wealthy Solly and the vulgar Sammy have prevented him and, while the former stands, portly and imposing in yellow vest and striped boxer pants, Sammy is under the shower, scrubbing away at his armpit with a cake of soap, as if conducting a personal vendetta against the celery (celery? It looks like celery) which grows there. His belly bulges like a well-filled shopping bag and his two brown nipples are door-bells. Ping! (Jack imagines himself pressing them) and then a two-toned Ping-Ping! The heavy vault of Sammy's chest swings open and a smooth young adolescent peeps out.

'What do you want?'

'What's it like in there?'

'Very cosy. So you wish to take up residence?'

'No thank you very much.'

'So all right already'—and clang! ribs and lungs vanish and a hairy panel conceals the hinges. Jack feels a mournful kind of nostalgia and sighs deeply.

'Wake up, Jack!' calls Sammy and rubs his cheeks with the palms of his horny hands. We can't wait all day for the drink you owe us!'

'Oh yes. That too. Of course.'

'Sammy?'

'Yes, old boy?'

'What were you like as a young man?'

'Young.'

'Oh.'

'God damn and blast the man and sod his bloody dogs!'
It's the Admiral of course, sailing into the dressing-room, with
the little tug-boat Vicar in tow. The Church (although
sympathetic) is more cheerful than the Navy. With God's help
and cautious irons off the tee it had won by three and two.
But it trips over naked Sammy's brown brogues.

'You all right, Rabbi?' asks Sammy. The Vicar fixes him
with a quizzical glance.

'Get thee behind me, Satan.'

'Not feeling so very ecumenical this morning then?' says
Solly.

The Admiral doesn't smile.

'A new fence, that we must have for a start, and, if I can
get my hand on the loose-wristed, jumped-up—Good God,
perverts, Negroes and Jews, is this the promised land? If Winnie
were alive today he'd turn in his grave.'

The others ignore him.

'The fence must be up within the month. If that Sparks and
his footling little German dogs interfere in the Hardinge Trophy
I'll not answer for the consequences.'

And so on. Let us not judge the Admiral too harshly. In fact
let us not judge him at all.

The Angell sisters were up. Guru lay in the big bed, hands
folded on chest like an effigy. They brought him tea and toast
and a hard-boiled egg, which he ate, shell and all.

Surprisingly, Abigail, so frail the previous evening, seemed
to have survived her unexpectedly busy Saturday morning,
survived and even flourished. There was colour in her cheeks.
She hadn't coughed once. Tessa was floating from room to room
in her lace peignoir, strangely like a sea-lion. As she passed the
dust seemed to dissolve at a flick of her wrist and such small
ornaments as had become disarranged during the course of the
dark hours (by the gravitational pull of the moon perhaps or
vibration caused by the great furnace in the belly of the earth),
magically righted themselves. Only Genevieve, sitting at the
stool in front of the dressing table and regarding the wistful
contours of her face in the generous mirror, one long finger
to her enchanting chin, seemed somehow ill at ease, dispossessed.

'Tell Guru.'

'Well, it's just that . . . you remember the telephone ringing when . . . well *earlier* . . .'

'Ah time and space . . .'

Genevieve's arched eyebrows arched even a little higher.

'Well . . . it was Rose-Marie and she sounded to be . . . well, in trouble, and I was wondering . . .'

Tessa came in. Abigail followed her carrying a bowl in which floated a single golden leaf.

Said Tessa: 'Rose-Marie troubled? Oh Genevieve, surely it is your gentle imagination?'

'Mine is gentle, too,' and Abigail sighed, 'gentler than hers.'

'Should I perhaps return her call?'

'Telephone? Bah! Rose-Marie is young lady?'

'Why yes, quite young.'

'Tell Guru of her.'

And Tessa it was who told. Of the chair and of the polio and of her lonely wandering eyes.

'We go to her.'

'But we don't usually venture out on Saturdays,' murmured Abby, 'and see how the trees are flirting with the wind.' She pressed the side of the bowl to her cheek.

'Poor trees!' Genevieve dropped a tear, a special one for the trees.

'We go to her.'

Tessa brightened. 'Of course we do. It's a kind thought.' A few minutes later, muffled and wrapped around with wool and fur, the Angell sisters astonished the Macfisheries Man (back at his post, a little cold and stiff, but not too badly off) by leaving their house, a few paces behind Guru, and walking resolutely down the gravel path in the direction of the Boggley Road. He let them advance some thirty yards and then mounting his loyal red bike, wobbled after them, doomed, turning the front wheel violently left and then right, but (alas!) running eventually into a fine old elm tree with hearts and arrows carved into its respectable bark. As he lay in the ditch, crawled upon by things, he laughed bitterly.

'Shall all my noble aspirations end thus? In a ditch!' A friendly hedgehog crawled up to him after a while and rubbed itself amiably against him. Then a toad and a couple of magpies. There were blackberry bushes between him and the heavens.

The blackberries were withered, cobwebbed, water-logged. Michaelmas Day was past. It was indeed the end of the old year. A few rogue drops of rain spattered his face. The sun had gone behind smoked glass. The front wheel of the red bicycle was buckled. His ankle pained him.

'I have found my niche at last. This is where I belong.' One of the magpies bit a button off his sleeve. Some nameless thing (otter? badger? mole?) muzzled his private parts.

Throggie on his way to a lonely lunch at the Chinese Restaurant stopped his battered Vauxhall and unwound the window.

'Y're all richt doon there?'

'Fine, Fine. It suits my mood.'

'Aye mebbe, but—'

'It's only this bloody hedgehog.'

'What hedgehog? I dinna see a hedgehog.'

'It's not given to everyone to see hedgehogs.'

'Clamber up, mon, the noo. We'll gang to the guid Doctor.'

'Ow!'

'Eh?'

'My ankle.'

'Aye.' The two men, arms round each other's necks, loved each other for a brief while, as they loaded the bicycle and themselves into the car. On the way to the Doctor's the Macfisheries Man told Throggie what he knew and what he had seen up at the house. Throggie was properly scandalised. He asked after Mrs Skullham. The Macfisheries Man spoke of her in unfriendly tones. And then of Albert, her father.

'He sits all day in front of the television. She puts it on for him in the morning and off when he goes to bed. He watches the test card.'

'Sad.'

'Yes. Very.'

The conversation was interrupted as they passed the Café Cappriccio, for a coffee cup came flying through the window, shattering the glass.

It was Cecil Sparks's coffee cup—or, rather had been—and it was flung at Rusty Motorcade, who *would* keep his hand on Caedmon's knee, when all Cecil wished to do was continue talking to the young man about playing Laertes. Eventually

Caedmon agreed on condition (Rusty's condition) that Rusty played Fortinbras and then, pacified, they all drank froth together to celebrate.

Outside in the street Cecil's dogs (having a grand walk this morning) were sniffing around the portico of the Burnt Scone when sulky-eyed Candida tap-toed out to offer them cakecrumbs. They raised their heads until they were pointed and thin like stork's beaks, sniffing up her long legs.

'Oooh, you sexy things!' giggled Candida, tickled and flattered even by dogs. Her legs and lips parted slightly as the Soft Meadows air raced around her curves. 'Oooh!' and then again, throwing her arms wide : 'Ooooooh!'

She waved provocatively at Throggie and his passenger as they puttered past. Both ignored her.

Doctor Bushey sat muttering to himself while his uneaten breakfast resented him from a chipped plate patterned with roses which had faded, but not wilted with the years. Liberals indeed! Wasn't a real Liberal left in the country, always excepting dear Jo. And they had had such high hopes. Himself, God and Beveridge in a Committee re-evaluating Marx. Some dream! And one by one his friends had bought sports cars, bijou residences, blonde wives, race-horses even. Liberals! Phooey! German cameras he could do without, Spanish oranges and Portuguese sardines, and as for spaghetti . . . poor Musso! If you were to be a dictator, you might at least dictate. And Hitler . . . once he had had a theory. Thyroid deficiency combined with a syndrome he had noted in certain cases of . . . A Jungian subject obviously, but where did that leave you? With his liberal principles and a theory about Hitler, he had dropped law for medicine. Socrates for Hippocrates. Since when there had been no more justice. And now this sublime injustice of Vietnam. He *had* to protest. He would *not* go out.

But it was a fresh morning. All the birds . . . 'Wring their pretty necks!' he said out loud. Doctors! Who needed Doctors in Soft Meadows Cross? Birds! Liberals! Doctors! Vietnam!

The door-bell rang. It was Throggie with the Macfisheries Man. Dr Bushey growled deep in his throat, just like a Tory.

Poor Rose-Marie needed a doctor. She had been reduced to staring out of the window at the birds on the lawn and hoping that maybe one of them would stare right back, when she was startled by the door-bell. Whom might it be? Her circle of friends was neither wide nor varied. Perhaps it was a huge Dartmoor prisoner with a hatchet-blade in his fist come all the way from the West Country by milk train especially to rape her. The idea was not totally repugnant but all the same . . . Perhaps he might creep round the bushes, putting the blade between his teeth to appear sweaty and libidinous at . . . this . . . very . . . window.

'Aaah!' A brown face pressed itself against the glass in front of her nose. She screamed again, appalled as much by the *unexpectedness* of the apparition as by the apparition itself. She was sure she did not wish to be violated by a brown-skinned gentleman. Or thought she was sure. Truth to tell, she had not given the notion that much thought.

She only screamed twice in any case, since three rather more familiar (though in this context equally unexpected) faces wafted into her field of vision. The Angell sisters! Out on a Saturday morning! She leaned forward, unlatched the French windows, and the small cavalcade entered.

'Good morning to you, Rose-Marie,' remarked Tessa pleasantly. 'We return your call.'

'You didn't half give me a start. Cooee!'

'I read a Sherlock Holmes book once,' murmured Genevieve in her quiet poetic voice. 'He knew, you see, that the other man was Australian on account of the dying man shouted "Cooee!" at him. At least I think that was it.'

They were all surprised at Genevieve's unaccustomed garrulity, none more so than Rose-Marie herself. But she was less concerned with Sherlock Holmes and his methods, than with . . .

'Won't you introduce me to your friend?'

'Oh.' Tessa turned her misty eyes downward. 'This is Guru.'

'Legs?' asked Guru.

'I'm sorry?'

'What she means is,' Tessa explained, 'she's sorry but she didn't understand what you meant when you said "legs" like that.'

Guru in his turn looked puzzled, then, with considerable emphasis, said again : '*Legs*!'

'Are they hurting you, poor Rose-Marie?' inquired Abigail.

'Yes a little they are, it's true, but—'

'Out!' said Guru pointing into the garden. In his high-buttoned brown costume he was a commanding figure in spite of his littleness.

The distant herbaceous border was like a football crowd and the blurred heads of the chrysanthemums followed their progress. Most things were russet. There was a damp but glistening lawn, with blades of grass which sparkled like slivers of glass, grass as sharp as glass, Rose-Marie had cut her tongue on it in summers past.

Guru waved his arms around. They took Rose-Marie out of her chair and laid her on her back on the lawn, but Genevieve became instantly concerned :

'Let me fetch a blanket, may I? It's so cold and wet for poor her.'

While Genevieve was gone, Guru walked a little away from the others and stood facing an overgrown forest of rhubarb. Into his cauliflower eyes came an expression of doubt and concern, but only the rhubarb was there to see it, the rhubarb and a fat tortoise with scaly, raffia legs, who lived therein. Guru returned to Rose-Marie, laid his warm hands on her forehead. The girl felt nothing but warmth and comfort then in his touch. His hands bore gentleness in their palms, and security lived in the tips of his fingers. She closed her eyes. The grass smelt sweet. When Genevieve tried to cover it with her blanket Rose-Marie waved her away. Thrushes hopped up to watch. A greenfinch perched on Abigail's shoulder. The birds were noisy but, birds apart, the garden was quite still and sweet. Guru removed clothing, uncovered legs. The Angell sisters assisted. Rose-Marie would not have wished to move, had she had the power.

Only Tessa asked :

'Rose-Marie, are you . . . ?' Dust particles flew like distant skaters in the oblique rays of the sun. 'All this dust,' said Genevieve, 'which never ever settles.' Poplars whispered. Guru rocked on his heels, set up a low murmuring, rocked forward and caressed the girl's legs, which, smooth and shapely but a little thin from disuse, became very faintly mottled through exposure and, near the rump, pricked out with goose-pimples. Rose-Marie (as might have been expected) passed from pleasure to ecstacy, from ecstacy to a kind of pain. The whimpers which issued from her throat claimed both pleasure and pain as ancestors. Guru stroked and then struck her thighs with the flat sides of his horny hands and this sudden rub-a-dub-dub pained Rose-Marie so fiercely that all at once she sat up and with the sole of her left foot in his chest pushed Guru right over on to his back.

With the sole of her left . . . pushed Guru . . . pushed . . . *her* foot . . . right over . . . with the sole . . . on to his back . . . pushed Guru . . . *her* foot . . . her left foot.

Guru breathed out deeply. His eyes were like helmet-spikes. Why should he have been so relieved? None of them spoke. Genevieve chewed the corner of her blanket. The blackbird pecked at Abigail's ear. Tessa, the practical one, thought nevertheless of the sea and how beautiful it was and how many colours it contained and how these colours came and went. Rose-Marie knew what she had done. Guru was the first to speak.

'Food!' he cried.

Rose-Marie dressed herself and walked indoors to see what there was in the larder.

The Admiral's wife was bored. Bored by Soft Meadows Cross, bored by Saturdays, bored by being the Admiral's wife. Time was striding across her country on seven league boots. Everyone and nothing changed. She wished she had had children when she was younger.

'God damn it!' she cried, 'I want immortality!' Then added as an afterthought: 'But if I'm not going to be immortal, let's have a bit of fun.' There was no one to answer her.

The sight of the damned pylon made her itch all over. Between her legs was a fish gasping for air. She found a number of pills in the medicine chest—no label on the bottle, but they looked soothing and she swallowed a handful, washing them down with cough linctus, and putting the remainder absent-mindedly into her handbag. Instantly regretted it. Began to worry. Other women would be happily employed cooking their husband's lunches. But Mrs Hessian was in *her* kitchen, beating the batter with *her* fork, peeling *her* potatoes, carving crosses on *her* sprouts.

She wandered moonishly into the kitchen, picked up a saucepan, put it down again, opened the oven, looked at the joint, picked off a piece and chewed it half-raw.

'Don't pick!' scolded Mrs Hessian.

She wandered to the drawer of the kitchen table, looked at the shiny, stiff knives until her senses began to reel. All those knives . . . and the effect of the pills . . . she needed fresh air.

Her steps, at first aimless, led her across the golf course, and then, more purposefully, she found herself taking the track which ran parallel to the Main Street, behind the Chinese Restaurant, the Midland Bank, and the School. When she was opposite the garden of the Farquhar's House (a fine old garden but not entirely shielded from prying eyes), she saw a vision. That crippled Farquhar serving baked beans on the lawn to the Indian fellow and the Angell sisters. And the birds singing symphonies. Well!

No wonder that her feet took her hastily on to Doctor Bushey's. But she hesitated at his door. The sight of so many rectangular and brightly coloured vehicles bustling along the motorway behind the house dizzied her so that she leant for support against the Doctor's door which had been recently left ajar by Throggie, when he ushered in the Macfisheries Man. She stumbled in, bumping against a fine Ming vase which rocked precariously (perhaps it wasn't Ming after all) before spitefully overbalancing and shattering into several dozen slithers of what might have been valuable crockery. The disaster had the effect (and it's hard to see what else would have accomplished as much) of bringing out not only the limping Macfisheries Man from the waiting-room but also the Doctor from his surgery.

'What do you mean by it, woman?' And to the Macfisheries Man whom he had himself absent-mindedly welcomed only a few minutes back. 'And who are you, and what do *you* want?'

Neither answered him.

'You've not come here to be married, I trust,' grumbled the Doctor, 'I'm not the right man for that, you know. You must

E

call on the Admiral, he's a sea-captain, he'll do it. Now leave me in peace.'

The Admiral's wife's confusion grew :

'I've not come to be married. I *am* married. And to the Admiral.'

'I'm the Macfisheries Man,' said the Macfisheries Man, 'and I've hurt my leg.'

'And what's wrong with *you*, madam?'

'I swallowed some of these,' said the lady producing pills from her handbag, 'and I feel strange and dizzy. Perhaps you'd like to examine me?'

Doctor Bushey snatched the pills rudely from her, chewed a couple.

'Pah!' he said disgustedly. 'Quells!' If you really are the Admiral's wife (which I doubt) what are you doing taking sea-sickness pills?'

'I was here first and what about my leg?'

'Take two of these three times a day after meals,' said the Doctor handing him the Quells.

'I most certainly shan't, and this isn't what I pay my taxes for!'

The atmosphere in the hall of the Doctor's House was deteriorating swiftly and becoming what can only be described as acrimonious, when the door opened yet again to admit Victoria, the Doctor's daughter, home from her school duties. She took command at once and it was no time at all before they were all sitting round an electric blower drinking coffee and listening to the astonishing story which the Admiral's wife was relating concerning the Angell sisters, the Farquhar girl and the Guru.

CHAPTER FIVE

The Reactions · *Saturday Afternoon*

The regulars in the Café Cappriccio sat blowing on their coffee-froth. A blonde with ferret's teeth was covered in badges and buttons. There was no money in that red plastic purse which she clutched so fervently to her heart; just a copy of Kierkegaard and a wistful toothbrush. A dark-haired waitress in a knitted sweater next her skin, swayed between the tables, solemnly, slender as the night. Three men and a girl were pricking each other experimentally with pins, while a young psychopath in a Fair Isle jersey contemplated a plastic chrysanthemum, and rolled his eyes.

Caedmon, Rusty and Cecil had made peace over a coffee, and were discussing the staging of *Hamlet*.

'I've always imagined it,' said Rusty, 'played to Mozart in the Empire style with eagles and King Charles spaniels and *you know* the sort of thing. A Hamlet in frills. There's too little self-indulgence in the theatre; what art is it if not the art of self-indulgence?'

'I like Brian Rix,' said Caedmon.

Ethie listened, making herself titchy small, upset that no part had been found in the play for her.

'Can't I even be the nurse?' she wailed.

'Don't wail,' said Caedmon.

'There isn't a nurse in *Hamlet*.'

'There is too. I did it for G.C.E.'

Cecil smiled at the other men, invoking their contempt and allying it with his: 'You certainly did, didn't you?'

'Oh, you are *grotty*. I bet there is a nurse.'

'If there's a nurse, you can be her,' said Cecil generously, 'I can't say fairer than that, love.'

But the girl looked suddenly downcast: 'Supposing there isn't?' Pause. 'Oh, you *are* mean.'

News came about Rose-Marie's miraculous cure.

Cecil explained that Rose-Marie was in his mind for Ophelia.

Surely her recent experience must have left its mark.

Rusty: 'This whole business about Rose-Marie raises once again the old controversy about miracles. Well, of course the girl wasn't paralysed. We all know (don't we?) of adolescent girls with hysterical tendencies (of course we do) who feel the desire to punish an indifferent world by some dramatic gesture. What's that? Oh, well I know she *claims* to have been paralysed since childhood, but whom would you choose to believe, a dubious Indian upstart or the voice of reason and experience?

'Jesus? His miracles? Oh well, if you're a fundamentalist there's no arguing with you at all, but as I see it, changing water into wine and sticking ears back on to high priests, it's all a bit of a stunt, isn't it, rather cheap, don't you agree? There's only one miracle s'far as I'm concerned, and that's the miracle of faith. I'm lucky that way.'

When he reached home Cecil went straight to his writing den where he tore up his Great Novel (both pages of it) and threw it in a ball to the floor, where it struck poor Irving on the snout. The dog's hackles rose like the Pennines. Literature is a dangerous weapon.

'Page One,' Cecil wrote yet again at the top of the page and 'Quadrille, a Family Saga in four parts,' beneath Page One. This could only be followed by 'Part One', so carefully and with tremendous flourishes he inscribed 'Part One' under the title. Conscious of having made a promising start he sat smugly back in his chair and lit a rewarding Sobranie. Ten minutes later he crossed through 'Part One' and replaced it with 'Part the First'. Ten minutes later inspiration sang in his ears. The muse descended like a meteor.

'Oh what an infinite creature is man,' he wrote (in green biro), 'and how petty his aspirations.' There, temporarily, it rested. Considering it in some detail Cecil was delighted with the morning's work. There could be no denying the loftiness of those opening phrases. Why, they were positively splendid! Although he *was* a mite unhappy about the 'and'. After all if man was infinite and the 'oh' surely indicated certitude on *this* point, then 'but' would be more appropriate for his petty aspirations. However there was something a little ... well ... jejune perhaps or grating about the oh ... but ... sequence as it now stood. 'Oh, what a noble creature is man! Oh, how petty his aspirations!' That was it—or almost. After a second Sobranie the 'ohs' lost their aspirates, and became all the more striking for that. Perhaps there was more he could do along these lines. Why yes, of course there was! Hastily the biro went to work again : 'O noble man! O petty aspirations!' No verbs! (And they say that the novel as an art form is dead!)

Suddenly Cecil was seized with the deepest depression and the words 'O petty aspirations' tolled a heavy burden in his head. That's all 'Quadrille' was, all he was, nothing but petty aspirations in a decaying carcass. He stared at the paper for a long, long time, then watched as his hand (quite hairless, almost translucent) stretched out ineluctably, seized the corner of the page and—

Wendy Pakenham bounced into the room with nauseating bonhomie :

'Have you heard about Rose-Marie Farquhar? It's truly amazing. Mrs Connolly was on the phone and *she* says that he laid her out, naked as the day she was born and practised some kind of black magic on her. Brown anyway.

'Who *is* he? That's what I should like to know. And lunch is on the table.'

None of the members of the club ever saw the week-end joint at the Royal Fairway. It was sliced invisibly behind green baize doors, then doused in gravy. Just as well perhaps. Oh, but the catering was lavish. To set off the meat, sprouts came in oval vegetable dishes, faded green sprouts, stewing in their own juice. And then there were chips, whose bevelled edges reminded one irresistibly of those elaborate combs worn by Spanish ladies in their raven hair.

'Splendid chow!' The Admiral smacked his lips. He felt better. He had shared several whisky macs with the Vicar; he especially enjoyed drinking when the Church paid. The Church resented paying, but the Admiral was not very forthcoming; he would offer, but never insisted, which was very not British of him.

As always after a few drinks the veins in the Admiral's face resembled one of those marine sunsets upon which he had stared so passionately so long. For that matter the Vicar had a little cross at the top of his nose, the stigma of his profession.

In spite of the Admiral's notorious anti-semitism, Sammy and Solly sat at table with him. Every time they cut their meat, rings flashed and the Admiral winced. He didn't like it but there was little he could do—none of the other tables was vacant.

Jack Rubin had felt the call of duty and absented himself. On Saturdays business was brisk at the betting shop and his presence inspired confidence in staff and clients alike. Before he left the club however he had taken the Vicar aside and, while feeding the fruit machine absent-mindedly, addressed him thus:

'Fancy a bet today, Vicar?'

'My goodness me, what a suggestion!'

'The poor are always with us.'

'Always with you, perhaps. That's why they're poor.'

'Let us not get personal. You and I both perform a function. I promise rewards on earth, you in heaven.'

'I don't *promise*.'

'Well, to be frank, neither do I, but I knew as how the fabric of the church . . . that is to say business is business but friends are friends . . .'

'Your train of thought is oblique. Try to be more lucid.'

'Well then, in a word, Vicar, Tongue of Flame in the 2.45 at Windsor.'

'What about it?'

Jack Rubin made an expressive Jewish noise indicative of disbelief in another's lack of opportunism. It is impossible to spell, but is full of Ss and Hs and Ms. It riled the Vicar.

'I don't see how any of this concerns me.'

'But what a name, Vicar! And what a tip!'

'Do you mean to suggest that I should invest the Church's money . . .'

'Good, young apprentice. Strong stable whisper. One hundred to eight.'

'It's certainly an unusual name.'

'I was so pleased when you rang me the other day.'

'But that was . . . well, a whim.'

'A charming one. A man after my own heart, I thought then and I have had no cause to revise that opinion. Between you and me, it can't lose. Ideal distance; ideal going, and *further-more*—'

The Vicar winced. 'No really, I'm much obliged, but—'

'Half a dollar.'

'Half a dollar?'

'Two and six, Vicar, to you.'

The Vicar took a deep breath.

'On the contrary, five shillings.'

Three bells flashed up on the fruit machine. Money poured out. The Vicar clutched his heart. It was still ticking faithfully.

'You're on, Vicar, at S.P.' and Jack Rubin had emptied all the shillings into his purse, and left.

It was rather a sad Saturday at the Rubin's house.

'Isn't Daddy coming home for lunch?' asked Ruthie.

'Course he isn't'—David was the know-all.

'I wasn't asking you, I was asking Mummy.'

'There's a spider on my dish,' said Little Jo.

'Daddy *never* comes home on Saturdays. He's busy.'

'He does sometimes.'

'Doesn't.'

'Does.'

'Love each other,' said Miriam. She had Rachel on her lap and couldn't be bothered much with the others. 'You are getting heavy,' she said.

'I'm a tiger,' said Rachel.

'No wonder then.'

'Mummy's got a tiger in her tank' sang Hannah. It was almost her birthday, so she did a lot of singing.

'There's a spider on my dish,' said Little Jo.

'Don't be silly, Little Jo, it's lamb stew.'

'I bet Daddy's good at golf.' Ruthie snatched another sprout. ('Oooh,' said David outraged) 'I bet he's the best golfist there ever was.'

'Don't be silly, Ruthie,' said David. 'All the best golfists in the world are Japanese.'

'They aren't, are they, Mummy?'

'Yes dear, David's right. Daddy's good but—'

'David's *always* right. Why'm I not always right?'

'None of us is right all the time, darling.'

'Not even Daddy?'

Under her breath : 'Specially not Daddy.'

'There was a spider on my dish,' said Little Jo. 'There was stew too. The spider was in the stew. I ate it.'

'If you eat spiders you die,' said David with the authority of the unassailably right. At which Little Jo began to cry.

Jack Rubin had promised to return to the club-house as soon as the day's racing was over, but in his absence Solly had invited the Admiral and the Vicar to sit in, 'for a few hands' with him and Sammy. In front of a blazing fire, on a November afternoon when the rising wind was blowing tattered fragments of the night in from the West, what could be pleasanter or more jovial than a few hands of poker? The rough caress of green baize on calloused hands blistered afresh from the morning's golf, on whorled and toughened finger-ends. Those amiable, two-faced kings and queens, so much more portly and colourful than real life royalty, and the sly knaves, so much more charming. And the knave of hearts especially with his curly moustache and caterpillar eyebrows, why one would trust him with one's daughter, of course one would, how could one deny him? And the queens, un-sexed, mere blank-faced allegories of a comfortable life.

A coffee and a brandy and a cigar and the clink of silver on silver; men amongst men; no feminine wiles; no feminine jibes; no need to reassure or flatter or flirt; men amongst men; chaps together; comrades; what God had made men for.

Of course there were a few women, had to be, in the club, but they at least wore tweeds and heavy shoes. Tactful. Kept away from the poker tables. Read *Country Life* and the *Field*. Looked at the pictures of dead birds with dead eyes and tight lips and let the unassailable masculine caul wrap them around. If men had wombs, they would resemble club-houses of golf clubs on windy November afternoons.

But for the Vicar there was that sermon to be composed. His head was hazy with brandy fumes, words and phrases jumbled together in perverse association. 'I take as my text this morning . . . straight flush beats five of a kind . . . the true meaning of the parable of the mustard seed . . . all twos are wild . . .

hymn number ... three tens ... provide the flowers for ... double the pot.' And all the time the spectre of Tongue of Flame hovered above his head. How long to go? How would he know? One hundred to eight!

They had been playing fifteen minutes. The Admiral was down, the Vicar a few pence down, Solly was level and Sammy a comfortable sum to the good.

Then suddenly the door was flying open and Jessica stood framed under the condescending portrait of the last captain.

'Buzz Buzz,' muttered the Admiral angrily, 'buzz buzz, buzz buzz.'

The Admiral's wife with one scything sweep of her leg overturned the table, cards and stakes and all and Solly went down too; all that could be seen of him was hairy ankles. People crowded round.

'I've got it!' cried the Vicar, meaning that, in a flash, he had his sermon for the morrow. The discomforting of the money changers in the temple ... with modern parallels.

In the temple, that is to say in Jack Rubin's betting shop, were such elders of the village as Mrs Skullham, Mrs Connolly and Old Porson, the caddy.

It was 2.30. There was a rush to back the favourite, Spoonfed, in the handicap chase at Kelso and Jack Rubin had to help his counter-hands, Marcia and Whispering Tim. Mrs Connolly and Mrs Skullham, bet heavily on Spoonfed, Caedmon Tomlinson, who had 'just popped in' fancied Lady Jemima at 6–1, while canny Old Porson, had a shilling each way on Rusty Dusty, an aged, plodding cart-horse of an animal. It was Old Porson's habit, after earning 15/– on the golf-course in the mornings, to spend his afternoons in Jack Rubin's shop ekeing out his capital on arthritic and dilapidated animals which surprisingly often chundered into second or third place and his evenings in the public bar of The Raven, drinking himself into an oblivion so total that death no longer held any terrors for him. And yet there was *something* in the old fellow's red and yellow eyes, some flicker of, yes, greatness that had never been fulfilled, splendour that had never yet been put to the test.

The betting shop was tiled like a public lavatory and hung

with framed pictures of Mandarin and Golden Miller and Nimbus and Mont Tremblant and Arkle. Also framed in gilt a remarkable winning wager as:

> '5/- win Yankee 55/- invested
>
> | GRIFFIN | 100–6 1st |
> |---|---|
> | MOONMAN | 15–2 1st |
> | RICHMOND PRINCE | 6–4 1st |
> | HOWZAT | 3–1 1st |
>
> = £792 8s. 4d.'

However, since there was no evidence of the identity of the lucky punter and certainly no one in the village (except Whispering Tim) willing or able to work out the wager, to compute the profit, this decoration was of academic and aesthetic interest only.

There were also cuttings from the morning newspapers in which the astonishingly confident predictions of the racing journalists were displayed to popular ridicule and contempt. There was no excess of joy in such a place. Whispering Tim never smiled. Marcia's brow was low. Losing money is a serious business.

'They're off,' cried a voice in the loudspeaker. 'And on the off they bet 6–5 on Spoonfed, 4–1 Jynxy, 11–2 Lady Jemima, 10–1 bar those three.'

Old Porson mumbled in his throat. When Lady Jemima fell at the fourth Caedmon swore fiercely and Mrs Connolly glared at him—though to hear *that* word, *actually* to hear that *actual* word, thrilled her no end—and hissed: 'No wonder your horses fall if you speak to them in such tones.'

Caedmon marched briskly from the shop.

Jack Rubin was content. With Lady Jemima out of the running and Caedmon out of the shop he had no fears about the 2.30.

Of the nine runners only four were left standing with a mile to go. Jynxy (the top weight) was making the running followed closely by Spoonfed, who was being ridden by 'Puppy' Garston-Jones the celebrated amateur jockey and co-respondent, with Worsted third and Rusty Dusty a distance behind the others. But Old Porson seemed quite content as lust stirred in the rat-infested crevices of his cheesy brain and he let his wicked left hand tickle up Mrs Skullham in a truly inexcusable way. Instantly, (almost, one felt consequently) the favourite (upon whom Doris had invested ten bob) slipped up and the general gasp and communal agitation which followed this disaster found her some little distance removed from Old Porson, separated at least by Mrs Connolly. Having recovered her composure the outraged landlady shook her fist at the old grinning goat, who winked gaily back, a wink intercepted by Mrs C who naturally took it as being intended for her. She remained puzzled when no further overtures followed, and blushed a deeper yellow.

The favourite brought down Worsted, leaving Jynxy a distance clear of Rusty Dusty. The nasal tones of the man from the Exchange Telegraph remained cool and uncaring as the end of the commentary drew near.

'And with three to go it's Jynxy a long way clear of Rusty Dusty. He's over that one, and Jynxy's going even further ahead—it's Jynxy, Jynxy, now a clear furlong ahead as he comes to the second from home. Over it safely, pecks on landing but it's still Jynxy a long way clear with one to jump—' his voice rose a full octave—'telephonic interruption. There's a telephonic interruption from Kelso.'

There was silence in the betting shop. Mrs Connolly and Mrs Skullham left to play bridge and drink tea with the Tomlinsons. Old Porson remained; cool as ever, his fine white head was like Popocatepetl, dormant but not extinct and capped with snow, his pin-stripe waistcoat a relic of wealthier, less happy days.

'Result from Kelso coming through. 2.30 at Kelso . . . Rusty Dusty finished alone. I'll repeat that—Rusty Dusty finished alone, and the price of the winner, 20–1.'

Even then Old Porson barely smiled. But Jack smiled and said with admiration : 'Cunning old monkey ! It's either black magic or I'm a Christian.'

Which, since he was patently not, compels us to regard Old Porson with a new respect. A dangerous man to have around a golf course or a betting shop. A dangerous man to have anywhere for that matter.

Twelve minutes later in the Nasal Novices Hurdle (Div. II)

(Two Miles) at Windsor, Tongue of Flame, whose light chestnut coat glistened like butter, the muscles in whose neck were like wavelets on a shallow beach, whose eyes were both gentle and resolute, whose ears were pricked with courage and circumspection, whose head was fit to lead the cavalry against the French, had won by a whisker from Doubting Thomas, and the Vicar, who had crept in heavily disguised, uttered a shrill cry of joy. Ah! Ill-advised Vicar!

'You're mad of course,' said the Colonel to his wife.

'No darling I'm not.'

'Why didn't you lead a heart back to me then. Didn't you see me signal?'

'I hadn't any hearts left, darling.'

'I appeal to you,' said Gilbert turning to Mrs Connolly.

'Indeed you do, you handsome thing you,' cried that coy lady, chiming with laughter like a square mile of London churches at Christmas. Mrs Skullham's stitched mouth did not easily smile. 'That's game,' she said, 'game all.'

'Perhaps we should stop for a cup of tea,' murmured Celia Tomlinson.

'Well, it would be rather nice.' Mrs Connolly thought how much the knave of clubs reminded her of Eduardo, that recalcitrant Neapolitan gardener of hers, who was always pulling up her salvias.

'Certainly not!' cried the Colonel. 'It's by no means teatime. Give me the cards, woman.' He dealt them. They fell as follows:

North (Mrs Skullham)
S   QJ9754
H   97
D   876
C   A5

West (Celia Tomlinson)   *East* (Colonel Tomlinson)
S   62   S   K10
H   AJ432   (Timothy)   H   KQ65
D   KJ1042   D   AQ95
C   J   C   Q94

South (Mrs Connolly)
S   A83
H   108
D   3
C   K1087632

'Have you heard the latest about this Indian fellow? It's all *over* the village?' Mrs Connolly picked up her cards with distaste. Her host frowned heavily, a frown which had cost a thousand brewery workers their livelihood three days ago: 'I will not have gossip at the bridge table. One no trump!'

Mrs Connolly mouthed something to Mrs Skullham, something comforting no doubt and placatory, about the Allowances that one should make for Men. Woman-talk.

'Are you passing messages? Good Christ, I will not stand for this!'

'Gilbert dear,' said his wife gently.

'Don't Gilbert me!'

'I said "One no trump!" I'm waiting.'

'No bid,' said Mrs Connolly.

'No bid,' said Celia.

'What do you mean "No Bid"?'

'Oh, I'm sorry. Three no trumps.'

'What am I to make of that?'

'Well . . .'

'Have you any points?'

'Oh yes, plenty.'

'Well support me then.'

'Three no trumps in that case.'

Mrs Skullham tightened her lips: 'Am I to call, Colonel?'

'Do whatever you like woman, but do it quickly.'

'We are free with our advice this afternoon, aren't we? I shall call "No-bid" then.'

'Four No-Trumps,' yelled the Colonel.

'Good heavens!'

'Asking for aces.'

'Acis and Galatea,' murmured Mrs Connolly. 'She was turned into a pillar of salt and he brought her back to life and taught her how to speak like a Duchess, but every six months she had to go back to the Underworld on account of she looked back at Sodom and Gomorrow. A beautiful story. Not like so much of this sex and violence you see on the television every night.'

'Is that supposed to mean "No-bid"?'

'Oh, yes. I do beg your pardon.'

'I've got one ace,' said Celia.

'Then call five diamonds.'

'Five diamonds.'

Mrs Skullham passed.

'Five no trumps,' and Tomlinson folded up his cards in a gesture of finality.

'Six diamonds,' said his wife, 'that means one king, doesn't it?'

Tomlinson said in his very quiet and ominous distillery voice: 'Please stop and think for a moment. *Stop* and *think*.'

His wife did so, then repeated brightly and much more confidently, 'Six diamonds.'

'No bid,' from Mrs Skullman.

'Six no trumps. And please let well alone.'

'We haven't finished bidding yet.' Mrs Connolly took a coy glimpse at Celia's cards which she held carelessly horizontal and exposed to view, 'I think I'll double.'

'Oh dear,' said that lady, 'we're vulnerable and I really don't know what to do now. Help me, Doris,' and turned to Mrs Skullham.

'You could redouble if you think it's all right.'

'It doesn't seem very hospitable.'

'On the contrary.'

'Very well dear. I redouble.'

The Colonel empurpled. Timothy growled in his sleep. Mrs Connolly led conventionally the fourth highest of her longest suit (the seven of clubs).

Gilbert looked at his partner's cards.

'Good Christ!'

'Gilbert . . .'

'But you haven't got a—'

'Ssh. Don't give away any secrets.'

'I wish I'd never married you. We'd have stood a chance in diamonds.'

'You kept taking me out, dear.'

'What's the use? Half a crown a hundred. It'll have to come out of the housekeeping, that's all.

Mrs Skullham took the club trick with her ace, and, with an uncommon flair for the potentialities of the hand, led back the Queen of Spades. Declarer ducked, but had to go up with the King on the next round, when it was taken by Mrs Connolly's ace. He swore horribly and the situation was not improved by dummy.

'You're not making many tricks,' it said, 'I'm disappointed in you. Spades and Clubs were run off and the Tomlinsons were twelve down for a penalty of 6,400 points.

'I thought you were being a bit bold going slamming,' said Celia, 'you really mustn't lose your temper like that dear.' For a moment the Colonel was truly speechless, then, with red rage spots coming and going in front of his eyes, he gasped: 'Stop in clubs! You had no stop in clubs.'

'*You* chose no trumps, Gilbert.'

'That's a penalty of seventy,' Mrs Skullham said.

'Oh dear, what about Macfisheries? I haven't paid last week's bill yet.'

'At half a crown a hundred that's eight pounds, fifteen.'

'Oh gosh!'

'Each.'

'No trumps indeed!' But Gilbert was sulking. And his wife knew long before he handed her the money that the battle was over, the dead counted and buried, the treaty signed.

'We'll not play any more,' she said. 'We'll have tea.'

'In that case there's a little matter of a further fourteen points.'

It was paid without a murmur.

'Each.' Once again the wallet opened and closed with a snap like a shark's jaws.

'Well, that *was* fun,' said Mrs Connolly, 'no, just one lump for me, if you please, and a Kup Kake. And have you heard the latest about that nasty little Indian fellow . . . ?'

Albert Skullham had no cucumber sandwiches for his tea. Doris his dutiful daughter, had left him an iced bun, with finger-prints in the icing. She must know he didn't like iced buns, they gave him constipation. She *must*. What was she trying to do to him? It never occurred to him not to eat it. 'No pleasure in it,' he mumbled aloud, 'one day she'll find me dead, that'll teach her. No pleasure in anything anymore. All these girls showing their fannies,' he was watching a pop music programme on the television—'an ankle was all we hoped for when I was a lad. Now I can see it all, it doesn't do me any good. Meat market, that's all it is, meat market.'

A group of young ladies in their flimsies sang to Albert :

> 'If you're ready, baby
> When I'm ready, baby
> We'll be ready, steady, go all night.'

A disc-jockey in a blond wig started yapping about the Detroit sound.

'What's that? What's that?' The old man cupped a hand behind his ear, anxious lest he missed anything of importance. 'I've not forfeited my rights, I'm not dead yet. You'll get old, you'll get old,' he shouted at the disc-jockey, and craned forward in his chair, upsetting the milk jug.

He never noticed the milk, and lay back in his chair, dozing off into a world he understood. Carpentier was fighting tonight and he had sacrificed half his weekly wage to be there. The cheers and music and applause from the television became the noise of the excited crowd at the ringside. The boxers stepped into the ring. The crowd fell silent. Milk trickled down Albert's ankle.

Oh how Rose-Marie skipped! Not for years had Soft Meadows Cross seen such skipping. In her yellow frock, as she pirouetted down the Main Street she turned the fading air golden with the blaze of her going. Her legs, which had been clumsy appendages, hummed and whirred with life, spun like propellers. The cold wind snatched tears from her eyes as she danced, while along the street lace curtains bucked in sympathy. All the citizens stood back to see her pass. O, she danced! How she danced! And above her head a coronet of magpies fluttered and dipped.

At length she banged up against Cecil Sparks, who was looking hopefully for inspiration towards the westering sun.

'You seem happy,' he said, draining happiness from her like a mop, and indeed she now stood still as a mop.

'Mayn't I be?'

'Silly girl, of course you may, but . . .'

The trouble was that Cecil failed to recognise her in her dancing mood, and when she reassured him that, yes, she was whom she was, in spite of being how she was, he still remained puzzled.

'Yes, I know what you're going to say, Mr Sparks, and it is strange; truly.' And she told him how it had happened except that she didn't know how it had happened. And he offered her the role of Ophelia, which she accepted happily, instantly. And imagine her feelings, too, when just then, as the light was beginning to fail in the High Street, her mother and father drew up beside her in their maroon limousine. Again she danced and pirouetted especially for them, glancing at her lovely gleaming distortions in the hub-caps of the Rolls.

'Oh, darling!' cried her mother and stepped gingerly out of the car, showing long, elegant fetlocks.

'Mind the paint work!' cried her father.

But behind his glass partition Du Pont was impregnable. The chauffeur had short, red hair and a red, short neck. He wore gloves. He had never known the proximity of a woman. Under his gloves his hands were smooth. He had never wished to. He wore gloves even to clean the plugs of the car, which he loved. He never remembered his dreams. That is all there is to know about Du Pont, chauffeur to the Farquhars.

The three Angell sisters sat around Guru like frogs around a mushroom and asked him questions.

'What is the nature of the universal soul, Guru?'

'The universal soul is a weathercock.'

'How so?'

'Through it may be measured the force and direction of man's inclinations.'

'But who can measure the wind?'

'Only the subtlest anenometrist.'

'Are you one, Guru?'

'I am Guru.'

Around Genevieve's neck hung a daisy chain. The sap had

F

run out of the daisies which were dry and wilting. Their little centres were yellow like cheetah's eyes.

'Where do you come from, Guru?'

'India.'

'Tell us about India.'

'There are mountains and many wise men.'

'Are there elephants and magicians?'

'There are elephants.'

'I've always thought of India,' Tessa remarked, 'as being like a sort of giant pear hanging from the Asian tree, and Ceylon is this nasty little wasp.'

'Buzz buzz buzz . . .' And Abigail was a dainty little wasp for fully a minute.

'I should love to bathe in the Ganges,' said Tessa, 'and dance on top of Kanchenjunga, the holy mountain of the Himalaya range.'

The walls of the house creaked and there was a wailing in the chimneys.

'Why did you come here, Guru?'

'How long will you stay?'

'What will happen to us all, Guru dear?'

But Guru was brooding, and did not answer.

CHAPTER SIX

The Party · *Saturday Evening*

It's dark. Rusty and Caedmon have been walking and have mistaken the route. Now that he finds himself in the familiar purlieus of the village, Caedmon slackens his pace. The sky is a black ocean; the stars fishes' eyes.

'They are trivial people,' says Rusty, 'you realise just how trivial they are?'

'They're people. One can't expect too much.'

Rusty puts his hand on Caedmon's. 'What do they know of life? Or of anything. They're not like us. They just ... breathe in air and breathe it out.'

'You surely don't hold that against them?'

Doubtfully: 'Well, no maybe not, but they *are* trivial. I couldn't stand to be like that.'

'They're only human.'

'No one is indispensable.'

'You would dispense with them then?'

As they walk away from a big empty oak their voices fade and the outlines of their bodies merge with nature. Up in the oak Little Jasper, who had been bird-nesting (in an *oak*?) spits disgustedly, then sneezes.

And not far away in the gracious living area of a detached bijou residence:

'Darling, what shall we do? It's already quarter to seven and we invited them for half past six.'

'Never mind, my love,' said Dick.

'But isn't there *anything* we can do?'

'Would you like me to go out into the High Street and blow a trumpet?'

Thelma picked at the peanuts, eyed the gleaming tray of cloudy cocktails, tried not to catch the eye of Du Pont (earning extra money as a waiter for the Worsleys) but let her stare rest on his clean, white jacket which she found so relaxing. Behind the cocktails a brigade of bottles; above them a

Canaletto print; in front of them, scampi, a greyish, yellowish dip, small cheesey footballs, anatomised sardines, and tinned asparagus tips clutching prunes.

'Not one guest. Not *one*.'

'They don't mean it hurtfully.'

'But it hurts.'

Silently Du Pont, moving as mutely as his Rolls, his fascia smoothly veneered, the ticking of his clock (84 to the minute) barely audible, brought round the tray. Thelma waved it away.

'Not yet! Not yet!'

'Very good madam.' He coasted off.

'I begin to wonder what right we have to bring our baby into the world.'

'What do you mean, dear?'

'Well, how could he learn to respect those parents whom society rejects? We shall have to move. The humiliation!'

'Be patient, my love, it's only a party.'

'But it's *my* party!'

'There's still time.'

The door-bell rang. Off darted Thelma, her silk cocktail dress (mauve and peach whorls and very fetching) billowing graciously behind her like a puff of smoke.

'Well, well, well, mazeltov,' and he kissed her with humid affection. It was Jack Rubin.

'Ah, Mr Rubin,'—disappointment in her welcome—'come in, won't you?'

'Miriam sends her apologies, but the kids, you understand— little schnorrers!'

He took off an Alpine hat with a fish-fly in it and a pile of betting slips fell out of the lining. Thelma hastened to pick them up.

'No, let me,' and he bent down, explaining: 'Bad debts. You'd be surprised if I told you who these related to. The rich are always with us on account of they will not pay their losses.' And he put the slips securely into a crocodile skin wallet.

Thelma and Jack moved through to the gracious living area. On top of the television a plaster of paris fisherman dangled his rod over a doily. The plastic flower-arrangement had been specially dusted. A green-faced girl with red tits combined prurience and mysticism above the mantel, and simulated smoke rose from simulated, indestructible coal.

'Nice place you've got here,' said Jack, testing the curtain material between his fingers. Du Pont approached him.

'Why, it's the Fairy Snow Man already!'

'Really, Mr Rubin, you mustn't upset him.'

'When he's got the drinks? I should live so long!'

Thelma looked beseechingly at her husband who was holding out a hopeful hand. Jack took it and shook it. Dick smiled gratefully.

'You know Dick?'

'I should say I do. How's trade, eh? Still soaking the rich and prosecuting the poor?' This reference to a recent shop-lifting case was not well received.

'I'm not sure I like the tone of that question.'

'No offence taken, I hope. None intended.' Jack Rubin took a drink from Du Pont. The door-bell re-rang. Thelma lowered her head and simpered: 'You will excuse me.'

'My pleasure,' said Jack. Which was no less than the truth, when the door opened to admit the Vicar, looking extremely jolly and smart, and wearing his dog-collar more like a neck-lace than a halter.

'Why Vicar, how nice.'

'Yes indeed. Yes indeed.' Then with enthusiasm, 'Hello Jack!'

'Hello, Vicar, a hundred to eight, eh?'

'I know, isn't it thrilling? And so simple. You tell me what to back, I put money on it and you pay me.'

'Well, something like that.' Jack Rubin was charmed by such clerical innocence but sad, too, that, like all innocence, it was doomed to destruction. The Vicar ignored his host and hostess (not hard to imagine how galling for them) and inquired of Rubin:

'And what is tomorrow's tip? Something good, I hope?'

Jack was profoundly shocked: 'But, Vicar, tomorrow is Sunday.'

'And do not the horses run on Sunday?'

'I'm afraid not.'

'But that is ridiculous. They can't come to Church.'

'A noble animal the horse.'

'Ah yes, Mr Rubin, but the Church is for sinners. Why by the way do you never take a pew?'

'My religion, Vicar, is Christ's religion. What was good enough for him is certainly good enough for me.'

'But surely Christ was a Christian?'

'No, Vicar, to be accurate he was like yours truly a Yiddisher.'

'Good heavens, this certainly bears some looking into. I can see I shall have to consult my Bishop on this most cardinal point. My Bishop, now he, I hope, *is* a Christian.'

'Vicar, my sentiments entirely. I hope so too. But in this wicked world can one be sure of anything? The only Hebraic Bishop I ever knew came to a very sticky end—three years to be precise, and yet, as I said at the time, he was a big man, he needed two religions. And if one religion is the true religion why should not two religions be doubly true? I may not have much faith in my fellow-man but I truly have faith in mathematics. Ah, Vicar, the world is full of bigots. Give me another of those cocktails. Are they frum?'

All this while Dick and Thelma had been hovering around the two men, desperate to be included in the conversation and vastly impressed with its tenor. They were talking of bishops! And of religion! Mrs Worsley looked at her salon with new eyes; saw it peopled with the rich and the famous, the beautiful and the witty. Eighteenth century minds in slender tapering bodies. All that was best in home counties society. People who had shaken hands with Prince Philip. M.B.E.s and M.F.H.s. And she reclining . . . somewhere (she didn't have a chaise longue—*yet*!) while the throng of notables paid her extravagant compliments while—

The door-bell. 'It's me,' through the letter-box shouted the Macfisheries Man.

Guru found a humorous invitation card on the doormat. It had been there a long time.

'Why, that is an invitation to a party, Guru,' said Tessa, 'on Saturday nights it is the custom for people to give parties, but we don't go out to parties much.'

'I went to a party once,' murmured Abigail, 'there were only three people there and one of them died.' Genevieve wept. 'Don't cry, Genevieve, he died beautifully.'

'Of what?'

'Of disassociation. They gave us seedcake and raspberryade and we played "Up Jenkins!" but there weren't enough of us to make it work.'

'We go.'

'We do?'

'We never answered,' said Genevieve.

'We never do.'

'We go,' said Guru, 'since that is custom.'

'It only said "Respond if it pleases you",' remarked Tessa, 'and it didn't please us. We never opened it.'

'We go.'

'But Guru—'

Guru's eyes flickered dangerously like tracer bullets. 'We go *now.*'

The Macfisheries Man was ill at ease. He had neglected his vigil of the Angell Sisters to come to the Worsley's party. It had been a terrible mental tussle. Besides, his leg was still painful. Yes, his leg was very rocky, and the Worsleys (optimistically catering for a crowd) had removed all the chairs into the bathroom and on to the porch. The Macfisheries Man was also ill at ease that he was not a sophisticated guest at such functions. He seldom went to an At Home, so no wonder he did not feel it. He stood against the wall, half-leaning on the radiator (it took the weight off his leg), with an empty cocktail glass in each hand. Since Thelma was clucking around the other two guests, Dick found himself obliged to endeavour to entertain his chief rival in the harsh world of Soft Meadows Cross retailing.

'How's business?' he asked in a friendly sort of way.

'I'm afraid I can't possibly tell you that.'

'Oh.' A pause. Du Pont circulated with the tray of cocktails. The Macfisheries Man, hands full, was unable to help himself. His dilemma communicated itself to Dick who took the glasses out of his hands.

'Have a third cocktail?'

'Thank you. What are they?'

'I'm afraid I can't possibly tell you that.' Ha, ha, thought his host, I'll play it your way, if that's what you want. And added after a silence: 'You are standing very oddly.'

'That is because I have hurt my foot.'

'I am sorry you have hurt your foot. How did it happen?'

'I'm afraid I can't possibly tell you that.'

'Does it hurt very much?' inquired Dick, resolving that if ever the room should become more crowded, he would take the opportunity of treading on the injured extremity.

'Yes it does, some of the time.' Silence. 'And your feet,' he inquired, 'are they well?'

Worsley chuckled briefly: 'I'm afraid I can't possibly tell you that,' he said.

The procession of Guru and the Angell sisters from the Boggley Road through the village to the Worsley's was spotted first by Throggie, lonely in the clubhouse lavatory, then by the Admiral and his wife from the discreet windows of Mon Chalet. Telephone wires hummed. They were spotted by the early Saturday nighters at the Raven, and Old Porson stared long and hard at the little Indian Holy man whose eyes were like pincers. 'There's a man,' he said mysteriously to his reflection in the stout which had splashed onto the table, 'there's a man that a man might follow.' He did not, however, although many did join the procession that night. It was strange and marvellous how many gossips watched them pass (from behind curtains, through chinks in doors, peering out between the crochet-holes of prejudice, lifting aside the lace curtains of distaste) and, when it was reported that Guru and the girls were visiting the Worsley's, it was strange and marvellous how many remembered that they too had received invitations which they (fortunately) had not answered in case of (well) just such an eventuality as this . . .

And that is how the procession became a procession, and that procession was, roughly, the first sign of communal agitation, of general excitation, of the unprecedented atmosphere which was to be an essential ingredient in the simmering stock-pot of Soft Meadows Cross. A blackbird whistled a Dies Irae and the rain beat itself against the thatch of one of the few remaining Tudor cottages in the neighbourhood.

And a little brown man slapped his horny paddy-pads upon the tarmac and looked neither to right nor to left of him, until Abigail whispered that they had reached their destination.

'Oh no, sister,' said Genevieve, 'surely our destination is a long way distant?'

When the door-bell rang, and scuffling was heard outside, Thelma left the Vicar and Jack Rubin who had got round to discussing the London Underworld. Jack knew a lot of villains and was assuring the Vicar that they were at heart upright citizens; the Vicar was maintaining that the Bishops of his acquaintance were at heart downright villains. In such conversations the generalisation often has the ring of truth and the particularisation the taste of slander. But the generalisation is generally the slander, the particularisation the truth.

When Thelma opened the door she did not at first notice Guru (who was quite short in stature) and found herself face to face with the three Angell sisters.

'Why, what a surprise! she cried and added hastily, 'a pleasant one, of course.' Then spotted Guru : 'Oh,' and vaguely, much startled, 'you must introduce us.'

'Guru,' said Guru, putting his hands up to the lady's cheeks, 'lady, you live hard. Relaxation, meditation, *so* good.'

'Won't you come in?'

After this the hall filled rapidly with the good burghers of Soft Meadows Cross. There was a sight for Thelma! Never in her wildest dreams (after an evening reading Michael Arlen or 'Chips' Channon) had she imagined, never had she dared to hope . . .

There was Cecil Sparks, so mysterious, his black polo neck sweater decorated now with a silver crucifix and accompanying him dear, cultured Wendy Pakenham, so unselfish, of whom it was whispered . . . There was Mrs Connolly with the number five iron which served as walking stick and would fend off reluctant rapists, should she meet any. There, the Admiral, vinicund face empurpled by the chill evening air, and his wife, flaunting her ruler. Colonel Tomlinson had brought his wife and Rusty and Caedmon and Ethel. And ooh! there was the Air Vice-Marshall, and ah! the lady who interviewed drug addicts and paederasts on TV.

The molehill of coats on Thelma's bed became a mountain.

Du Pont's fins flashed, his tray was held aloft like a banner at Agincourt.

The bell!

It was the Farquhars, no less. They owned race-horses.

'How good of you to come! How truly kind! Let me take your musquash. The butler will give you 'un queue de cock!'

'But it's Du Pont.'

'Oh, of course, how stupid of me.' Thelma's sunshiney face darkened with anxiety. 'You didn't *mind*, did you? He said he had the evening free, and so of course I—'

'He who steals my chauffeur steals trash,' said Farquhar, making a rare literary quip, but he didn't seem pleased.

Thelma took two steps into the living-room (one day she would have a *dinette*, and a *sun-room*, and—even—a *gun-room*) and then the door-bell rang once more. Mrs Skullham and others.

'Come in! Come in! Dick, come and welcome your guests. Oh, where *is* the man? May I call you Bill and Elsie? Oh, Frank and Edith then. How good to see you.'

In the centre of an awe-struck circle stood little Guru, beaming, which was uncharacteristic.

'How do you find our country and our remarkable climate, Mr ... er ... ?' inquired Wendy Pakenham, spacing the syllables with thoughtful condescension.

'Guru,' said Guru.

'I beg your pardon?'

'I think,' said Farquhar, 'he said Uhuru which means Freedom.'

'Oh,' said Wendy and floundered rather. 'Britain, you know, has the oldest working democracy in the world. If we wish to express an opinion, any opinion, we can go to Hyde Park Corner and—'

Du Pont offered Guru a cocktail. Guru took it and sipped it and spat it out. Farquhar, imagining this to be a local custom of ... wherever the devil it was the little brown chap came from ... followed suit and soon several of the guests were smiling, bowing and spitting out cocktail.

'Oh,' cried Thelma, running up distraught, 'what is wrong with our lovely cocktail? It came out of the *Sunday Times Colour Supplement*, you know. They said that Princess

Margaret liked it. Perhaps I didn't get it quite . . .'

The door bell.

'Oh my goodness me!' and she was away.

Said Mrs Connolly: 'In my humble opinion the cocktail is quite delicious.'

Guru's eyes snapped like tiger's teeth and he made for the formica-covered bar.

'Come in, come in, make yourselves at home! Welcome to Thelma's salon! Coats over there in my boudoir!' It was Rose-Marie (whose changed status was not remarked by the hostess) and her friend Victoria Bushey, dark-browed and intense.

'How nice of you to come, and did you bring your brother?'

'Alas, no,' replied Victoria, an only child.

The Tomlinsons were talking to the Admiral's wife about the servant problem.

'There's no loyalty any more, that's the price we have to pay.'

'Not the only price either, by George!'

Jessica quite agreed. 'I'd change places with my Mrs Hessian any day. Two days a week off and I'd like to know when I last had two days off.'

'No loyalty. How different from the 'thirties.'

'I mean she gets board and lodging and eight pounds a week and won't allow me to wash up the knives.'

Tomlinson looked up sharply: 'Eh, what's that?'

The Admiral's wife was surprised herself at what she had said. With the ruler in her right hand she slapped the knuckles of her left hand. 'Silly me. But really servants are the limit.' This was a view halloo to Mrs Connolly who caught the scent and came galloping up, 'cross brush and 'cross briar.

'Exactly what I always say.'

'What?'

'Servants.'

'Oh. Yes.'

'Eduardo, for instance. My Neapolitan. Do you know how he spends his time? (And my money come to that).'

'Woman-talk!' Disgruntled, Colonel Tomlinson went off to swop man-talk with the Admiral who quite understood. 'Buzz-buzz,' he said, and smiled a welcome.

'He will pull up my salvias.'

'You don't say?'

'I most certainly do. No sooner do I put another lot in than—'

'I'm surprised you persevere,' said Jessica.

'One must be very patient.'

'Why we put up with it I don't know. It's not just incompetence, it's malice pure and simple.'

'Simple, yes. Not so sure about pure. What with that and the electricity company, life is fast becoming intolerable. You've heard about my pylon?'

'Yes,' said Mrs Connolly severely, 'and mini-skirts!'

Celia brightened: 'There I *am* with you'—and cast a look at Ethel—'showing their bottoms for all the world as if—'

'I know what I'd do if I were a young man.'

'My goodness yes. I have told her, but she won't listen to her mother, of course.'

'That would teach them some modesty!'

'I'll say it would!'

Stretching across the room the Admiral's wife brought down her ruler on the back of Ethie's thighs.

'Leave her alone!' cried Celia Tomlinson, outraged and reserving the right to thrash her own family.

Cecil Sparks was talking to Rose-Marie and Victoria was horning in. Rose-Marie had been explaining (as she did to everyone she met) how Guru—over there—toying with the bottles—had mended her legs, and Cecil had seemed impressed but sceptical.

'It's psychosomatic,' he said.

'It is?'

'Yes indeed. Your legs were always all right, but you just didn't believe it.'

'You really think so? They did hurt awfully, actually.'

'You mean, you thought they did.'

Victoria said: 'You can explain anything that way.'

Sparks ignored her: 'Alternatively, it could possibly have been a Freudian reaction to infantile repression or a traumatic sexual experience when young.'

'I'm sure it wasn't that,' said Rose-Marie, shocked.

'You've read the case history of Little Hans, of course?'

'We had to read Freud at Roehampton,' added the Doctor's daughter, 'even the dirty bits.'

'Oh yes. Of course I intend to incorporate a great deal of Freudian and Jungian theory into my novel.'

Victoria hadn't known. 'Ooh, are you writing a novel?'

'He's been writing it for quite a while now. It's a Saga, isn't it?'

'Well yes, it is in a way, but it's not old-fashioned at all. All that Galsworthy crap. Oh no, it's intended to portray the shallowness and emptiness of present-day bourgeois existence.'

'Can't be shallow *and* empty, can it?'

'I beg your pardon?'

Victoria was a logical girl, as are so many unprepossessing girls. Logic cannot explain why they should not be beautiful. So much the worse for them, so much the worse for logic. But logic does impart to a girl its own fascination. Victoria, logical as she was, represented a challenge. It was not welcome. Angrily Cecil turned to the less demanding and more appealing figure of Rose-Marie.

'I must read you a chapter or two some afternoon.'

'You're always saying that, but you never do.'

'Well the fact is that I want it to be perfect or—because I mustn't be arrogant must I, duckie—as perfect as I can make it before I share it with anyone.'

'Honestly, I can't wait,' gasped Rose-Marie. Cecil Sparks's crucifix jangled against his wishbone.

Caedmon and Ethie were listening to Rusty Motorcade expounding on the colour question. He was impressive.

'The first thing to remember is that we're all the same under the skin. Oh, it's never been proved of course, I know that, but it's an assumption one has to make in dealing with this whole tortuous subject. Otherwise one lays oneself open to the whole Riefenstahl thing, you see. No, as I say, I assume that, and then go on from there.'

'Where to?' asked Ethie reasonably.

'Well now. This is a small crowded country and that's a fact of life, whether you like it or not, and we're not exactly riding along on the crest of the economic wave, are we? I mean how would you feel if, after thirty years faithful service in the mines, you were made redundant and then found all the other jobs had been taken by the blacks? Then there's the housing problem; just because these foreigners are prepared to live in crowded squalor (and I don't except the Irish), lowering the value of property, urinating on the stairs, spreading disease and cooking these extraordinary meals—well, I mean, you can imagine, can't you, the effect this has on people who've been waiting for a house for ... Well the thing is one's got to be practical, and however liberal one's attitudes the fact remains that they aren't the same as us, are they, I mean, how could they expect to be when they've so little experience of civilisation and democracy? Mind you, I don't hold it against them. On the contrary we'd be the same if we were in their shoes, only, of course, we'd still be white.'

'They don't always wear shoes,' said Caedmon looking in the direction of Guru.

'My point exactly. The bare-foot syndrome. No, the point is this, it's not fascism to want to send them all home. It's ...'

'Democracy?' suggested Ethie. Rusty Motorcade beamed. She felt herself opening like a cabbage in the glow of his approval.

'Exactly,' he said.

'Are you by any chance a Scrabble player?' the Colonel asked Farquhar.

'Not quite my line, old chap.'

'Oh, I expect you play Monopoly then. And talking of Monopoly, I always wondered (and perhaps you can tell me) what *is* the Community Chest?'

'That is'—Farquhar nodded in the direction of the Admiral's wife—'or would be. So they say.'

'Pay a ten pound fine or take a chance, eh?'

'Precisely.'

'I'd pay the fine.'

The men chortled, boys together chuckling over an illustration in the biology text book. Earthworm, rabbit, Admiral's wife. Formaldehyde. Nice to be boys together. Tomlinson pushed his way over to the Admiral.

'How's life up at the Club?'

The Admiral tried a cute look. 'No better for some of the riff-raff who're taking over the village.'

Tomlinson raised his distinguished eyebrows and pointed his nose in the direction of Guru.

'Not only him,' replied the sailor, 'although, God knows we can't be doing with too many of that stamp.'

'I expect God already knows. Try telling Buddha. Who did you mean then?'

'The . . .' And the Admiral made a long nose with a curved finger.

'So bloody rich, that's the trouble.'

'So bloody *English*.'

'Well exactly. Chosen race indeed.'

'Bad as the Welsh.'

'Oh, I wouldn't say that. The Welsh stay in Wales. Some of them anyway.'

'Not enough.'

'There I agree with you. Horrible little men singing all the time.'

'The Jews?'

'The Welsh. One simply doesn't know where to turn.'

'Bloody bad sailors.'

'Are they? The *Welsh*?'

'And the Jews, come to that.'

'Hope we don't.'

'What?'

'Come to *that*.'

'So do I. *So do I*.'

'And as for these long-haired—'

'You mean at the Café Cappriccio?'

'I do indeed.'

'There was some kind of a riot going on there this morning. Crockery flying about. Disgraceful.'

'Really? Well, that won't do at all.'

'Indeed it won't. Indeed it won't. Can I be confident of your support in any action I feel compelled to take?'

'Yes, of course.'

'Good. I shall set the ball in motion then.'

'Ball rolling.'

'I beg your pardon?'

'Or wheel in motion.'

'What?'

'Mixed metaphor.'

'Oh. I wouldn't know about that.'

'I thought you were a Scrabble-player.'

'No.'

'Monopoly?'

'No.'

'Oh.'

Celia Tomlinson and the Macfisheries Man were uncomfortably close. The crush had forced the latter to the wall and there he stood with the broad green leaf of a rubber plant sprouting between his legs like some exotic African disease. For some minutes they faced each other in silence, each aware of the unpaid account in Mrs Tomlinson's name, neither able to broach another subject since the debt was really all they had in common.

Eventually the lady opened her bag and took out her cheque book.

'Would you take a cheque?'

But at that moment their host came by.

'What's this? What's this? For services rendered, eh?'

'You may live to regret that remark,' snapped the Macfisheries Man.

'I may,' Dick agreed, stepping heavily on the other's injured foot.

Angrily Celia pushed her way towards a big tweed back, which might have belonged to Gilbert. She intended asking him to take her home. Then they could play Scrabble. She tapped on the back, which failed to respond. She knocked harder.

'Are you my husband?' she inquired. The Admiral turned round and snapped:

'Talk sense, woman! We're both married.' Then the sight of her pretty little duckies made him hesitate. With a touch of pathos in his voice he murmured: 'Not that I don't appreciate the offer.'

Guru had taken over the bar; was mixing occidental drinks with oriental concentration.

'Oh, how sweet of you!' carolled Mrs Worsley, 'really you shouldn't bother, although no doubt you have an exciting eastern surprise for us. How thrilling!'

Guru's eyes were like sunflower seeds, and he seemed to

grow taller. The room grew silent and all faces (sunflowers) turned towards him. He stirred a jug and added a little white powder from an envelope. But it was really his eyes which . . .

The cocktail fizzed and bubbled. Thelma peered in.

'My, how simply *mar*vellous! Whatever can be in it?'

'Goat's testicle, 'said Guru. Colour drained from his hostess's face. 'Taste!' he cried imperiously. The etiolated lady raised a limp hand, feebly dissenting.

'Drink! Is not Madhu nor Aireya nor Sara nor Assawa, but drink!' At Madhu he put the cocktail to her lips, at Aireya he tipped it, at Sara she choked and at Assawa she spluttered. In Thelma's salon the silence became complete, like locusts going. Guru ladled out the concoction generously into glasses which Du Pont distributed. Only Thelma, clutching her freckled throat with one hand and a plaster swan with the other, was aware of the ingredients, and she was too faint to speak. The swan plunged to the ground and shattered.

'Drink,' cried Guru, 'for Nundi and Shvetaketu and Babhravya and Dattaka and Chanayana and Swarnanabha and Ghotakamukha and Gonardiya and Gonikaputra and Kuchumara! Empty your glass for Vatsyayana!'

This, the longest speech Guru had made since his arrival in Soft Meadows Cross, was also, unquestionably, his most influential.

Everyone drained his glass.

Epexegetically the cocktail was like a python uncoiling itself slowly in one's guts. First it was as if the python were breathing heavily, emptying and replenishing its lungs at the expense of one's own; the heat of its body caused a somnolent kind of callor to permeate the stomach. At the same time the dryness of its squarrose body rubbed viciously against the soft lining of the belly. Then it began to uncoil. Phew!

There wasn't room for it to uncoil. As it stretched its full length its head was forced up through the oesophagus into the brain itself where it breathed its flatulent fumes directly (it seemed) into the nerve centres. As for its tail that was earthed away down in the bowels, where it wriggled and twitched among the coprolitic rubble, loosening and dislodging and creating chaos generally. The usual avenues of respiration were

G

almost completely blocked by the serpentine coils—hence the puffing and panting and calling for air that turned the room into a black hole of Calcutta. Naturally the size of the reptile and its restlessness had the effect of contorting its several land-lords—hence the leaping up and down in the air on all sides.

'Myself, I wouldn't trust the Indians further than I could spit 'em,' gasped the Admiral, 'but they make a bloody fine cocktail.'

If on a windy day you watch the sea breaking on a pebble beach you become aware after a while of a certain lunatic rhythm, a certain pattern in the sequence of events. A few moderate waves will be followed by a series of larger crests which in their turn lead to what fishermen improperly call the 'seventh' wave. This wave is catastrophic, and leaves the sea (with a great sucking and heaving) tired and wan. Thus the Worsley's living-room after Guru's cocktail had been drunk. And suddenly, it was hot.

Dick flung open the window, Thelma blew down the front of her dress, the Macfisheries Man threw off his jacket.

Heat flowed out into the garden, and the coolth that replaced it was not cool for long. Only Guru seemed unaffected by the stifling humidity, and he was smiling benignly about him as if all the guests were his family, which of course they were. Oh, he was a superior paterfamilias! Transfixed by his quivering eyes, people began to behave oddly.

The schoolmistress, Victoria Bushey, had deep, deep pools of unexplained grey beneath her eyes, lines etched above the nose. Her black hair was swept back behind and above her ears like a gorse bush. Rusty Motorcade put his hand on her upper arm and quoted:

'In pe d'un Papago s'allieva un'Oca,
In pe d'un Cagnolatto
Ghe un Porchetto zentil, che basa in boca,
Lascivo animaletto.'

'Don't be silly,' said Victoria, 'I've been to Majorca too, you know.'

'Let's have some music!' cried one of the guests, switching on the radio.

'I'm an ordinary man,' sang Rex Harrison.

'Ooh!' yelled Cecil Sparks, 'listen to her then, isn't she a caution?'

Jessica shut it off. Cries of: 'Leave it on!' 'We want to dance!' and 'Show us your legs, lady!'

'Maybe I will show you my legs,' said she severely, 'and maybe I won't, but I'm sure as hell going to sing.'

'You're beautiful,' Wendy Pakenham told Cecil, 'and he's beautiful too. I can keep it to myself no longer. I may be just a stupid middle-aged woman but I want you both.'

'Silence everyone. I am going to sing a song of my own composition entitled "Little Billy Bender".'

The Admiral's wife sang. Her voice was perhaps a little shrill, but mostly they listened:

> 'Little Billy Bender
> Hadn't got a penny
> When he came to my house
> I wouldn't give him any.
>
> Little Billy Bender
> Hadn't got a tanner
> They told him "Take your thingy out
> And use it as a spanner!"
>
> Little Billy Bender
> Hadn't got a shilling
> Said he'd earn it easily
> If only Poll was willing.'

Mrs Connolly began lifting the bottles off the shelf above the bar and letting them drop and splinter. The Vicar was licking up the liquid and picking cut glass off his tongue.

'Don't think too harshly of me,' he kept on saying, 'I don't make a habit of this, you know.'

It became apparent that the party might develop in many directions.

'Little Polly Pepperpot
Went and told his mother
She cut his little thingy off
And gave it to his brother.

Sir William Bender KCB
Renowned throughout the nation
Is now a striking tribute to
Infantile Castration.'

The applause was sparse.

People walked about distractedly, their hands in front of their faces. Some stood on tip-toe eructating; others crouched down and farted.

Doris Skullham stood facing the wall, swayed slightly, and looked at herself in a mahogany-framed mirror. 'That picture is crooked,' she said, 'An' it keeps getting crookeder. The least one should ask of a painter is that he paints his stupid picture straight. Why doesn't he keep it still?'

'It's an action painting,' said Cecil Sparks.

'What's that? It's a horrible painting anyway'—and she stuck out her tongue at it. 'Ooh! Did you see that? It insulted me! It ins—I will not stand for that; I tell you I will not'—and she tore it off the wall and dashed it to the ground. As she stood over the broken mercury, splintered segments of her face lay on the floor. She sat down and tried to piece them together : 'I feel quite shattered,' she mumbled.

'The thing about parties,' Rusty Motorcade was saying, 'is that they are a desperate attempt to find an answer to mankind's solitary condition. Every party is, in effect, an orgy, by which I mean a merging of personality, a pilgrimage via drunken forgetfulness and promiscuity to the promised land where everyone is faceless, where the great universal consciousness hangs over us like the moon. But the basic objection of anthropomorphic monotheism to sex of any kind is—'

A salted cashew nut hit him on the back of the neck. It stung. He turned sharply. The Macfisheries Man was using his braces as a catapult and Wendy Pakenham was handing him ammunition, nut by nut. They made a thoroughly abandoned twosome.

'Oh really,' Rusty shouted, 'be your age.'

'Daddy, Daddy, I don't want to go to bed,' cried Wendy, tucking her skirt into her knickers and sticking her tongue out at him.

'Don't mind him,' said the Macfisheries Man limping over to her, 'I shall always remain faithful to you.' But Wendy knocked him down.

'More of that cocktail and quickly,' cried Gilbert waving a menacing shoe at Du Pont. 'I am one of the leading exporters in the country, I'll have you know.'

Du Pont filled his glass.

'I could have a dozen OBEs if I were to raise my little finger. I supply Her with gin, you see.'

'Don't boast, Daddy, please,' begged Ethie.

'I'm a frequent visitor at the Palace. I have breakfast with David Frost and I'm quite rude to him sometimes.'

'Daddy, *please.*'

'Gilbert!' cried his wife sharply, 'that's enough now!'

'Suddenly'—and Ethie's nose began to run—'you don't seem like my Daddy any more.' Her father began rumpling her clothing as if she had put the idea into his head.

'What's *happened* to him, Mummy, have you ever seen him like this before?'

But the unnatural mother merely pinched her daughter's nose and giggled: 'Leave me, darling, I want to be alone.'

'Mummy!'

'I'll have her.' And there was the handsome American Air Force Man from the Latchvine base diving out of the clouds with the sun behind him. And a Spitfire on his tail.

'Pat,' yelled Candida, training her gun-sights and firing a short burst, 'I'm your date.'

'Baby, we've all got our problems.' And with his hand on Ethie's tail fin he navigated her to the punch-bowl.

'God bless America, Land of the Free!' cried Ethie.

'Don't blame me, ma'am, I voted Democrat.'

Suddenly Celia Tomlinson collapsed on the floor. Dick proposed giving her the kiss of life: 'I'm a married man.'

'Go ahead, be my guest,' said the lady's husband, at which the lady herself sat up suddenly wide awake and appalled at their brief exchange.

Meanwhile the Angell sisters had got hold of Caedmon and

were wiping his eyes with anything that came to hand. Wisps of gauze, sleeves of dresses, curtains, the lining of the Macfisheries Man's jacket.

'Girls, girls, what are you doing?' asked Mrs Connolly in her customarily nosy way. It was a strange spectacle.

'He says he's got something in his eye.'

'We think it's a mote.'

'It's all red and swollen.'

'It's like sunset at sea.'

'It's so sad.'

'Perhaps we should loosen his clothing.'

'Ooh yes, let me.'

'Let *me*.'

They got his trousers open and delved around. In vain Caedmon tried to make himself understood; there was nothing wrong with him at all; nobody would listen. And the Macfisheries Man watched, taut with jealous frustration. He cried:

'My eyes hurt something awful,' but nobody cared.

Guru made more cocktail. It was seized upon and swallowed with enthusiasm. The party got under way.

To Albert Skullham in front of his television, the cries of the party guests were a faint and soothing accompaniment to the clever juggler who kept spinning those clubs or apples or saucers or whatever they were. Although Albert was too deaf to recognise the voices from the party next door, the buzz of them, the distant laughter, was a comfort and a consolation. He felt less lonely.

All the same he was somewhat bothered by his daughter's absence. She had not warned him that she was going out, and such sudden alterations to his routine disturbed him, well, of course they did, and she had said specifically when challenged that she would be back in time to boil him an egg for his supper. Jugglers were all very well, but a man needed to be fed, and with every minute that passed his anxiety, for himself rather than for her, increased.

The juggler juggled—a hunchback juggler, funny, you didn't see many of them these days—the party hummed and tinkled until finally the old man could wait no longer. It was not such a challenge the boiling of an egg and the making of a piece of toast and the slicing of it into soldiers and the heating of the milk for a milky drink. When she made it, she always contrived to produce on the top of the cup, skin which stuck to his lips as he drank, clung like the tail of a determined mermaid— horrid! There should be no skin on the milk tonight.

He pushed aside the coffee table on which lay the remains of the iced bun. He wedged the rubber tip of his stick against the chair-leg and levered himself upright. (The juggler un- concernedly continued.) He made his painful way into the kitchen.

Found an egg, a brown one—*she* always kept the brown ones for herself—spooned it into a saucepan which he filled with water. *Salted!!* He hummed to himself as he unwrapped the sliced bread. Bread?—he'd never call *that* bread! Bread? Blow yer nose on it! Hummed to himself:

'There's a little white cottage perched high on a cliff
Which I'm yearning and longing to see,
At the end of the day seems to stand there as if
It were waiting and longing for me.'

Would need butter for the bread and a knife to spread it, and a saucepan for the milky drink. What a lot to remember! And oh, the strain on his poor old feet!

What next? Oh sit down, that next! Nowhere to sit. No time to sit. He heard his stomach bubbling like a cauldron; acid, too much acid. Must eat. Must light the gas; the egg must be boiling while he was busy with the rest. The full five minutes this evening, none of that runny white, like snot . . . Skin on the milk and iced buns and runny eggs . . . a crash and a tinkle from the party next door, as if someone had broken a mirror . . . bad luck for seven years if they had.

'And the nearer I get on my long journey home
To my heart brings a joy so divine . . .'

The matches were there and turn on the gas, hiss, hiss, remem- ber those snakes in the basket in Bengal, how they hissed, and that stupid, *stupid* young subaltern, what more could he have done, what more *could* he have done? And light the match, there the bugger, it had snapped and was on the floor, still alight. He put down the stick and cautiously lowered himself.

'And the joys left behind and the love I shall find
In that little—'

Crash! His feet were simply not up to it and his stick had gone slithering way, way across the floor. What a wide expanse of floor when you were on it! Military two-step! There was the match! He had put his hand on it, put it out, silly! It would have gone out anyway.

Well, he couldn't get up, knew that without even trying!

Hiss! Bengal. A nice, but *stupid* young man. Just wait till she ... nothing else for it. Funny smell though. Smelt like chutney.

'And the joys left behind and the love I shall find
In that little white cottage of mine.'

The floor was cold. Quite soothing. And applause from the television. Well danced! Rest his cheek for the minute. She'd not be long. Pity about the supper though. He was hungry. And she'd never let him try again, not now. Yawn. Big yawawawn. Cough. More like a choking fit. Better now. Sleepy though. Hiss. Smell of Bengal. Martha. Sweet smell of Martha that first ... little white cottage of ... laughter ... away we go ... such a storm, such a rough sea ... little white ... toast ... rather have a brown one any ... juggler ... chutney ... sleepy-time-girl ...

The death by misadventure of an old widower in the home counties is of little importance in the scheme of things. Old men will die. Only by failing to die would Albert have achieved what aways escaped him in his lifetime, notoriety of any sort—but Albert was mortal.

Caedmon lay naked on his back exhausted from the struggle. The three Angell sisters crouched over him blowing on his bare chest. He would have moved, but with Rusty Motorcade's knees heavily upon his biceps he was pinioned as conclusively as a butterfly in a show-case. He was very beautiful. It was possible to trace a line from the upper arm, outside and round the breast, into the navel, and then up the other side, a line already etched by sinew and muscle and bone in strict and perfect opposition. Genevieve traced such a line. Caedmon squirmed. The tuft of hair under his arm seemed almost the colour of platinum, the texture of velvet, and his flesh was full of juice. Cecil Sparks peeped from a distance, chewing a mauve lip with jealous, ochre teeth. Jack Rubin also watched. And his mind, Jack's amiable, forthright mind was flooded with nostalgia for what he had never known. The figures of his dumpy wife and amiable, chattering children receded, became mechanical, while in the forefront of his vision arose the image of a young man in P.V.C. . . . Nothing would be the same again. He glanced at Guru. Guru nodded.

But Cecil snapped: 'The hell with it!' and turned away. The lovely Candida was waiting, took his hand and bit it. Cecil felt a pleasant quivering in his loins. Manly. He almost felt manly. As for Caedmon: 'The hell with it!'

A rather less idyllic disposition of limbs was apparent in the fireplace. To assign limbs to their proper lease-holders was almost impossibe. One arm, a little loose-fleshed, seemed to belong to the Admiral's lady. At least the hand still clasped her ruler. And a leg which was booted and suspendered in a transatlantic way could surely have only been a USAF leg. For the rest silk and nylon, buttocks and breasts, ears and toes, rose and fell, heaved and panted, most unattractively.

Victoria Bushey, assailed from behind by an invisible—to her —satyr (the Admiral, breathing heavily), was barking aloud from the *Chambers Encyclopaedia* (which she clasped in front of her) the section on Attila the Hun, while Ethie was chasing Rusty round the sofa touching him, while he cried:

'No, that's naughty! No, really, you go too far! Ooh! Please! Not there! Not *there*!'

The Vicar, much moved, was consoling Doris Skullham for the broken mirror, but his big, blue eyes coursed round the room like whinnying dogs in a hare-filled wood:

'Of course I've never been one of those churchmen who— see there!—but the dividing line between social responsibility and individual—good heavens!—Even I myself at times—no, that is *too* much—and seventy times seven is an arbitrary figure—woof woof! Woof woof!'

'For my part,' said the Mayor of Gruntham coolly (he had heard that there was free booze and just happened to be passing), 'I don't know what's got into you all. Irresponsible and childish behaviour, I call it.' But then unexpectedly he exposed himself, which weakened his argument no end.

The Farquhars and the Tomlinsons, turn and turn about, were bouncing up and down on the sofa, whose springs sang a Kyrie Ellison, but Solly Schneider led a splinter group upstairs and organised on the landing a game of nude grandmother's footsteps. Thelma, Wilfred, the Church Organist, and a handful of others played, and Mrs Connolly was a coy grandmother. Oh, what a pile of lace and wool and whalebone!

And Rose-Marie stared out into the night so full of happiness that she felt she would burst and scatter a new constellation of stars into the sky. She, she alone, was the expanding universe (and how it would expand!); she, she alone, was the big bang. Bang! She, she alone? She turned her elegant head so that her hair was flung like spray across her figurehead, and looked across the rude room to where Guru sat cross-legged under a fine Vernon Ward. She smiled at him, but he didn't seem to notice. He looked tired. For a moment she thought that the fire in his eyes had burned itself to cinders. But then majestically he roused himself and managed some kind of a smile in return.

'No wonder you're tired,' Rose-Marie said quietly, 'it must be exhausting putting the world to rights.'

CHAPTER SEVEN

The Dust · *Saturday Night*

The orgy burned itself out. So repressed were the good citizens of Soft Meadows Cross by decades of straitened lace and bound hide that the climax came swiftly and the pleasure was brief. By three in the morning the party was over. One by one the guests pulled themselves together, reassembled their limbs and adjusted their clothing, staggered into the rain and tramped the sad crusade home.

Gears shrieked like banshees and gateposts wilted. The Macfisheries Man, his foot stiff and sore, rode his bicycle into a different ditch and lay amongst the festering vegetation. Familiarity breeds content. He was comfortable in his ditch. He murmured sweet nothings to the wild life.

As the guests left they threw distasteful glances at Guru, who was still sitting, pensive and cross-legged on the floor. They were not grateful for the pleasure he had afforded them. People are grateful to those who awaken their consciences, before their real benefactors. The Stafford Crippsesses before the Marie Stopesesses. The Angell sisters collected Guru and took him home. They at least were grateful.

'You have expanded our horizons,' said Tessa, 'you have made us aware.'

'Through you death has become a guest in my house; no longer a thief in the larder,' said Abigail inconsequentially. She was a voracious reader of Emily Dickinson.

But Genevieve just wept.

The Vicar laughed as he climbed into bed, but his laughter had a strident note, close to hysteria. The bedclothes felt clammy, and the pillow was hard as a rock. A small covey of rats disturbed by his inquisitive toes, scuttled for shelter under the mattress. The darkness was cold as religion. The Vicar forgot to wind his alarm clock.

And Doris Skullham smelt the gas as she unlocked the front door. 'Oh, the gas bill!' she thought and simultaneously: 'Oh,

—Dad!' As she flung open windows and entered the kitchen she knew what she would find, what she would have to live with.

She didn't see him at first, but felt him with her toe and looked down. His dear face was dirty from the kitchen floor. The bottle of milk stood on the kitchen table. She poured milk over his face. She salved his face. He *was* dead.

She shouted for the Macfisheries Man who didn't come. She rang Dr Bushey, who didn't answer.

She rang the police station.

All that night the rain fell like a shroud over Soft Meadows Cross. There was a hissing and a dripping. The hissing was all the rain, the dripping was each drop. The dripping was higher in pitch than the hissing. Leaves—such November leaves as still remained—quivered when the rain whipped them and everything that man had constructed creaked as the wind leaned across the county.

People slept. The Macfisheries Man slumbered damply in his ditch. And even in their dreams, people heard the rain as— maybe—pattering feet (a woman's dream) or rustling money (a man's dream) or whispering elves (a child's dream) or discontented audiences (Cecil Sparks's dream).

And as they dreamt they left their bodies and joined Albert Skullham who was dreaming too; of his life, and lives before that life and lives yet to be lived. Only 'before' and 'yet' meant nothing to Albert Skullham now. He had jack-knifed into the fourth dimension. The ripples of his re-entry soon vanished.

But it rained that night in Soft Meadows Cross. And the dust was laid.

CHAPTER EIGHT

The Ashes : *Sunday Morning*

Miriam Rubin lay awake and mourned the end of her marriage, of 'life, as we know it, on this planet'. For all her six children whom she loved with a generous impartiality, for all the security which Jack had given her after her empty windswept adolescence in the Yorkshire dales, whither she had been evacuated from the Commercial Road, for all her friends and possessions she was deeply grateful. Fifteen years of happiness, on and off, with but intermittent intimations of mortality and frequent holidays by the sea, had spoiled her perhaps for the disillusion of middle-age. Hers she could handle. Jack's, well that was something ese.

He had come home at three in the morning, from a cocktail party, yet! Had said nothing, *nothing*! When he looked at her these days, his eyes were crooked and full of distaste. Now he was asleep and she bent wistfully over him. Softened by sleep, his face was boyish with just a patina of weariness and experience. His hands were clasped under his cheek ... Shalom aleichem. She wanted above all to be allowed to mother him too, and might have, had not Rachel thrust her skinny little body into the room.

'I'm a tiger!'

Grunts from Jack, who opened his eyes, saw Miriam, and turned away.

'Shut the door, darling.'

'I am a tiger,'—but she did not shut the peppermint door.

At breakfast it was David who caused the trouble.

'My egg's all bloody,' he said. Ruthie was shocked.

'You're not allowed to say that, is he Mummy?'

'No dear,' said Miriam.

'It's rude, isn't it?'

'I don't want it anyway.'

Miriam sighed: 'All right, give it to me. I'll have yours, you can have mine.'

109

'I don't want yours.'

'Why not?'

' 'Cos it's yours.'

'Silly silly David, hasn't got a spavid,' sang Hannah.

Although this particular ditty didn't mean anything it always had the effect of infuriating her brother.

'I want Hannah's egg,' said David, taking it, 'she can have mine.' Hannah burst into tears.

'Mummeeee, he's taken my ee-egg!'

'Cry-baby,' said Ruthie smugly.

'David, give Hannah her egg back.'

'Shan't.'

'David's showing off, isn't he, Mummy?' said Ruthie.

Little Joe made fish faces for a while, then stopped.

'I feel sick,' he said.

'That's it,' Jack announced. He'd had enough. 'I've had enough. I'm off to the Golf-Club.' He had been going anyway.

'Oh darling,' said Miriam, all thought of Little Joe chased out of her mind by terrible misgivings, 'you know what happened yesterday. You *did* promise.'

'So I promised,' Jack shrugged. 'This morning I unpromise. I'll be home for lunch.'

'Kiss me then.' He did—with lips like padlocks. Miriam watched him go with a heavy heart. When she got back to the breakfast table Little Joe had been sick and David had eaten Hannah's egg.

Miriam didn't say a word, but started to clean up the mess. She couldn't really find it in her heart to blame Jack. Women must be blamed.

As soon as the Vicar awoke he knew that he should have woken earlier. It scarcely needed a glance at the alarm clock to tell him that it was...4.45. *What?* Oh, it had stopped. Well, in that case... His watch was still loyally ticking and its bland face informed his volatile one that it was twenty past ten. And Morning Service—there were the bells now—would be about to... What about the bloody verger then, why hadn't he—the *what* verger? The nothing verger. It wasn't the verger's job to bring him his morning cup of tea.

Anyway what right had he to lie in bed castigating the

verger, when he should be all ready in the vestry. But as soon as he stepped gingerly out of bed the weight of his head hurled him to the floor. And his sermon . . . for Christ's sake! He stood up. Every sinew shrieked. What had happened last night? Images in scarlet and mauve, devil's pictures were flaunted before his weary imagination. Oh no, not that, must have been a dream, after that how could he preach?—But how could he preach? How *could* he preach? How could he pre-eeach?

Dick and Thelma Worsley surveyed the detritus of the previous night's party. It was appalling. Articles of clothing, broken crockery, vomit, chair-legs, soured wine-glasses stained with ash, even (inexplicably) an artificial limb.

'Well,' said Dick unconvincingly, 'the price of success. Now we belong to the ages.' Thelma didn't reply. Her face, usually glowing like a Christmas tree that children have blown on, was fused.

'I'm so unhappy. The disgrace.'

Their middle-class misery sat between them, steaming like the Maxwell House.

'Dick?'

'Yes, dear?'

'We can't stay, can we?'

'Well . . .'

When Jack reached the Golf Club he found the car park abandoned. The village itself was uncommonly quiet. No one was anywhere. Little Jasper was on the putting green pretending to be an Aston Martin and Old Porson was there in danger of being run down, but that was about the extent of it. Pity, because it was a lovely clear morning after the rain with the sky a pale water-colour blue, and perfect for golf. Jack changed his shoes and wandered into the Pro's shop where Throggie was listening to Children's Choice.

'A lovely morning, Throggie.'

'Aye, that it is. Lusten, wull ye, it's Andy Stewart.'

'What is?'

'On the wireless, mon,' Throggie raised his eyes to a clannish God in a tartan heaven. 'Dud ye iver heer unnathung si grand?'

'No,' said Jack. 'Where is everyone already?'

'Och, hist, mon, hist.' Jack histed until the end of the music.
'If theer's a hiven, Andy'll be sungin' theer.'

'They must have all overslept after the party.'

'Dinna ask me.'

'Well, it's very mysterious.' But Throggie was no longer
available for comment; he was in his second ecstacy.

'Lusten, wull ye, it's Jimmy Shand and his band.' Jack
returned to the clubhouse, and telephoned the Admiral.

The Admiral's wife surfaced slowly from a memorable dream
in which she had been sailing alone and naked in a five-masted
schooner. All night long sharp-finned, wet flying-fish had slapped
into her stomach and plopped against her titties and she awoke
tingling all over. To find herself lying on the floor under the
open window, damp from the overnight rain. She shivered,
hauled herself upright, caught sight of the pylon, drew in her
breath, seized a wrap, cossetted herself in it and staggered to
the phone, which was half off its hook and shrilling plaintively
to itself.

'Whosit?'

'Jack Rubin speaking.'

'Oh.'

'Can I speak to the Admiral please?'

'I've no idea.'

She stumbled into the next room. Her husband had not
undressed. He lay across the bed like a stranded water-buffalo.
She poked him. He let out a single, huge, terrifying snore. She
poked him again.

'You're wanted on the phone.'

In the clubhouse, Jack waited several minutes and fed his
entire collection of sixpences into the pecunivorous machine
before he was finally reassured by the gruff rudeness of the
old sea-dog.

'Bloody hell, what d'yer want, Rabinowitch?'

Jack inquired, were they not to play their regular Sunday
game of golf.

'D'yer know what the damn' time is, eh?'

'Twenty-five past ten, isn't it?'

'Exactly.' The Admiral promised to come up for a drink in
an hour or so but would be in no condition for golf. He rang

off. Jack studied himself in the mirror behind the bar. He looked as if he had spent a couple of nights paddling in the Styx.

Dr Bushey laid the Sunday papers open on the breakfast table. Tears blurred his eyes so that he was unable to decipher the print. He heard scuffling in the wainscoting.

Victoria was not yet up, which was unlike her. From time to time the good doctor threw a slipper at the ceiling, but to no effect. He brushed away his tears, studied the press. To begin with he was encouraged by them, but they flattered to deceive —there it was in the Sunday Express, a mass grave, a whole Vietnamese village. He sighed deeply and buried his head in the newsprint. He could hear bombs. He could smell burning flesh. It was getting worse; everywhere. But he was still alive.

The old man was dead. Albert Skullham was dead.

The police had been. They were very young and fiddled with things. They had broken an ornament. They did not consider that Mrs Skullham had done her old man in. They thought it improbable. They told her so and waited to be thanked. They brought mud in with them.

Anyway, they said, if the time of death could be established, perhaps she could provide them with an alibi. She did.

'Heard it was quite a party,' they said wistfully. Then they became practical: 'Have you had the doctor in to sign the death certificate?'

'I phoned him, but he didn't come.' Her eyes were red.

'Well, let's phone him again now, shall we?' They dialled the number.

Dr Bushey let it ring. Scuffle, scuffle, buzz, buzz. Victoria was woken by the phone but by the time she had stumbled down the stairs, the instrument had stopped ringing.

'Oh Pappa,' she said, 'you're impossible. I'm sure they'll take your stethoscope away.'

He didn't answer her. She forgave him and kissed the top of his head. He shrank from her. 'I'll go and put the coffee on. What's the time?'

'Time?' The Doctor looked up, looked weary, looked down. Victoria grabbed his wrist and consulted the watch thereon.

H

'Gracious heavens! I'm late for Church. I'm sorry, Daddy, but you'll have to wait for your coffee,'—and was away. Alone, Doctor Bushey covered his ears and screamed silently. He looked as though he was yawning.

On November mornings the sun, low in the sky, shone more or less straight through the East window of the Church, illuminating the Christ figure and all the appreciative saints, touching their halos with gilt and lifting a fine bouquet from the rich, leaded dyes of the stained glass. Thence infused with colour, it permeated the whole church with patterns and shades and hues; it lit on the brazen candlesticks at the ends of the wooden pews, striking a sparkle from them as if they had just been cut from the centre of the earth. The wings of the eagle lectern glinted like a real eagle cutting the edge of the morning with its wings, and the horizontal saints of the brasses seemed almost resurrected by the warmth and the glow. On such mornings it could have been His House. Such mornings were rare.

There were not many regular church-goers amongst the villagers. Mrs Connolly sat primly there, hands folded like billets-doux in her lap. There too Wendy Pakenham, whiskers twitching as always, and there the Tomlinsons, very much the worse for wear. Ethel and Caedmon had stayed in bed but the Loins were there. As regular hippies they cowered a bit in their pew and tried to look sneering. Behind them sat Rusty, who displayed his independence by never kneeling or standing when he might sit, and by ostentatiously failing to say 'Amen'. In spite of studying to be a saint Rusty Motorcade was determined not to be seen to be a slave to religious attitudes and conventions. He talked of one day founding a new sect, 'The Specific Church of Christ Pragmatist'. There were many precedents for saints who offended the orthodoxy of the day. Besides which Rusty had been appalled, after he had made a special effort to be up in time after his late night, to discover that Holy Communion could not be celebrated since there was no Vicar to administer it. Why should he say 'Amen' to such an incompetent's pronouncements? Certainly not! When he got to be a saint he would surely tell the Bishop about such a betrayal of Christian practice. He might not even wait that long. Near the back under the organ loft Rose Marie had her eyes tight shut. She was giving thanks. Rather than diminishing, her gratitude was swelling and overwhelming her. To wake up and find that it was not a dream, that her legs were still real legs, why that had been an awakening! Victoria, very puffy from her run, sat down next to her and squeezed her wrist. When Rose-Marie saw who it was, she smiled and didn't mind.

The restlessness in the congregation, the insecurity of having no intermediary through whom to speak to God, began to spread like hell fire. Mrs Connolly whispered mean nothings to Wendy. The Tomlinsons chatted away merrily about I.C.I. Until, at length the Vicar arrived, hair awry, cassock billowing, unshorn and unmistakably agitated. Playing for time, he gasped: 'Let us sing—' but, since he had no notion which hymn number to announce and was unable to focus his eyes, lamely concluded: '—a hymn.' Some sort of Christian compromise was reached.

The Macfisheries Man woke up in his ditch. The ditch was a bunker on the eighteenth fairway. He felt sicker than he had ever felt in his entire forty-two years. Sun was spread like custard upon the Soft Meadows but there was no sun in the bunker. He was so cold, so wet. He felt as if his blood had turned to semolina.

'The wages of sin are death,' he muttered and a frog croaked. He shivered uncontrollably, a shiver that caressed him from top to toe. Sand clogged up his scalp. His finger-nails felt like emery paper. 'I am a wart on the face of creation. It would be better for me that—'

But just then Jack came by, having seen him from the club-house.

'Good morning, Jack,' said the Macfisheries Man, but then such a fit of the shakes overtook him that his man-of-the-world air left him entirely. Jack helped him up.

'I was waiting for the Admiral,' he said, 'but let me see you home, shall I?'

'Do you remember,' inquired the Macfisheries Man, 'do you remember last night, and what, that is to say, whether—'

'Not a word more, I implore you. I understand. Sleep under the stars, why not? "A wandering Aramean was my father"!'

'I'm glad to hear you say so.'

'Do you think you can walk?'

'I can try.' But the Macfisheries Man's ankle had stiffened and he could barely limp.

'Not far to go. Make an effort, eh? Be a scout, be a soldier.'

'Ow! I wonder what old Guru put in the drink?'

Old Guru had been roused by the Church bells. The girls were already up. They brought him food and coffee, and Genevieve caressed his shoulders softly with her long hair.

'Why bells?' Guru inquired.

'For prayers,' Tessa explained. 'To raise the good people to Church.'

'You go? All go?'

'We don't go ourselves, no. We have our own worship.'

'We read poetry,' said Genevieve. Abigail added:

'Not only poetry, philosophy too sometimes. Last week it will be J. W. Dunne and next week it was C. S. Lewis.'

'That's a serialist joke,' Tessa thoughtfully explained.

'I like the poetry best,' said Genevieve, 'often it makes me cry. Specially when it's about faithful animals. That's the best poetry of all.'

'Guru go to Church,' said Guru.

Tessa: 'But Guru we shall be too late. The Service is short and it is quite a long way to walk.'

'We go now.' And Guru brushed the toast and egg into the bedclothes. They held his clothes for him while he climbed into them. Abigail nibbled his bony shoulders, but her sisters slapped her gently. She had no right to take advantage of them like that; and time was short.

J. W. Dunne would not have agreed that time was short, and neither did the Church choir:

'As it was in the beginning, is now, and ever shall be, world without end, Amen,' clinging desperately on to the Amen like mountaineers to their ropes, but they had in the end, one by slippery one, to slide into the deep crevasse of silence.

The pulpit was empty. Wilfred, the organist, played a few bars of an anthem but didn't feel like pulling the stops out. The Vicar, in desperation, prayed for eloquence, but was answered by a tirade of coughs from the congregation. Why do people always cough in Church, he wondered. It would be all right if they were to pray every time they coughed. The Vicar climbed the steps to the pulpit which seemed as high as a martello tower.

'Em . . . I was going to preach to you today about the turning out of the money-lenders from the temple and the . . . em . . . overthrowing of the tables . . . but . . . em, em, I don't really have anything of value to say on the subject.' A long silence. *Get me out of this God, and . . . and . . . I'll believe in you, God! There, how about that?*

At which moment the heavy church doors crashed open to admit Guru, followed by the Angell sisters. All heads turned. Shock, resentment and distaste were written on every brow as the girls ushered Guru into a pew.

The interruption saved the Vicar. He found the words: 'Wash me and I shall be clean; purge me in hyssop and I shall be whiter than snow.'

'He's no Christian,' murmured Mrs Connolly to Wendy Pakenham, referring to Guru and not the Vicar.

'Some of them are you know, dear. It was the British Army that—'

'Some of them may be but this one isn't. You can tell it just by looking at him. And those girls—'

'I know, dear, who'd have believed they had it in them.'

'They should be ashamed of themselves.'

'It's a bit blatant to bring him to Church.'

'Bit blatant? My dear, I'm surprised the Vicar allows it.'

'The wages of sin are death!' cried the Vicar.

'Quite right, quite right,' whispered Mrs Connolly, whose hands itched to applaud, 'we know very well whom you mean.'

'We live in an age which has forgotten the meaning of sin. We live in an age in which there is no such thing as individual responsibility. If we do wrong, why then it is not ourselves but our upbringing that is to blame and if we bring up our children badly, it is not our fault, but the fault of our parents. We believe in rewards but not punishments, but I say unto you that God gave us free will and in giving us free will He gave us a choice of good and evil. If we choose right we may be rewarded; if we choose wrong we must be punished. Now there are many people today who feel that the scientific advances of the present generation represent a threat to religion. We go up in rocket ships—if God is up there why can't we see him? We build giant telescopes with which we can probe the corners of space, only to discover that space has no corners. And when our telescopes fail us we cry that we cannot find Him, where is He hiding? But I say unto you look inside yourselves, there shall ye find Him. He does not hide from you; yet you think you can hide from Him.

'That you cannot do; neither from Him nor from His punishment at the Terrible Day of Judgement.'

'No,' said Guru, standing up. 'No punishment. You do not understand.'

Candida, the waitress at the Burnt Scone, lay late in bed, luxuriating in her nakedness and rubbing her smooth limbs gently against the striped sheets. She hugged the pillow to her and pretended it was Steve McQueen. She lived on the Gruntham Estate where film stars were few and far between. She was a norphan and had recently left the norphanage, which establishment had found her employment at the Burnt Scone. She hoped one day to go to London and be corrupted. It didn't seem too much to ask. She thought that if she had fifteen pounds it would be enough to be going on with, since corruption might well be combined with profit. If only a few more kind elderly gentlemen would come to the Burnt Scone for coffee, but the kind ones weren't rich, and the rich ones weren't kind and oh, if they didn't come soon she would toast their tea-cakes and butter their scones, make no mistake! In the meantime she had her smooth limbs (my thighs are like junket and my breasts like baked apples with cherries on top. She would have liked to taste the cherries but couldn't quite reach with her long lubricious tongue) and her dreams of London. Maybe she'd be a notorious model, doing super wicked things with the international set and take drugs and demonstrate against things.

In the meantime it was Sunday and she could stay in bed for hours.

'No,' said Guru, standing up, 'no punishment. You do not understand.'

Caedmon, who had been dreaming guilty dreams (and no wonder), was woken up by the telephone, through whose mouthpiece came the prissy voice of Cecil Sparks.

'I don't think any the worse of you for last night, you know.'

'Whassit?'

'So we'll say no more about it, shall we? I'm just ringing to remind you that this afternoon at old Sparky's we are reading through our little play.'

'Shakespeare's.'

'What? Oh yes, well, it's ours now. So see you at half past two eh? 'Bye now.'

'Grunt.'

'Who was it?' asked a dishevelled and bed-raggled Ethie gloomily round the door. Her eyes were like tinned apricots and her hair was ratty.

'Cecil Sparks.'

'He's always waking us up.'

'Yes.'

'My God, I need some coffee, etc., etc.'

'Yes.'

'You don't *like* him, do you?'

'No.'

'Good lad.'

A pause.

'You're *not* queer, are you, Caddie?'

'No.'

'You're very strange all the same.'

Inspired by his conversation with Caedmon, Cecil Sparks sat in his black pyjamas in front of his novel thinking deeply, scratching Irving's ears from time to time, then scratching his own.

'Quadrille, A Family Saga in Four Parts. Part the First.' So far so good. No question, it had dignity, and an old-fashioned air of leisurely seriousness. Not yet in the Henry James or Conrad class, but well on the way, well on the way.

A sudden burst of creative energy illumined his soul. Swiftly but with careful spacing and in a handsome script he inscribed:

'Chapter One'

'No,' said Guru, standing up. 'No punishment. You do not understand.' All heads turned.

'Really,' said Mrs C.

'Ssh,' said Wendy P.

'The thing is...' said the Vicar beginning to climb down from the pulpit into the arena.

'Explain punishment,' said Guru, approaching the Vicar as he pattered up the aisle, 'when day of judgement, *when*?'

The Vicar dug a thumbnail into the eagle's head in frustration. He could see members of his congregation encouraging him with nods and becks and half-suppressed gestures of the hands, but encouraging him to what? It was easy to nod and beck and gesture, harder to ...

'And so in conclusion,' announced the Vicar, but the hesitancy in his voice indicated that so far as conclusions went he had no stall in the market-place, nor even a booth in the desert for that matter.

'No,' said Guru again, 'no conclusion. An answer rather.'

Mrs Connolly who loved the Vicar for his broad shoulders stood up and pointed at Guru.

'Leave the Church immediately. Go on, off with you, you tiresome little man!' (The tone was the one you hear in Swiss ski resorts when ageing English ladies present cups for ski-ing prowess to local boys in ornate turn-of-the-century hotels on occasions when Things Go Wrong and People are Hurt).

Guru of course, didn't move. He was bathed in stained-glass sunshine. The Vicar was not. But the Vicar was after all, a man of some parts; had taken correspondence courses, realised that he should (but didn't) relish a theological debate. Then Rusty Motorcade took a hand.

'Answer him, Vicar,' he cried, 'stick to orthodoxy and you'll be all right.' This finally persuaded the Vicar to the joust. He started however with rather a limp lance.

'What was your question again?'

'No punishment,' Guru repeated, 'when day of Judgement?'

'Well, in a way, I'm *glad* you asked me that, glad of the opportunity to clear up what is a muddle in, I feel sure, the minds of many worthy Christians, whose faith is unquestioned, but the rational grounds of whose faith is, like an old tin can, a little rusty, a little bent, a little unserviceabe through misuse. But such folk, good folk, honest folk, should not despair. Help is on the way. A little oil, a little polish, a little—'

'Answer!' thundered Guru. 'How punishment?'

The Vicar took a deep breath. Clung on to the lectern for support. It was not easy to marshal his arguments. If only he felt a little less weary; he was not fit to be an emissary of the Lord, at least not without his regular eight hours a night. The words of an unregarded and long-rejected little missal came into his mind. 'Flowers of St Cuthbert' leapt to his aid.

'To argue that man is immune from punishment because of his special relationship with God is an indignity to both and a totally disreputable position to maintain.'

'Bravo!' cried Rusty. But Guru seemed unimpressed even by St Cuthbert and remained where he stood in the coat of many colours shed by the East Window.

'And Judas? Did he have free will?'

'Certainly he did.'

Guru quoted quietly: ' "Behold he is at hand that doth betray me".'

'Matthew Twenty-six, Forty-six,' said the Vicar.

'Free will? And St Peter?'

'He above all. Of all the apostles Simon Peter was the one most fallible, most free.'

' "Before the cock crow, thou shalt deny me thrice." Free will?'

' "And he went out",' sighed the Vicar, ' "and wept bitterly".'

'And Jesus Christ? Free will?'

'Enough of this! The devil cites scripture.'

Guru spread his arms blandly wide. 'Devil? Where Devil? Punishment? *What* punishment? *Free will?*'

'You must have misunderstood me,' said the Vicar, 'in modern theology it is suggested that punishment, or hell as it used to be known, consists in the consciousness of missed opportunities. So I believe. Hell,' said the Vicar, who had never thought of it before, 'is reliving your life, unable to change it for the better.'

'How relive? *How?*'

'I think I understand what you are getting at,' said the

Vicar, 'it would be wrong to take my words too literally—'

Rusty Motorcade: 'Oh no!'

'—when I say relive I do not mean that in the literal sense, I mean a kind of mystical rebirth, a kind of—'

Guru seemed no longer to be listening. With considerable contempt he said: 'Day of Judgement, *when*?'

'Ah, if man knew that, if man could tell the day of his death ... But we must be ready, we must watch and pray, watch and pray ...'

Guru left. The Angell sisters followed him out. Rusty Motorcade was reading in his prayerbook a list of all the relations that a man must not marry. The congregation stretched their legs and ceased to worry. It had been a stimulating service.

Jack had taken on more than he had supposed when he offered to walk the Macfisheries Man home. It was a longish walk to the Gruntham Estate and the poor, lame Macfisheries Man stumbled frequently. Occasionally he gasped out some such phrase as: 'You needn't have gone to all this trouble' or 'It's really most kind of you' to which Jack, unused to compliments, would reply: 'It's nothing. Don't mention it.'

Thus they reached Mrs Skullham's. Two milk bottles and a *Sunday Express* sat outside the front door.

Jack propped the Macfisheries Man against the door-post under the little wooden hat that such houses wear over their entrances. The elbow of the Macfisheries Man pressed against the bell-push.

Mrs Skullham, her eyes a little less red, but her hair flying in Medusa wisps, came to the door. As she opened it her lodger fell in and knocked over the umbrella stand. This small and unimportant event affected the volatile Mrs S. who at once broke into tears again.

Jack tried to expain. Doris, not understanding, looked blankly at him.

'Good-bye then,' and Jack hurried back to the Golf Club, puffing out his cheeks with relief. Mrs Skullham, with her dead father in the kitchen and her sick and feverish lodger prone in the hall, had slow hysterics. Then, since no one cared, she pulled herself together and helped the Macfisheries Man to bed. She would have liked to have made him a hot, milky drink, but Albert was still in the kitchen. The police had sent for a surgeon and left; the undertakers had not yet arrived; she draped her lodger in a clean pair of Albert's pyjamas, and opened the window.

Leaving Church, Wendy Pakenham pondered only briefly upon the issues raised by the impromptu discussion she had just enjoyed. A discussion, to her way of thinking, made a pleasant change and she had heard nothing to shake her belief in a benevolent creator. Or a destiny which would reward the aristocracy for the tribulations it suffers in this vulgar world. But Mrs Connolly was complaining about Guru's behaviour, which she took to be a personal affront.

'Ever since he arrived in the village it's been nothing but trouble, trouble, trouble. I think—' and here she lowered her voice so that a passing blackbird should not hear, 'something shall Have To Be Done.'

Mrs Connolly's eyes turned into scorpions as Guru came trotting past with the Angell sisters chuffing in his wake, but she delved into her bag for a tattered envelope and followed him at a distance.

He seemed impatient and almost, for him, surly. He walked up the very middle of the main street. Fortunately as it was Sunday, there was not too much traffic, but what there was hooted at him in shrill complaint. Occasionally he muttered 'No punishment' and shook his brown head violently from side to side.

'He's angry,' said Tessa, 'I know. I can tell.'

Abigail, for whom the brisk trot might at any moment prove too much, asked, 'What can we do?'

'We could give him buttercup wine and wash his feet in spring dews.'

'Wrong season, darling.' Such abruptness from Tessa was unusual and clearly indicated that she was anxious about their holy man. Perhaps even jealous? Usually she encouraged Genevieve in her fancies. It was Abigail and Genevieve who had slept either side of Guru after the party. And she, Tessa, the eldest and wisest, had not slept at all, but had lain bitterly awake, resentful of the scuffling to her right. She did not blame Abigail for Abby was *not* strong, but Genevieve at times was a little too apt to take things for granted. Of course they made allowances for her and of course she had a poetic nature, but sometimes she seemed to use her poetic sensibilities more as a weapon than a gift. It's not easy to have two younger sisters, especially when those sisters are sharing the man you love. Tessa on the whole was very kind and patient; a good girl.

The fierce Mrs Connolly jumped out from behind a clump of rhododendra and thrust an envelope into Guru's soft paw. A starling's head emerged from her clenched, left fist. She glared implacably at the Angell girls and was off like a panther through the undergrowth. Guru, crumpling up the note, permitted himself a smile :

'Water of the Ganges is deep and muddy, yet it cleanses the whole world.'

'Oh how true !' cried Abby.

The road ran parallel to the twelfth fairway of the golf course. Opposite the tee Guru stopped and pointed.

'What?'

Jack Rubin was driving. He had fixed to play the last nine holes with a visiting Japanese industrialist. The Jap was very polite, very clean; a very polite, clean Jap. Old Porson, caddying for Jack since the Admiral was not playing, watched.

Leaning over the fence, Guru inquired of Jack : 'What?' in a low voice. The unfortunate golfer, distracted in mid-swing, sent the ball out of bounds into the road where Abigail caught it and threw it back.

'Oh very, very bad luck, old fellow,' said the Jap.

'Aie, aie, aie,' said Jack stickily. Old Porson looked at Guru with simmering eyes.

'This is Golf.' Tessa put her hand on Guru's arm, seizing a sudden and unexpected advantage over her sisters. 'It's a game in which the players must hit the white balls into eighteen little holes in as few strokes as possible.'

'Easy,' remarked Guru.

Jack's second drive followed the first. It landed on the bonnet of a passing Sunbeam Talbot. Ping !

'Oh *awfully* bad luck, old chap,' said the Jap.

Guru inquired : 'Why here?' and then, pointing towards the green, 'Why not there?'

At which Jack pulled out a cigar and lit it with ferocity.

Meanwhile the Jap struck an inscrutable two hundred and twenty yard floater. This seemed to settle some question in Guru's mind, for he leapt over the fence and seized a club.

'No, Guru, no,' said Tessa. 'Not here. We must go to the Club-house.'

'Then go.'

Candida, beautiful as she was, was still young enough to make Impulse her God. Discretion remained for her one of the very minor angels. When she looked up the London trains in the ABC, or compared her sweet body with *Playboy*'s 'Play-mates' or *Penthouse*'s 'Pets' (she had no staples across her stomach and plenty of body hair but otherwise did very well), there seemed to be no reason why she should not enjoy a life of elegant sensuality in the metropolis. But such a life should begin elegantly, and not on the back of a lorry, so she kept in her room a Burnt Scone menu card to which she had added under 'buttered scones, toasted tea-cakes, sundries' the words 'I will do anything legitimate for £15'. This card she would keep by her and flash in front of incredulous commercial travel-lers, American tourists, or any other males who ventured into the tea-house expecting innocent home-made sponge and goose-berry preserve. But of course they all laughed and tipped her ninepence, so that was that.

Cecil Sparks only came in for pastries for his *Hamlet* re-hearsal. But Candida, who made Impulse her God, was an opportunist . . .

They came to take Albert Skullham away. Fitted him with a wooden waistcoat and brass buttons, all ready to go under-ground and meet his Maker amongst the moles.

The Macfisheries Man lay in bed upstairs, tossing in delirium, spitting out the names of the Angell sisters with a strange kind of affectionate venom.

And for the first time for . . . ever so long, Doris Skullham found herself thinking obsessively about her sometime death and dissolution. She had time to think. She had not a great deal, poor lady, to compensate her in life for what she feared from death. She wondered about all the lonely people who survive for so long without going mad or taking their own lives. How do they manage? And do they? Do they?

She also wondered whether the instinct for self-preservation might not be morbid rather than healthy; and had other, blacker thoughts.

'Sometimes,' she said to the hall clock, 'I feel like a character in a bad novel, the servant of a stranger's whim, living another's reality and suffering unjustly to satisfy their pique.'

'Tick tock,' said the clock.

CHAPTER NINE

The Match · *Sunday Afternoon*

The Admiral, as befitted the Captain of the Royal Fairway, warmed his bum before the Club-house fire. His legs astride, a whisky mac in his mighty hand, his plus-fours drooping over long, woollen, check socks, he positively steamed.

'Bloody scandal,' he grunted several times. Colonel Tomlinson agreed. 'What's that? What's that?'

'I said I agreed with you, Bertie. It is a Scandal.'

'What is?'

'This Guru fellah.'

'Wasn't that what I said? Make sense, Tomlinson, good God man, try and make sense.'

Celia joined in : 'You know what happened in Church?'

'Certainly not. Never go there myself. Dreary place. Nothing to eat, nothing to drink, all that bowin' and scrapin'.'

'Guru was there,' said Gilbert.

'Who?'

'The Indian fellah.'

'Oh him. He's the one we were talking about.' (A second whisky mac found its way into the Admiral's paw; smoke began to rise from his Harris Tweed gusset.)

'Well, yes. He was in Church.'

'Where?'

'Church.'

Again Celia broke in : 'Admiral, your trousers are on fire.'

'Nonsense, nonsense, they're plus-fours. Had 'em for years. What was this Indian doing in Church?'

'Arguing.'

'Was he? *Was* he? Splendid!'

'And what about last night?'

'Last what?'

'Night. At the Worsleys. What a brute he is!'

'Splendid! Quite splendid. Not been a night like it since Aden in 'forty-four.'

127

'Don't listen to him,' shouted Jessica from the fruit-machine, whose shiny handle she was caressing tenderly, 'he never was in Aden.' She pulled the handle. Two grapes and a cherry came up. 'Ooh, grapes,' she said, 'ooh.'

'Terrible fellow,' muttered the Admiral.

('You really are on fire,' said Celia, 'actually.')

'Who? Worsley?'

'No, no, no, no, no. That Guru or whatever he is.'

Solly arrived at the Club-house, was greeted by Jack Rubin. 'What's yours?'

The Admiral spied Jack and Solly.

'Shalom!' he cried offensively, 'what's new in Tel Aviv?'

Said Solly: 'They're circumcising British tourists now, Christopher Mayhew, yet.'

The Admiral's trousers burst into flame. Feeling warm the old sea-dog moved away and sat down. Lack of oxygen extinguished the conflagration. Somebody brought him another whisky mac. The Jap crept in, but was sent to drink with the artisans, and smiled gratefully all round. Jack, who was a popular figure when buying drinks, bought drinks.

'Where were you all?' he asked.

'How about a few hands of stud this afternoon?' Solly's invitation. Jack's eyes blazed up briefly, then sank to embers.

'Really, I don't think I—'

Solly did his favourite parody: 'So alright already. My life! Vot's zis? Vot's zis?' Jack changed the subject. 'Who do you think I met on the twelfth?'

The Angell sisters glided in. Surprise, surprise! From the Admiral grumpily: 'Bloody women!'

'Whom?'

'Guru.'

Obediently on cue Guru entered.

Victoria Bushey, increasingly anxious about her father, had invited the Vicar to lunch. But the Vicar was not expected at the Doctor's for twenty minutes. He had removed his cassock and brushed his hair. He had tried to settle to *The Sunday Times* and their artistic colour photographs of the starving millions, but could settle to nothing, for his brain was whirring like a big clock about to strike.

He left the Vicarage and walked in the orchard. Through the arthritic branches of the old apple trees he could see the gravestones in the Churchyard, stones whose legends he knew by heart, but could not always understand. Little Cathleen Brown, taken to Christ at the age of six months, now there was a puzzler. Maybe Mr and Mrs Brown had reasoned it out in 1824; under the date they had caused a legend to be placed. Did it contain eternal truths? The lichen knew. The lichen had clung to it and kissed it and annihilated it. And Cathleen? In Abraham's capacious bosom.

When the Vicar turned southwards he could see the Soft Meadows, but they held no consolation for him now. *No punishment*. If it were true . . . ? Cathleen Brown, surely not a child . . . better for us, but *was it*, that a millstone should be . . . because if Cathleen were not to be punished . . . should not be punished? Or could not? *Could* not. But what then? Could, should we be punished for having grown up? We never asked for that, or for . . . *could* not, it wouldn't make sense otherwise.

Born innocent . . . corrupted by children. Or born corrupt like . . . little Cathleen Brown? No!

And who should punish us? And how? Pitchforks. Come *along*. What had he said in Church? Latterly the words had come readily enough. *Words*. What had he said? 'How punishment? Because free will.' Free will? What did he know of that? (Trod on another rotten apple, no free will there, and look at his shoes! Not fit to go out to lunch in.)

And punishment for what? The Vicar was only human; and Judas; and Simon Peter; and little Cathleen Brown . . .

It wouldn't do at all.

'When Day of Judgement?' A fair question. *Really*. Well? Decorations will be worn. So many in the dock. Even a computer, programmed with every act of man's ingratitude . . . but God had no need of a computer. (And vice versa). So many to judge, and not only humans. Rhubarb leaves. In the overgrown kitchen garden the Vicar plucked a rhubarb leaf and hurled it into outer darkness. When Day of Judgement? He must talk further with that Guru.

The Admiral gruffly accosted the little Indian.

'Look here, old man, are you a member of this club?'

'Member? Yes.' The bright reply confused the Admiral who took refuge in a cough.

'May I ask how long you've been a member and who proposed you?'

'Yes,' said Guru, and, glancing at the bar, he ogled the Admiral and added: 'Cocktails, yes?'

'Good God, man, have you *no* sense of shame?' The Admiral's angry whisper brought Jessica from the fruit-machine. 'We can't go through all that again.'

Said Jessica nostalgically: 'It was beautiful. All grapes and cherries, but once I got a pear.' The Angel sisters were playing a private game of their own invention, which involved standing quite stock still, then making unexpected snaps at each other's faces with their pointed little teeth.

'How they've changed,' said Celia. 'Before he moved in they would never have come to a place like this.'

'Babylon,' said her husband, 'Sodom and Gomorrah.'

'I wonder if they played golf in Sodom and Gomorrah?'

'Played the course backwards,' said Solly, who had been eavesdropping.

Meanwhile Guru, dissuaded from concocting another cocktail, was making plain the object of his visit.

'Golf. Guru play golf.'

'Perhaps, Guru,' said Tessa, who appeared to have won the game, 'you should take one or two lessons first and then play. I'm sure you'd be very good.'

'Why lessons? Easy golf.'

At this the Admiral had a splendid idea. He would toast Guru's toes for him once and for all.

'Look here, Guru, I'll play golf with you myself after lunch and, if you put up a good showing, old man, you can join our club and we'll know that you're a white man at heart. There! You can have a stroke a hole. Can't say fairer than that, can I?'

Guru smiled quietly to himself: 'Easy golf.' The Admiral beamed too. ''Course it's easy. Concentration, that's what you need. You're good at that, aren't you, you darkies? Old Gandhi sitting in the road contemplating himself, splendid fellah, taught us a thing or two, I can tell you. There was a real Englishman, one of the best. Oh yes, it's a bloody easy game, golf.'

The other members susurrated in appreciation. A show-down with Guru, that was the answer. Humiliate him on the golf course, and all the rest would follow.

News travels fast in Soft Meadows Cross. Celia met Mrs Connolly and told her. Jack phoned home, said he wouldn't be home to lunch and told Miriam. Jessica went putting and told Throggie, who, she staunchly believed, was not as impartial as he seemed. (But his putts went in for all her flirting). Soon the whole village was vibrating with the unprecedented news that the Admiral and Guru were matched at golf.

Rose-Marie, skipping and leaping in the air, knew nothing of the impending drama. No more did poor Mrs Skullham sitting desolately amidst the debris of her status quo, nor the Mac-fisheries Man, shaking and sweating with fever, conscious only of delirious dreams and, in waking moments, his aching head and his pained foot, nor Cecil Sparks, whose soul had been blistered by Candida's unexpected offer but who was running through the final arrangements for the read-through of *Hamlet,* where they should sit, how he should address them, which magazines should be left carelessly scattered, as if nothing had happened, nor his dachshunds.

But just about everyone else in the village knew. Like foot and mouth disease, the story was whispered by the wind and sparged by the birds.

Tomato soup, roast lamb, roast potatoes and macedoine of vegetables, tinned fresh fruit cocktail, none of it to Guru's taste. They brought him an apple. It was green. It sat on a white plate, looking up at his brown face. Light reflected off each on to each. Oh, green Guru! Oh, brown apple!

Delicately as if for an appendectomy or a Caesarian he sliced the apple. The flesh was milky-coloured. The knife dissected a pip. Within the pip the kernel was milky-coloured. He ate the kernel. Apple juice sparkled on the blade of the knife (Wallace Brothers, Sheffield). The flesh of the apple turned brown.

Jack leaned across the table. 'Myself, I'm Jewish,' he said. Guru nodded politely.

'We have more in common, you and I, than all those . . .'

'No punishment. When Day of Judgement?' asked Guru.

'No, Guru,' hissed Tessa, 'not *him*, not *here*.'

'Pardon?'

'No punishment,' thundered Guru. The Admiral choked over a square of white carrot, which popped from his mouth into his lap. 'When Day of Judgement?'

'Judaism,' began Jack, hastily thumbing through in his mind all those index-cards marked in the top right-hand corner, 'Judaism, tenets of, to inform the goyim,' 'Judaism does not emphasise the after-life, but lays stress on the living of this one.'

'No punishment?'

'If one lives one's life as fully as possible and in joyous anticipation of the coming of the Messianic age when all men shall be—'

'When Day of Judgement?'

'I'll have to look that one up,' said Solly. 'Better than that, I'll give Rabbi Keitelmann a ring this afternoon. He's *very* progressive. He watches the telly on Friday nights. He'll know.'

'You not knowing?'

'Well, let's just say I shouldn't like to commit myself.'

'What are they talking about?' the Admiral shouted over the condensed milk at his wife, 'Because if it's politics . . . Am I or am I not captain of this club?'

'It's not, dear, and you know you are.'

'We're talking religion,' said Jack, 'I'm converting Guru.'

'Religion? Superstitious poppycock! I've never bothered my head with all that bollocks and look at me now.' They all did, without comment. Genevieve sang a sad little song about the last snow-drop in spring. Somebody burped and somebody farted. The steward's wife brought in a lump of cheddar.

Wendy Pakenham was an artist and a cook. Her paintings, modest and discreet, had none of the strong, bold lines of her treacle tart or her Irish stew. Her cooking leaned more in the direction of Mrs Beeton, even Florence Greenberg, than Elizabeth David, Robert Carrier or Desmond Briggs. No un-weaned lambs in nests of chervil for her. But an infatuation, even when the subject is middle-aged and the two objects indifferent, is inclined to add savour to any recipe, and her Sunday lunch, plain as it was and interrupted as its preparation had been, triumphed. The crackling of the pork was brittle, the potatoes crumbly and golden with grease, the apple sauce fluffy and the broad beans a succulent, buttery, yellowy green. She looked for no thanks from Cecil. The scratch of his fork as it scraped the last of the potato and gravy from the porcelain was sufficient reward.

'What do you know of that creature at the tea-shop?' asked Cecil Sparks, wiping his epicene lips with a mauve, silk handkerchief.

'Which creature, Cecil?'

'Oh . . . you know.'

'What does she look like?'

'Too absurd. All crotch and eyes.'

'Oh. Oh I see.' Jealousy hopped like a toad in Wendy's breast. 'You mean Candida, the waitress?'

'Yes, yes.'

'Why do you ask?'

Cecil looked ruffled. 'I am studying her. She might do for the younger sister in the novel. Bring her up here one evening.'

'But how? It's not as if—'

Airily : 'I give you carte blanche.'

'In her case cart is the operative word.'

'Oh la. I do believe you're jealous. At your age too. *Or because of it.*'

Wendy spooned deep into the greengage crumble, hurled it venomously on to a dish.

'You can be very cruel sometimes, Cecil.'

'But it's for art. For literature. For that I would sacrifice anything.'

'Even me?'

'Would you pass the custard?'

'Why isn't Daddy home for lunch?' asked Ruthie. Miriam sighed and answered bitterly :

'I expect he's got better things to do, darling.'

'I bet,' said David, 'he's gone to Texas to fight the Eskimos.'

'Eskimo, Eskimo, Eskimo,' sang Hannah, delighted with the new word.

'I'm a pussy-dog,' said Rachel.

'Pussy-dogs don't put their feet on the table.'

'Mummy,' said Ruthie, 'isn't Rachel *naughty*?'

'I shall think so if she doesn't put her feet down.'

'Daddy's naughty,' said David. 'Daddy's very, very, *very* naughty.' Ruthie flared up at this. She had been intended to.

'Daddy is *not* naughty. David mustn't say things like that, must he, Mummy?'

'Eat up your carrots, Little Joe.'

'Must he, Mummy, must he?'

'I'm a pussy-dog,' said Rachel.

'I thought you were a tiger.'

'I'm a pussy-dog-tiger and Teddy is a pussy-*cat*-tiger.'

'Daddy isn't naughty, Mummy. He isn't. He *isn't*.' Miriam sighed.

'Carrots, Little Joe.'

Little Joe considered his plate for a while with great seriousness. Four is a serious age. Finally with an air of abstracted finality he pronounced:

'Carrots don't matter.'

Old Porson stood on the first tee of the Royal Fairway with Solly's clubs, which Solly had loaned Guru for the occasion.

'Bloody hell, who's caddying for *me* then?' roared the rabid sea-dog.

'Little Jasper is, sir. I thought I could be of more use to the Indian gentleman, sir.'

'You did, did you? Where's Throggie?'

Throggie appeared from his little shop, all greased and shining. He was singing.

'Throggie, what the hell is the meaning of all this nonsense?'

' "Cambleton Loch, I wush ye wur whusky",' sang Throggie.

'What?' the Admiral cupped a hand behind his ear.

' "Cambleton Loch, och aye",'

'Can't understand a word you say.' The Admiral, cutting his losses, growled at the terrified Little Jasper: 'Tee up the bloody ball, can't you?'

A vast gallery of local people had foregathered to watch the Match. The spikes of their shooting-sticks tormented the turf and their bottoms spread wide like vegetable marrows. The Admiral was 'loosening up'. That entailed swinging his clubs ferociously around his head, occasionally clipping Little Jasper in the pit of the stomach with the practical end of his driver, behind the ear with the sharp-edged face of his wedge.

Guru meanwhile was sitting on the tee in the Lotus position, his forehead resting gently on his ankles. What was he thinking? There were many who wondered.

'We can *never* know,' Tessa explained quite severely to her sisters, 'what people are thinking. Only from books may we sometimes tell—if we are lucky and the books have been both eloquent and sincere (such as the works of Norman Douglas, Mrs Gaskell and Proust)—what they have thought. You may maintain, sisters, that it is possible to judge from somebody's actions that their thoughts are such or thus, but I confess that I often act quite other than I think. This it is which makes the task of the novelist so onerous, as Huxley puts it : "The trouble with fiction is that it makes too much sense. Reality never makes sense." But Huxley put these words into the mouth of one of his characters, as if the Chinese box of literature were to him a consolation rather than a frustration . . .'

Tessa might have continued in similar style for quite some time (there were days when she did) but . . .

'Shut up, woman, for God's sake!' bawled the Admiral. 'How in heaven's name can I be expected to play golf under such conditions?'

To tell the truth (or a fictional approximation of it anyway) Genevieve and Abigail were grateful for the Admiral's impolite interruption. They thought Tessa supremely boring when she was in one of her moods, but never liked to tell her so. (Abby hadn't even read Proust. For shame!)

The Admiral addressed the ball with a waggle, swung with a wiggle, and struck it with a thwack, his choler finding expression in his golf. The ball sailed, ooh, it must have been two hundred and fifty yards.

'That good?' asked Guru, 'that right?'

'Of course it's not right, you brown ape, it's out of bounds!'

Guru seized a club from Solly's bag. 'No, not that one, sir!' cried Old Porson. It was a putter. Guru ignored his caddy's advice. Put a ball on the ground; struck it. It travelled some fifteen yards. Guru set off in pursuit, struck it again with the same result.

'Hey!' yelled the Admiral, 'come back here! I'm playing another.' Obediently Guru returned. The Admiral played another. A good one this time. Guru put another ball on the ground; struck it.

'You can't do that,' squeaked Little Jasper. The Admiral's cronies wagged their heads at Guru sternly.

'He play two. I play two. Is only fair.'

Throggie was instructed to follow them round in an official advisory capacity. He persuaded Guru to stick to the one ball. After eighteen putts the Indian had reached the edge of the green. The Admiral playing four, was offered a putter by Little Jasper.

'Why new club? I new club!' cried Guru and, seizing a sand-blaster from Solly's bag, strode excitedly on to the crew-cut green turf. Throggie wrested it from him, handed him the putter.

'Ye dinna ken muckle, ye gawk!' Guru looked pained and confused. He sat down and practised civil disobedience for a while until the Admiral holed out and informed him that he couldn't win the first hole anyway.

'Perhaps I hunger-strike.'

Genevieve helped him up, saying: 'But you've only just had lunch.'

Crows sat on the fairway of the second like reactionary politicians impeding progress. 'Caw, caw!' they cried and they flapped their lazy wings and leant into the breeze. Crows would make good politicians. They do no harm, crows.

In his rehearsal tights, over which he wore long woollen leggings, Cecil Sparks strutted like a turkey cock. Although his body was soft, his mind was hard and active as a laser beam, and he was determined that the company he had assembled should interpret his will precisely. He *knew* what he wanted; knew all he had to do was connect.

The doorbell announced the arrival of the first of his actors and it was no surprise to Cecil that it proved to be his Auntie, the J.P. Such a reputation had she for punctuality that he called her his 'Auntie Clockwise' and, if punctuality may be considered a character defect, in her it was a vice.

'I'm early, I know, but' (she said, sweeping aside her heavy fur coat for which a whole battalion of small vermin had lived and died, sweeping it aside from her burly shoulders as if it were no more than Brussels lace) 'I wished to have a word with you, Sparks, about my proposed interpretation of the role. I've played Gertrude before, you know. It is, as I see it, essentially a *mother's* play.' She was a large woman, well built, the sort of aunt the most confirmed materialist might wish to possess. Like a noble Bugatti or haughty Cadillac. Truly she appeared as if fine and dedicated engineers had worked long hours in her extravagant manufacture. Overtime too; and Sundays.

'But Auntie—'

'And, I wish to be reassured that I shall not be frittering away my histrionics in the company of talentless and amateur ... butterflies!'—This unexpected noun conveyed very precisely to Cecil Sparks both what she feared and expected was all she was going to get.

'But, Auntie, butterflies can be turned into—'

'What?' she snorted contemptuously, 'moths?'

'No, but they can at least be pinned and mounted.'

'*You* are to do the pinning, Sparks? You are not trifling with me, I trust?'

The very idea of trifling with so formidable a lady could never have occurred to the actor/manager and he said as much, always couching his compliments in the most subtly obsequious way. The only thanks he received was a sceptical grunt; yet how gratefully he seized on even this.

'I knew you'd see it my way, Auntie.'

'I have not as yet seen it *any* way, nor do I intend to see it, until I have seen *them*. And seen them pinned.' And as if she had the power to attract, to magick people to her, the doorbell rang a second time.

'Answer the door, Sparks. We shall discuss niceties of inter-pretation later.'

Lunch with Doctor Bushey was not exactly a duty, nor yet entirely a pleasure, for the Vicar. The old boy was educated and that, in Soft Meadows Cross, was something. His daughter was a splendid cook and that, in Soft Meadows Cross, was something too. But the Doctor had become very strange, so distrait recently that conversation with him was an Alpine, indeed sometimes a Himalayan ascent, requiring courage, steadfastness, crampons of concentration and the ability speedily to improvise when an uncharted crevasse yawned suddenly in front of one . . . and that was something else.

Over the apple crumble the Vicar, conscious that a guest should in some measure entertain his host and conscious too that the Doctor had not spoken for twenty minutes (when he had flung the one word 'Anaemia' at his long-suffering daughter, quite without justification so far as the Vicar could tell) remarked in a cool, pale, high-pitched voice :

'How strange that so frequently the autumn wraps up its colourful gifts in a warm bundle of unseasonable sunshine !'

The Doctor seemed indifferent to this promising conversation piece until suddenly, pushing his bowl of crumble and custard ferociously to one side, he muttered :

'Keeps the bombers off.'

'I beg your pardon?'

'Bombers. Bombs.' And, to illustrate his thesis, he let fall the pepperpot on to the dining-room table from a great height. A side-plate was shattered. Morosely : 'Direct hit,' the Doctor added.

'Oh Daddy, you know you shouldn't.'

'But why should anyone bomb us?' asked the Vicar, all clerical innocence.

'They won't.'

'But I thought you said . . .'

'Too clear. Visibility you know. So much for your warm bundle of unseasonable sunshine.'

'I don't understand.'

The Vicar took another sip of water. His host continued venomously : 'Then there's the things under the floorboards.' At this Victoria looked up :

'What things?'

'Bugs. Beetles. Little, black, busy things, eating away at the framework of our lives.'

'Oh, it's a metaphor,' said the schoolmistress, much relieved.

'It most certainly is not. I've seen them. So would you have, had you eyes to see.'

Victoria muttered to the Vicar: 'This is something quite, quite new.'

'Wood-worms, shreves, cockroaches, woodlice gnawing away with their sharp little teeth, nibble, nibble, nibble, gnaw, gnaw, gnaw.'

Quietly Victoria inquired: 'Tell me, Vicar, who is to treat the doctor when the doctor's sick?'

To this sad question the Vicar, whose tongue was gouging crumble out of the crevices of his back teeth, asked an equally sad one of his own:

'And for that matter if God is dead, who shall instruct the Vicar?'

Suddenly Victoria clutched the reverend gentleman's arm. 'You don't really believe that? Surely you, of all people, can't?'

'You give me no chance to answer, my dear.'

'I'm giving you a chance now.'

'In that case I must admit that there was a time when I could have dismissed the contention out of hand, but recent events . . .'

'You don't mean that you've lost your faith?'

('Nibble, nibble, nibble, gnaw, gnaw, gnaw,' continued the Doctor.)

'No, not that perhaps, but when you ask whether God is dead I would now insist upon a definition of those two big words. Who is God? What is dead?'

'So you cannot answer me?'

'The modern way,' chuckled the Vicar, trying to appear so very old since it was obviously hopeless to try to appear so very young, 'yes or no; in or out, up or down, black or white.'

('No, out, down and black,' grunted the melancholic Doctor.)

'But tell me how you instruct your children about God.'

'In the school? Well, they tell me. They know all about Him. He's usually a combination of their father and The Saint.'

'And why do you suppose that I should know any better?'

Half to herself Victoria said: 'I just thought you would. Excuse me, father, and you too, Vicar. I'll go and wash up.' Much distressed the girl swept out. The atmosphere between the two men became a mite easier. The Vicar stirred his thick, rich coffee with an apostle spoon.

'If you really think you have dry or wet rot or vermin in the woodwork, Doctor Bushey, I can recommend some thoroughly sound church restorers. They'd be only too happy to do an estimate for you, I feel sure.'

'Oh.'

'They advertise in *The Times*, although even that is no guarantee of respectability any more.'

'Napalm,' said the Doctor, 'and a mass grave.'

By the time they reached the short fifth the crowds of spectators had begun to weary of the contest. The Admiral had been playing for him undistinguished stuff and Guru had scored 91 for the first four holes. Frequently he had stopped to meditate, occasionally he chanted a sad snatch of some oriental incantation but in the world of golf he remained an innocent. Oddly enough, while Guru himself appeared careless as to the course of the match, Old Porson was evidently taking it very hard indeed, grumbling away to himself like some old-fashioned water geyser. But shy. Although desperately anxious that Guru should improve and match stroke for stroke with the Admiral, he was still unable to shatter the bars of his prison of self-consciousness and tell Guru what was wrong. Not hard to tell him. Firstly that he should keep his head down and watch the ball, not stare into the distance and invoke Gandhi. Second, that he should swing a little more slowly, a little more easily —for he attacked the ball as if it were a dangerous serpent about to strike at him. The faces of the clubs were covered with grass, the ball with mud and Old Porson with confusion.

At the short fifth where the Admiral drove the green, Guru hit his ball straight into the Admiral's golf-bag, which he then carried off in the direction of the pin. But did this half-heartedly, as if he knew all along that it was against the rules. The Admiral taunted him :

'Bad luck. Bad luck. *Bad* luck !' every time he struck the ball.

'All my life,' said Tessa, 'I have been looking for a hero, and I sometimes think that in spite of all the strides which women have made on the long rutted path to total equality with all that that implies, they do always and shall always—if they mustn't have gods or devils—require heroes . . .'

(Guru's ball rested coyly under a bramble bush. 'Bad luck. Bad luck. *Bad* luck!')

'It is not pleasant when one has eventually chosen one's hero to find him a figure of fun, his big red nose a source of scoff to the local children, his sores a communal licking place for stray dogs.'

'Indeed you go too far, Tessa,' said Abigail.

('Plenty of golfers could be found who would call *that* unplayable,' said Old Porson a little sourly, as Guru hacked away at the ball energetically like a boy whipping a top.)

'But I shall not falter in my allegiance to my hero. I may—indeed I know that I shall—stumble on the weary pilgrimage, but I shall not turn back. Rather shall I keep my head steadfastly turned to the East, and pausing not a whit for refreshment, pursue ever my only master.'

Guru's ball trickled across the fairway and into a little stream where it pretended to be a pebble. Guru splashed down through the water with Solly's brassie and struck a pebble which had been pretending to be a golf ball. The head of the club was shattered.

Genevieve ran up to Guru, caressed him for a while, then kissed him. In spite of the scant encouragement she had received, she returned to her sisters glowing happily.

Grunted the gruff Admiral: 'While you're dredging the stream and corrupting the young, I'll go and putt mine out. I begin to wonder whether it's worthwhile continuing with this damn' apology of a golf match.'

Guru left his stream and walked over to his opponent. He stood very close to him and didn't blink.

'Shall not lose,' stated Guru with finality. 'Shall not be allowed.'

Crates, boxes and parcels were piled up, like deserted Egyptian tanks in the small front hall of the Worsley's mournful little house.

'You think we are doing the right thing, Dick? Running away like this?'

'Not running away, dear, running to . . .'

'But what is there in South Africa?'

'A *natural* aristocracy.'

'How do you *know*? I'm not trying to be difficult, Dick, really, but we had *such* hopes . . .'

'We shall have servants.'

'You mean that?'

'Of course. They're two a penny out there.'

'Black ones?'

'Four a penny.'

Thelma laughed: 'But do they have . . .' and searched in her mind for the precise image.

'They have gold and sunshine and tennis clubs and . . .'

'No, but do they have . . . *fingerbowls*?'

Dick was thoughtfully silent. He took the pencil (with which he had been checking off their possessions on a list) from behind his ear and put it in his breast pocket.

'Do they?'

'We shall take our own with us just in case.'

'Oh yes! We shall teach them *every*thing. But—' her brow crinkled—'do they have a queen?'

'They have our queen, Thelma dear.'

'They do? What are we waiting for then?'

'The taxi.'

'South Africa, here we come!'

'A-one a-two, a-swing a-two, and out and two, with press and two, and press and press and breathe and breathe and up and up and down and down.'

Cecil watched with satisfaction as *his* company of actors rose and fell in *his* sitting-room (reluctantly) to *his* command.

'And now I want you all to try and imagine that you're in a beautiful garden full of flowers. Beautiful flowers, lupins and delphiniums, and . . . no, not yet dear. But I want all the flowers in your gardens to be the faces of your friends around you. Walk around, yes, all of you, you can start now, and smell the flowers and touch the flowers and *love* the flowers. Touch, touch, touch, there, that's spiffing!'

'It's nothing of the sort!' Aunty Clockwise (a peony probably) said, 'I thought this was to be read through. Really Sparks, sometimes I think you're potty.'

'But, Auntie, *please*—'

'Only one thing matters in the theatre, Sparks, and that's projection.'

'Voice exercises; yes, indeed, we were just coming on to them.'

'Sir Frank Benson used to tell me that my projection was quite astonishing. I can remember him saying to me when a small group of we actors were boating on the Avon. "If you were to whisper the soliloquy of the heroine of the Scottish Tragedy into the ear of the lion that stands guard at the South-East corner of Nelson's column," he said to me, "the whole of London from Tower Bridge to Harrods would stop whatever it was doing to listen." And that was not shouting, mind you, that was *projection*. Give me your hand—' and she turned to Rusty Motorcade, who was most readily available—'place it just . . . there.' And she put his hand approximately over her diaphragm. 'And now—"Brek-ek-ek-ex Ko-ax Ko-ax" —there, what did you feel?'

'Well really, I—'

'Oh come on, don't be self-conscious, this is the theatre, darling, and we, why we are dedicated Thespians.'

'How remarkable,' murmured Ethel Tomlinson, confusing Thespians with Lesbians.

'Well?'

'Corset.'

'Oh really!'

'Perhaps, loves,' said Cecil Sparks quickly, 'it is time for us to get down to business, by which I mean, of course *Hamlet*, about which I intend to make a few introductory remarks before we commence our reading.'

'Excuse me, but I simply *have* to go to the loo,' cried Ethel. Her nervous excitement was pressing upon her bladder. She was to play Cornelius. Cornelius! She didn't remember the play too clearly (she had been *sure* there was a nurse in it somewhere) but, wow!, Cornelius sounded important actually, super actually. Charles, the Loin, who had brought her along and fully intended, in the other sense, to *bring her along,* which required gratitude on her part and patience on his, barked sharply (the pattern of the relationship must be quickly established and understood): 'You're always going,' adding with a touch of philosophy : 'Women are impossible creatures.'

'Actually no, Charles. I read it in a book. It's not true.'

'What's not true, Ethie, and what did you read in a book?'

'That women go more often than men.' Giggles. 'Oh, aren't I awful, talking like this in front of everyone? Sorry, everyone.' And off she dashed.

'I don't know where she gets such books,' said her father.

Auntie Clockwise had regained her professional poise:

'The call *was* for two thirty. It's half past three and we've not even started.'

'You're perfectly right, Auntie,' said Sparky, 'we will all try to be more punctual in future, won't we, loves?' And smiled brightly upon the assembled company. No visible or audible response unfortunately.

And then *Hamlet*.

He explained to them how Laertes was in love with the Black Prince and offered in evidence Act 1, Scene 3. Why, he asked, was Laertes so anxious that Ophelia should 'be wary' and 'keep within the rear of your affection'? Why? It stood out a mile. Jealousy. That was all. Jealousy of his sister's place in Hamlet's affections. And why was Hamlet so sulky throughout the first act? Why, it stood out a mile! Because of Laertes' going back to France without so much as a by your leave.

'In that case,' asked Rose-Marie—and of course it did concern her—'why does Laertes go at all? Did he have another little friend in France?'

'Certainly not, ducky.' Cecil Sparks seemed quite shocked. 'He was a nice young man. Loyal too. But ask yourself another question. Why was Hamlet so easily persuaded to leave Denmark after killing Polonius when there was surely everything to keep him there? Ophelia if, as the commentators claim, he really loved her. Gertrude if, as those other commentators claim, he loved *her*. Claudius, whom he had sworn to kill. Well, I mean, it stands to reason that Engand was the last place he should want to go. And yet look at Act 4, Scene 3:

' "Claudius :   Therefore prepare thyself.
                         The bark is ready, and the wind at help,
                         Th'associates tend, and everything is bent
                         For England.
Hamlet : For England?
Claudius : Ay Hamlet.

Hamlet: Good."

'Really, there was his duty plain as a pikestaff in Denmark; why *should* he be so pleased to go to England?'

'Well it doesn't make sense, Mr Sparks, if Laertes was in France—'

'Were,' said Sparky.

Rose-Marie drew breath. 'I beg your pardon. If Laertes *were* in France why should Hamlet want to go to England?'

'Precisely.' Sparky smirked at his cleverness.

'Well, tell us,' asked someone.

'Because he never intended to go to England at all! There! How about that? And Ophelia goes mad because she learns the truth about the man she's in love with. "Lord, we know what we are, but not what we may be." How true! How very true!'

'How does she learn?' asked someone else.

'Well really, Shakespeare couldn't tell us *every*thing. But Laertes had already as good as told her. Now, you see, what Hamlet meant to do was overpower the pirates and go not to England, but to France and join his Laertes there. But remember—Hamlet had killed Laertes' father—well, naturally if Laertes had heard about it from someone else—no, no question, Hamlet had to go to France and explain.'

'Why didn't he then?'

'He would have, he *would* have. But there were those pirates, you see. And Laertes had left France anyway, gone back to Denmark, to a dead father and a mad sister. Not a very pleasant home-coming, I think you'll agree. Now I shall not be dogmatic about this, but it is very possible that Hamlet knew whom he was killing when he killed Polonius and killed him because the old boy didn't approve of his, Hamlet's, association with Laertes. Well, he wouldn't, would he? So there we have it, my dears. Hamlet loves Laertes. And because of his love drives Laertes' sister mad, kills Laertes' father and finally Laertes himself. For each man kills the thing he loves, eh? Yes, Hamlet really loved Laertes, and he reciprocated it, this is what we must portray in our production and it's all'—here Sparky paused and pointed dramatically in his aunt's direction—'Gertrude's fault!'

'I think,' said Colonel Gilbert Tomlinson offensively, 'your theories are rubbish.'

K

'Oh, that's nice. That's very nice.'

'Just produce one concrete piece of evidence, one quotation will do, to show that Hamlet loved Laertes or Laertes Hamlet!'

'Well, of course,' said Cecil Sparks, 'I'm not one of your pseuds, you know. When Hamlet's dying, Laertes comes up to him and says—and I want this to be a big moment in my production—"Goodnight sweet prince". What could be clearer, or more affecting?'

'But I thought it was Horatio said that. I mean, Laertes is already dead.'

'Details, details, I can only concern myself with the grand design. Anyway, it's time we started reading the play.'

It was at the long eighth, a dog-leg to the left, with the Admiral seven up but tetchy, that the cow appeared. Well, no, the cow didn't appear, because she had been there all the time, but, as the largish party breasted the rise to the eighth tee, the cow hove into sight. She hove, heavy and contented on her short legs, and chomped the cud and swished her tail seductively. There were seldom cows on the golf course. One could go further; there were *never* cows on the golf course, or had never been, but this was certainly no mirage. Mirages don't moo, and this cow did. It was a reassuring moo really, a moo of a generous spirit, an outgoing moo which seemed to say: 'Glad to see you, boys; nice to know you're still around.'

'Well, I'll be jiggered,' said the Admiral (who never had been) and then, appreciating that outrage was surely expected of him : 'Get that bloody cow off the course!'

No one spoke. No one knew whose cow she was.

'Come up and see me some time,' helved the cow.

'Very well. We'll just have to ignore it and if we hit it, call it a man-made hazard under the local rules.'

'Man-made,' murmured the Admiral's wife, 'whatever next?'

The Admiral teed up, took a few virile waggles with his wrists, was put off by a moo, addressed once more the ball, tapped it off its tee, cursed, was answered by a moo, cursed again, finally swung the head of the driver back and up with a curl of the shoulders and a frown of the brow, and swish down again—only the ball was gone ('Moo!'), snatched away by a swift and wicked brown claw.

'Fuck!' cried the Admiral under grave stress.

'Cow,' said Guru lucidly, pointing.

'Well, of course, it's a cow! Didn't I say it was a cow? If you intend to interrupt me every time I drive to point out features of the damn' landscape . . .'

'Sacred Cow!' said Guru and trotted off. Two hundred yards away stood the cow. Guru trotted briskly, diminishing fast, seemingly (it was difficult to tell from two hundred yards) held some conversation with the cow and returned considerably more slowly, since he was leading the cow. Leading the cow? Well, the cow was following him obediently to heel.

'Oh really,' said the Admiral with as much feeling as the roundest curse, but he was not truly crotchetty, not at core crotchetty, since there was some pleasure to be had from being seven up after seven holes against an uppity and wily oriental.

Oh, but, it was hard to concentrate with a cow on the tee! She was so *big*. And smelt. And the flies! She swished her tail. The Admiral's drive landed in a clump of dead nettles. An otter sat on it.

As Guru, learning fast, teed up and took his driver, the cow muzzled him. Old Porson and Little Jasper tugged on her tail and, when she did take a step backwards, found themselves all of a heap on the ground. The cow leant gently upon them while Guru drove.

And a fine drive! Off into the sun, slicing the air into yellow bananas, one below and one above, then hanging poised, a black spot upon the sun's surface—a drive of ninety-two million miles. Everybody shaded their eyes with their hands. Hazily reluctant, like a child leaving the beach at six o'clock on an August evening, in front of him supper and bed and dreams that can never challenge reality, behind him sand dinghies that resisted the tide for a full five minutes, and star-fish and the smell of sea-weed and the pop which it made and smooth flat pebbles that daddy skimmed upon the calm, purple sea, especially like those pebbles, the ball splashed back to earth.

'Aye,' said Throggie, splitting the word into two syllables. This 'aye' was the greatest compliment he had ever learned to pay. Guru spoke to the cow. The cow mooed. The limpid eyes of the Angell sisters glistened with love.

'Aie, aie, aie,' said Jack Rubin.

'Aye,' repeated Throggie.

The gentlemen in the crowd of spectators exchanged low whistles of admiration. The Admiral's wife fondled the knobbled handle of the Admiral's golfing umbrella.

And the cow seemed to have a remarkable effect on Guru.

Insofar as the Admiral was unnerved, Guru was inspired. His six at the eighth was quite good enough to win the hole from his rattled opponent. At the uphill ninth the cow trod the Admiral's ball half-way into the soft turf and Throggie, who was a greater respecter of truth than persons and had in any case a live sense of the irony of life, refused to deem it unplayable. The Admiral hacked away manfully for a while before picking it up. At the tenth, the Admiral, much vexed, played Guru's ball from the tee, which, together with the stroke he had to give, proved too heavy an impost.

But the eleventh hole saw the crisis of the match. The Eleventh Hole at the Royal Fairway is only 265 yards from tee to tin. It runs alongside the path which borders the entire estate, on the other side of which path sits Cecil Sparks's house, whence the three little dachshunds make their forays on to the fairway. But this is not the only hazard at the Eleventh. There is Solly's Doom, the big bunker that guards the right of the green and which Solly would have moved long ago had he been allowed to have his way. He could, of course, as director of Yom Tov Properties Ltd. have carried out his threat to build bungalows on every fairway, but should such a drastic step be induced by one bunker, however bad? It was nobody's secret that Solly had his eye on the captaincy and then perhaps . . .

Well, for a captaincy . . .

Four down at the eleventh with eight to play, and Guru's honour. His new confidence, inspired by the miraculous appearance of the Bovinity, had created in him the relaxed rhythms that are the secret of the classical golf swing. So that now when he swung (and the cow mooed) the ball travelled a respectable distance towards the green. While Guru played the Admiral chopped surreptitiously at the cow's shins with a sandblaster until peremptorily stopped by Mrs Connolly who sold cruelty to animals flags every Easter in Oxford Street. The cow reacted philosophically.

The Admiral's drive rolled to within a couple of feet of Solly's Doom and stopped. A simple chip shot and a putt should be sufficient to stop the rot, and five and seven . . . well, if he lost after being five and seven, then the Senior Service was not worthy the title, nor the Admiral worthy the Senior Service.

The Parade marched up the Fairway, the sun gilding the bottoms of Admiral, Guru, caddies and cow.

It had been apparent from the moment that the Colonel, in the character of Bernardo, stood up to deliver the first line of the play that Cecil Sparks had more than problems of interpretation with which to concern himself. For as Gilbert folded one white hand across his chest, cleared his throat and inquired, 'Who's there?' it was as if he were asking his secretary at head office just that question. Wilfred, the Church Organist, on the other hand had taken it into his Welsh head that for the role of Francisco, which he was doubling with the First Player, he should adopt an unnaturally deep voice. With resonant majesty he bellowed: 'Nay, answer me. Stand and unfold yourself.' But addressed to the head of a brewery 'unfold yourself' sounded so incongrous, so *obscene*, that one could sympathise with Rusty Motorcade's choked laughter. As for Auntie Clockwise, she simply raised one of her most ominous eyebrows and held her ground.

Things had been progressing satisfactorily with only one temporary embarrassment, when Ethie, having spoken, and rather superbly actually, Cornelius's one speech: 'In that, and all things, will we show our duty, etc. etc.,' began to riff through the pages of the play to discover with a sea-bird's screech that that was approximately *all* that Cornelius had to say, and even that was said in unison with Voltemand. Voltemand, played by a chauffeur! It was all very well his, 'I do my best to give satisfaction, Miss Ethel,' but she *wasn't* satisfied. One line—only half a line really—in the whole play. It was nasty while it lasted, but Cecil with great tact and some reluctance mollified her by offering her the double role of Cornelius and the Player Queen. 'I bet *she* doesn't say anything either,' Ethie sulked.

'Indeed she does, plenty of lines, luv, and significant ones too'—though Cecil fully intended to keep the Players to a minimum and include only their dumb show. There would be time enough for cuts in due course, and the girl must learn discipline. 'It is the loyalty of sword-carriers through thick and thin, which has made the British theatre what it is today,' Auntie Clockwise was in the habit of maintaining.

Then came Act 1 Scene 5 and the Ghost's first lines. Taking a miniature trophy from the mantelpiece (Dorking and District Drama Cup, 1948) and putting it to his lips, Cecil Sparks began a dialogue between Hamlet (normal vocalisation) and the Ghost of Hamlet's father (an eerie echo effect induced by the silver trophy). There was bound to be discontent at such an unexpected device; indeed there was; consternation even.

'You're not suggesting for a moment that you—'

'Really, Sparks, I didn't come all this way to take part in a charade you know. Invention and imagination is *one* thing, but—'

'Please, please, ladies and gentlemen,' cried Hamlet's Ghost, holding up a flabby white hand not unlike a buttered scone, 'let me at least expatiate a minute upon what isn't, you may be sure, an arbitrary or playful effect, but a genuine attempt to communicate the essence of the play. I first considered doubling Hamlet with the ghost of his father when—'

But at that moment unaccountably Irving, Garrick and Gielgud began leaping up and down like scampi in a pan, yapping their small-brained heads off, until Cecil was inaudible. Cushions were flung but to no effect and then the reason for the disturbance materialised, mooing. Outside the window on the eleventh fairway a large brown cow sauntered into sight. Ethel, still humiliated, opened the window. Dogs leapt out, yelling like mandrake-roots.

The Admiral, after a fine recovery shot from the dead-nettle clump, was chipping to the green. The ball floated in a lazy parabola and was caught by Garrick who started earnestly to chew its outer casing. Irving and Gielgud seized each a mouthful of cow-udder.

Cecil Sparks took a few resentful but elegant steps to the window. Chose to ignore the rumpus. Recommenced reading.

Not so the cast. Gertrude and Claudius, Horatio and Laertes, waving their copies of the play, walked as fast as their dignity would allow them out into the garden, followed by other members of the Danish Court and a few assorted Scandinavians.

'Call your bloody hounds off!' cried a familiar voice, and the Admiral's face, contorted into a mask of naval outrage, appeared over the hedge. The cow, from whom depended like leeches (or lychees) two little dogs, was bouncing up and painfully down.

'I'll get you for this, Sparks!'

' "Fat weed!" '

'Eh?'

' "Go and root yourself on Lethe wharf".'

'This time you've gone too far.'

'But it's *Hamlet.*'

'I don't care if it's the Archbishop of Canterbury.'

'Philistine!'

'Lounge-lizard!'

Cecil Sparks took up his position at the head of his troupe; the golfers lined up, shooting sticks at the present. The actors hurled Shakespearean obloquy over the hedge at the golfers; the golfers made impolite gestures in return.

A dog choked over a mangled golf-ball. The cow gave an anguished moo like the all-clear siren. Cecil called the Admiral 'that incestuous, that adulterate beast', and the Admiral marched through the hedge as if it were buttercups and daisies (it was holly). Heads fell off dead dahlias. Rhododendron bushes wilted. Vultures (rarely seen in —shire) circled overhead.

Cecil found his forces deserting and retreated indoors, whence he cocked a snook through the window. When the Admiral prepared a salvo of Dunlop 65s, Auntie Clockwise, with the presence of mind of an old stager, pulled the cord that released the Venetian blinds.

'Oh, art and science! Implacable as ever!' cried Rusty Motorcade from the gloom.

Mrs Skullham was no mystic. To her it was inconceivable that Albert could exist other than in that wrinkled, ill-fitting skin. She knew herself well enough to be convinced that she no longer stood any chance of divine revelations, mediumistic messages, and would be receiving nothing further from God or Daddy. The pattern of the tapestry was all too apparent. They had taken him away. She sat down on the bed and put her hand on the brow of the Macfisheries Man.

The Macfisheries Man tossed and turned. He cried out several times. The fever was at its pitch, and his stripey pyjamas were hot and damp. His collar-bone was as prominent as the handlebars of his red bicycle and the skin hung loose now on his belly. He still smelt faintly of fish. Mrs Skullham neither loved nor pitied him, and, at the moment when she decided to nurse him back to health, with all that that implied, the decision was a selfish one. Yet not entirely. Wherever he went on his moonlight jaunts, it was an indication that he was, as she had liked to suppose, a sad, wandering spirit. Surely no man would choose to spend his days in dreams and his nights in ditches, which he certainly must have done to judge by the look in his eyes and the state of his clothes. Any man must—*must* respond to the offer of a warm byre and slippers by the fire, no more need to roam, no more dinners for one from Oxo-stained cookbooks, and clean clothes and no buttons dangling, and a good, good woman. He need carry obsession on his humped shoulders no, no longer. No longer. No longer.

The Macfisheries Man opened his eyes to a world which was for a moment sharply in focus.

'Oh,' he said nervously, seeing the gaunt lady sitting on his bed, and then, 'oh, it's you', and relapsed into a health-restoring sleep.

'Since I want him and he needs me,' the lady said aloud, 'nothing shall stand in our way.'

And she went downstairs to make thin soup, rich in health-restoring protein.

The Doctor and the Vicar sat staring at each other across the congealed wreck of the lunch. Neither spoke for a long time. The Doctor's eyes were sparkling blue, bluer than cornflowers in his harvested face.

'Burning themselves, imagine that,' he said at length, 'pouring it over and . . . desecration . . . dedication . . .'

And the big, square moulds of cars roared past on the motorway, veneer and rubber, oil and metal, and in front of their facia sat moulds of men, veneer and blubber, oil and a hollowness inside.

An hour passed. Words, devices, suppositions curdled in the Vicar's brain. His skull was a basket full of snakes. Again the Doctor spoke.

'Vicar?'

Hopefully. 'Yes?'

'Nothing.'

It must now and finally be admitted that it was a combination of circumstances, natural and supernatural, which led to the defeat of the Captain of the Royal Fairway Golf Club by an Indian holy man who had never before touched a golf club. To take the supernatural first, since the supernatural has an impolite habit of frequently jumping its place in the queue: there was the cow.

The cow's appearance at such a timely psychological moment in the match can scarcely be considered a coincidence. Coincidences imply a random element in life, and that cow was a Freisian and certainly not random. And with the cow one must bracket the dramatic improvement in Guru's game. He was fit and wiry, yes. He had strength and a sufficiency of instinctive intelligence, yes. But is this enough to explain his sudden astonishing aptitude? Or should we not in this too see the hand of something above and beyond human agency? Poor Admiral, unaware that he was being out-driven by history.

Of natural causes there were several. The appearance and subsequent actions of the cow played their part in unsettling the rhythm of the Admiral's swing, breaking the intensity of his concentration. His unaccustomed exertions the previous evening began to take their toll of his stamina, and overconfidence, induced by the commanding lead he had built up during the first nine holes, sapped his determination. Complacency was the ruin of empires, ours especially; how much more so may the same insidious worm whittle away an early lead of seven holes. Finally, and more directly, there was the uncharacteristic behaviour of Old Porson who missed no opportunity, especially when Guru began to win back some of his early losses, to aid destiny in its grand design by such means as kicking the Admiral's ball into an unfavourable lie; persuading Little Jasper —persuading? suborning rather—to hand the Admiral the wrong clubs; a timely cough; a subtle fidget; and thus, and thus, and thus.

Man and Superman, Nature and History, Brahman-Atman, these were the forces which individually *and together*, combined to cause the downfall of the Admiral.

And there he stood on the seventeenth green, his whiskers curling with humiliation, like Gogol the giant bear baited in a pit (the seventeenth green nestled in a green declivity of land), beaten three down and one to play, by a sniggering Indian who was shaking hands all round in an obsequious kind of way. And the Admiral seized his clubs one by one and shattered them over his knee, all except his steel-shafted brassie which would not shatter but which shattered his knee instead (and Jessica grabbed the brassie and fingered it nostalgically). And all the merry good folk of Soft Meadows Cross, who had watched dispassionately the downfall of their champion, Solly Schneider and Mrs Connolly, Jack Rubin and Throggie, the Farquhars and the Admiral's wife, the lovely and serene Angell sisters, vanished into the Club-house for a drink. And the baited bear bellowed at the dusk.

And the bellow echoed faintly across the green Royal Fairway and wafted in through the windows of Cecil Sparks's living-room where, in spite of interruptions, Hamlet had just died and boring old Fortinbras, played with ineffable contempt and a pompous Keble manner by Rusty Motorcade, had bulldozed in too late as usual with typical Shakespearean inefficiency.

'What a strange noise,' remarked Wilfred, the Church organist.

'A bruit,' said Colonel Gilbert Tomlinson.

'Like a wounded bear.'

'A bruin.'

'I think, Sparks,' said Auntie Clockwise, 'that I shall play Gertrude as a younger woman, sensual and provocative. That's the joy of *Hamlet*, isn't it? One may interpret any role to suit one's personality.'

'Yes, Auntie.'

'What is your opinion, Voltemand?' and she turned to the chauffeur who blushed scarlet from bonnet to axle.

'What me, Madam?'

'Certainly.'

'Well, Madam, you could be sensual and provocative. You could be anything, Madam, you're a fine, handsome lady, you know that.'

'Enough, enough,' carolled Cecil Sparks, smiling at his now mild Auntie and letting his hands roll around like propellers on his wrists. 'You are all to go home, dears, and on Tuesday we shall have our first rehearsal proper. But I want you to know that I'm very pleased with you. You've been terribly and jolly good and I'm sure the Bard himself would be proud of you. Off you go now, loves, shoo-shoo, shoo-shoo, and start studying your lines.'

When they had all gone, all but Auntie that is, Cecil remembered that he had omitted to serve the brandy snaps. He and his Auntie chewed them up together notwithstanding, while silence dropped around them like poison from an upas tree. Finally :

'Oh, Auntie, you are wonderful. I do admire you so.'

But the Aunt smiled chillily like a frosty magnolia with wilting outer petals.

'Not wonderful,' she said, 'just a professional, Sparks, that's all.'

Long after the guests, long even after Auntie had gone, Cecil Sparks sat staring at the last of the brandy snaps. One line of Hamlet's rang in his ears : 'That is Laertes, a very noble youth.' For nobility was what distinguished, what particularly distinguished Caedmon Tomlinson. His lustrous, green eyes were all very well, his husky voice passed muster, but all that was nothing to the nobility of the lad. He, Sparky, meant him no harm really; had received no peculiar signs of reciprocal affection—rather the reverse—would not for the world and all its secret wonders besmirch that nobility, that distinction of mien, those lustrous, green . . .

The brandy snap, its Fallopian tube, accused him. His private desires danced in lurid images before his eyes. 'Something, something, lemonade, and round the corner chocolate's made.' For God's sake, close your eyes, go limp and think of cricket ! Cricket ? Coverpoint . . . long leg . . . sneaky Chinamen . . . and . . . Hah ! Was he a hypocrite, or was he . . . ? All he hoped for was to protect . . . that was it, *protect*, and, at the same time . . . no ! With a scything sweep of his arm he knocked the

pile of *Hamlet*s off the coffee-table. Picked one up, opened it
at random, with closed eyes pointed a finger at the middle of
the page.

The bard would understand. He who loved the 'onlie begetter'
of the sonnets. That great universal soul. The wide-winged
albatross of literature. The bard, who loved men *and* women,
the bard, the beard, the bard would understand. He opened his
eyes and read: 'A little more than kin and less than kind.'

In desperation Cecil strode from room to room, but in each
some inanimate object accused him. Mirrors reflected his guilty
secrets, walls shut out the sun. He put his hand in his pocket
to—and found a menu card! What? A menu card! With
what written under 'sundries'? 'I will do anything you like for
£15.'

Good heavens! Good gracious! Great Scott! Good grief!
Oh ducky!

Candida, the waitress at the Burnt Scone. He had quite
forgotten her. The hussy! And yet... What would Proust have
done? No, not Proust, de Maupassant. Cecil pulled book after
book from the shelves in desperation. Walt Whitman con-
tradicted Thomas Hardy. Samuel Johnson fell upon D. H.
Lawrence. Oscar Wilde said one thing, Galsworthy another
(Firbank a third).

Books! What was he doing consulting books? What would
Marshall McLuhan have done? How would Fellini shoot it?

'I will do anything you like for £15.' *Anything?* Was that
possible? Anything was possible. Read Dale Carnegie. Was
anything possible? Not with Caedmon, but with Candida. £15.
What was £15? Or rather, where was £15? He went into
Wendy Pakenham's room and looked under the mattress.
Everything conspired together. *Anything?* Wendy had Sunday
afternoon off.

Cecil, feeling more determinedly virile than he had for
years, stole the money and left the house.

'Daddy, Daddy,' cried Victoria, bursting into the room like
a lion through a paper hoop, 'I've got some wonderful news.
They said on the wireless that the peace talks—'

'Ssh, child,' said the Vicar, 'your father is not well.'

'Not well? What do you mean?' And then she saw him,

scrabbling on the floorboards with paper and paste, quite mad. She ran to him but he didn't respond. He kept making inconsequential noises and tut-tutting, but he had withdrawn entirely from the Vicar, from Victoria, from the human race.

'They're sending an ambulance from the cottage hospital in Boggley. I thought I'd better stay with him, though I had intended to be at Cecil Sparksissis.'

Blackly said Victoria: 'I'm sure you acted in the very best interests.'

The Vicar smiled vaguely and shifted his position. With a modesty born of ineffable arrogance he murmured: 'I only did my duty.'

Victoria went to the phone.

'My poor child,' said the Vicar, 'for whom are you telephoning?'

'Guru.' Gently the Vicar took the receiver out of her hands and replaced it on its rest. 'You must seek consolation within the Church, Victoria.'

The Vicar kissed the unfortunate girl manfully. Victoria flinched. The sound of the kiss became the ambulance bell and men in white uniforms hopped out of their mouths, pulling stretchers out from under the blanket of their tongues.

They took the doctor away.

When Guru reached home, followed (in Indian file) by the Angell sisters, Little Jasper and the cow, there was a huddle of village gossips buzzing under the porch. He smiled benignly upon them and touched a brown forehead with pinkish fingers. There was much pushing amongst the ladies. Gulls skimmed above their heads. Guru halted, his retinue close behind him. Mrs Connolly started forward nervously, like a subaltern, and the other ladies closed ranks, cutting off her retreat. There was a certain amount of whispering.

'Did you read my note?' asked Mrs Connolly, first at the waterhole.

Guru took her indoors. The other ladies clucked angrily together. *Their* problems were just as acute, *their* lives as empty, their . . .

'The thing is,' said Mrs C., having talked about the weather, 'I have these dreams.'

'Good. Dreams are good.'

'I'm in this long corridor, this tunnel it really is, and you see I want to get through this tunnel because there's the sea at the other end of it, and all the time I know I can't because—'

'Aargh!'

'I beg your pardon?'

'Aargh! Bloody English dreams!'

'Well really, I must say . . . I only came to see you because I thought . . .'

'Did *not* think; *never* thought; and that is reason you came. Guru teach you to think.'

'But my dreams, Guru?'

Guru stood behind the sad, sharp, selfish lady and touched her neck. She stiffened.

It was some twenty minutes before she relaxed sufficiently to gain any benefit from the insidious movements of Guru's hands upon her exhausted frame, and as many minutes before the word which he so studiously repeated acquired any kind of hold over her pettish mind (and the sisters made tactful tea and the other ladies and Little Jasper and the cow went impatiently home) but in time she began to imagine that she was deriving some kind of benefit from his treatment and to hope (which counted for more) that she would be further improved in due course, if she did this and this, according to his secret instructions; and in any case she came to imagine (since he had expended so much time on her) that her life was of some small importance—which, if anyone's wasn't, hers wasn't—and then she went home with her word and her hope for the future and her posture slightly improved.

And then Guru and the Angell sisters went into Boggley to see 'Carry On Doctor' at the Rialto.

Seeing dear Cecil taking that common young gel from the Burnt Scone into his bedroom, Wendy muttered with bitterness: 'Love Brooks No Compromise', and placed a toothmug against an important adjoining wall. With her ear to the tumbler she could hear nothing at first. Except a kind of shuffling.

Candida was dancing for Cecil. And Cecil was aghast.

The girl's limbs twisted and coiled and glistened like Medusa's locks; she had forked tongues on the end of her fingers and her pubis was a hive of bees. Her head spun and rolled on the pillar of her neck, her cartilages buzzed like helicopters and her breasts opened and closed like fans. Cecil was astonished, *astonished*.

Girls had bodies like these? Their skin smelt as sweet, did it? and it was a reassurance and a consolation to put your arms around their waists (kneeling with your head against their stomachs) and be held; *was* it?

Candida's clothes were no more than the inner skin of the shelled egg. She had sloughed them off so cleanly you'd never have believed it. And that was what it was like (was it?), golden-pink and shining and plain and perfect with the cleft of the jaw and the hollows of the collar bone and the thin branches of the arms and the buttoned navel and the half-hidden zip in the fur and the proud, clenched bottom with its double dimple and the legs of frozen milk? Was it?

Oh Candida!

'Well?'

'Yes!'

And Wendy's ear was white against the glass as the cries died down and the murmurs grew:

'I'm all damp.'

'That's nice.'

'I *was* surprised.'

'Why?'

'That . . . well, of all people . . . well, that you . . .'

'I hope you don't think . . .'

'What?'

'That I make a habit of . . .'

'What?'

'Well . . .'

'What's it matter what I think?'

'Well, then, I hope you don't feel . . .'

'What?'

'Well . . .'

'I feel nothing.'

'Then why . . .'

'*What?*'

'*Well, why . . .*'

'Oh. To get to London.'

'Nothing?'

'Hardly anything.'

'Oh. Pity.'

Long pause.

'You *have* to go to London, ducky?'

'Oh yes, I have to go to London.'

'Oh. Oh.'

'I really believe you mind.'

Candida seemed to feel almost sad. Cecil was such a sad man. Had been, with his plays and his books.

'You've got your work.'

'My work!'

'Well surely it's something.'

'Oh, it's something. Can I visit you in London?'

'Cost you fifteen pounds.'

'Let us say ten.'

'Very well.'

'Promise?'

'Promise.'

'Promises butter no parsnips.'

'I'd better go. What do you want? It was fun while it lasted. No strings.'

'Don't go.'

'You mean ... ?'

'Yes.'

'If that's what you'd really like.'

'Yes. Oh yes, yes. How could I have been so blind? Art. Boys.'

'Boys?'

'Give me women every time.'

'Give?'

'Ten pounds.'

'Let's say twelve and a half.'

The glass fell to the floor and lay shattered. Wendy Pakenham looked down at the fragments, shook her head unhappily, bent down to pick up a piece of glass. Reflectively she chewed it. Blood trickled out of the corner of her mouth. How *could* he? She asked the room: 'How could he?' and the walls and the windows and her innocent easel. Her what? Her easel. She stared at her easel with intensity.

An easel with a pretty landscape, all fireflies and herons and evening mists, a landscape she had been so proud of a week ago. She hurled it to the floor and jumped on it. Stamp on yon firefly, crush yon heron, smear and grind yon evening mist.

But then she stopped, intrigued rather by the perverse pleasure she found herself taking in this carnage. Stopped and considered. Crossed thoughtfully to her tubes of oils. Threw a red and a purple and an ochre on to the painting and leapt after them. Her sensible heels penetrated the canvas but her toes exploded the tubes and with those toes she made whorls and smudges and a bloody great mess. Then exhausted and out of breath she stopped to admire the result. She knew at once. It was the first work of art she had ever created.

After tea Jack had taken Miriam and the older children into Boggley to see 'Carry On Doctor'. In the circle they found themselves next to a stern-faced Guru and the Angell sisters, whom the shabby Rialto and jealousy had yellowed.

The children yelled with laughter whenever funny Frankie Howerd came on and shrieked at Hattie Jacques. And when Barbara Windsor took off her blouse the boys gurgled for sheer joy. Guru seemed little moved; and Abby and Genevieve on either side of him watched Guru quite as much as they watched the film. After a while the little Indian went to the lavatory (it surprised the girls that he had not been able to subjugate the demands of the body as did the Monarchy); Jack followed him.

'I wanted to talk to you,' said Jack. In the cubicle Guru read the graffiti and remained silent. 'At least I wanted to talk to somebody, but it's not easy . . .'

'Pencil?' asked Guru.

Jack handed one over. 'I thought that perhaps you . . .' (Scratch, scratch, scratch, went Guru's pencil. For want of anything better to do, Jack relieved himself, wishing that he *could* relieve himself, trying to do just that.) 'You see, I don't . . . well, I don't any more, that is to say, *get on with* my children, and, as for Miriam, well no man could ask for a better wife, but recently I have begun to wonder, that is to ask myself, not

L

that I need to ask myself, since the answer is plain enough, and I tried to tell Rabbi Keitelmann—he's a good man, with a lovely singing voice and a great Talmudic scholar—but well, he's a busy fellow, whereas you ... at least I wondered whether ...'

Guru stopped writing and turned his beautiful eyes (gentle like blue rhododendron flowers) upon Jack Rubin.

'You know well what to do,' he said, or his eyes said.

'It's true that I do,' murmured Jack, tucking away his faithful old immortaliser,' so why do I want that you should tell me what I have known for years?'

When he returned to his seat, Jack kissed Miriam with such unusual affection that she knew it for what it was—a kiss of farewell. She had, of course, known for years, but it was still a shock, and she had to do all she knew to keep from crying.

She was even unable to laugh at Frankie Howerd.

CHAPTER TEN

The Fire · *Sunday Evening*

'Aye, 'twas a Scot who fust invented alcohol,' cried Throggie nostalgically, swivelling the golden blend around the lovely bowl of his glass. 'Alcohol, indeed it wus.'

Solly shook his head mournfully. 'A Scot invented alcohol? I should live so long to hear such tales!'

'Colquhoun. Aye, Alasdair Colquhoun, och aye, that's the wee lad. Al Colquhoun, Alcohoon, Alcohol, d'ye bear with me?'

'Colquhoun, was it? Cohen, more likely. Albie Cohen, the sweetest little schnorrer in all Shoreditch. I remember the day he invented it. "Alcohol, schmalcohol," said his friend Morrie, "tomorrow's Yom Kippur." "All right already," replied Albie, "so next year I should atone!" '

Sammy laughed and Solly smiled as Jews must smile at Jewish jokes when there are goyim present. The sandstone cliffs of the Admiral's face looked more than usually bleak. Another round of drinks was ordered and consumed. The Farquhars went home to supper and the television and the Admiral's wife shovelled placebos into her mouth like anthracite bricks into an Aga.

Then the evening turned a little vicious.

Hard liquor, without love or friendship to justify it, lack of sleep, and the memory of an ineradicable humiliation created bitterness in the Admiral's heart, and the spray of his bitterness splashed over the others, so that they brooded silently too on senility and injustice and dyspepsia. The Admiral roamed the carpet of the club with his stormy sea-legs, as if vainly trying to re-establish his right to the place. He shook his head from time to time violently and angrily; fish flew out of his hoary locks and scuttled into the wainscoting. He touched things. The green baize of the notice-board, the stained white jacket of the steward, the edges of the pages of the sporting magazines. 'This is still mine,' he seemed to be saying, 'and this, and this,' but the chairs wilted under his touch, the window-panes dissolved, his wife shrank from him, and turned into a chicken. Something had to be done. What would Drake, Nelson, Jellicoe have done? He bought his crew (Solly, Sammy, Throggie, Jessica, and a half a dozen social members of the Club) a double ration of rum and spoke to them eloquently about Nombre de Dios bay and bowls and the Nile and the River Plate and Philip the Second.

'Though I have but the body of a weak and feeble woman,' cried Jessica, inspired, although it was not entirely true.

The Admiral's appointed second-in-command was Throggie, in spite of his being a Scot. He had a cousin by marriage who lived in Bideford (he said). It was enough.

'To the hatches, Number One!' and the professional led them to his shop, whose door he kicked in with a hefty Scottish boot. They were each provided with clubs (putters for the ladies) and a generous supply of balls, then sailed off northwards in the direction of Boggley and the enemy.

But were overseen.

Sitting on a tee-box on the eighteenth tee, Old Porson had been thinking private black thoughts. Some worm of concern had been gnawing in the arcane recesses of his heavy old brain, some verminous, irritatingly nagging itch of truth and purpose which both worried and exhilarated him. He looked at the stars, which had never been more to him than holes in the sky; they blazed and dazzled him. He looked at the curvilinear moon, until recently a processed sliver of cheese; its edge looked sharp enough to cut diamonds with. He looked at his hands, hands which had until now only weighted his arms and lifted his food and drink; suddenly they seemed eloquent utensils, servants of his will and his desires. He tried out his voice, caterwauling into the night; it sounded not so gruff, nor so low as of late. He was a little plumper, a little taller, a little younger, a little stronger. His eyes a little clearer, his heart-beat a little faster, his breath a little sweeter. Above all he was discontented.

And then he saw through the night and heard through his discontent a group of rough people breaking into the professional's shop. Last night, or any night past for many years he might well have shrunk off to the Raven and inundated his conscience with warm, cloudy beer. Not tonight. Not now. Guru would not wish it. He crept closer until he could distinguish voices and faces. They were talking such sodding nonsense. All about ships and the sea. And they were mean. They had it in for some poor rating. He, seemingly, would be no able-bodied seaman by the time they had finished with him. They started to climb the hill which would lead them to the six-masted House. They semaphored with their arms and the early frost under their feet rattled back in morse.

Old Porson tilted his head into the wind and followed them discreetly. He had never been to sea. He couldn't imagine what it would be like. Not, he imagined, like this. He spat, however, rather in the manner of a sailor.

The House loomed up, riding at anchor calmly in the security of the night. None of the lights was on.

'Tee up for a broadside fusillado,' cried the Admiral. 'And Number One—'

'Aye, Aye,' said Throggie.

'Lend me your cigarette lighter.'

Old Porson sidled round the house in a cautious parabola. He kept a brown hand in front of his silver face; trod carelessly on a stoat which squealed and scurried off into a clump of Old Daddy Man's Beard. Adrenaline lubricated all the caddy's old joints, and cogs, which had not revolved for years, turned noiselessly. Puffa-puffa-puffa; wisps of steam rose from his heels, his bottom twitched. Meanwhile the Admiral was soaking his handkerchief (very pretty; embroidered with a border of lilies of the valley) in lighter fuel.

Old Porson reached the window through which the Mac-fisheries Man had used to peer, but it was latched. He tapped his knuckles on it for a while; no response. He tried other windows; the back door. He heard the fusillade of golf-balls striking brick and wood and glass and saw the brand. The grass and undergrowth was coldly damp, but they had rags with them. A second broadside and a tinkle as the window of the downstairs lavatory shattered. He could see no virtue in security any longer, so lumbered round to the front of the house and climbed through the broken window.

A chorus of barks and yelps from the fire-raisers bounced of his bottom as he jumped over the sill. They had obviously mistaken his identity.

'One little Indian, one little Indian, one little Indian boy,' they kept crying. He turned on all the lights he could find. There was a smell of chutney and a smell of . . . something else. Dusty mirrors and faded velvet.

'Guru,' he shouted, 'Gooo-Rooo!' Only a crackle answered him, a crackle and a hiss. He plunged through room after mysterious room. Books shed their dusty knowledge as he brushed by, all that truth and beauty hung in the air like lime-tree fluff. 'Gooo-Rooo!' Another fusillade thundered against the clap-board and the smell of something else became unmistakably the smell of fire. Doors yielded to him, corridors yawned before him, he ran full tilt into a grandmother clock, which chimed disorderly. Its door flew open and a dead mouse came rolling out and squelched on the floor.

'Gooo-ooo-Roooo-oo!'

Cries of triumph from the distant outdoors, as the flames took a hold, licking the timbers—vile fellatio! Wardrobes, full of taffeta and lace, swaying pomanders and faded inexpressibles from an old, lost generation. Old Porson blundered on, until he felt sure that he had essayed every room in the house. There was much creaking now, and a kind of sucking, gulping noise. Only no girls, no Guru. He found a skylight, climbed on to a chair—a rocker, which hurled him to the ground. Another chair and a bruised old man dragging it, limping with it through the deserted house, gasping out 'Guru' now, less a warning than a blessing. Strange transformation.

Solly and Sammy, inspired by the flames and who knows what ancestral memories, improvised a hora—the Admiral took it for a hornpipe and cheered them on, hauling an imaginary rope through his horny, salt-bitten hands. Jessica was imploring Throggie with her lustrous but rather barmy eyes to do something, anything to her, hurling her knees at the sky, and shaking her pink slip at the bewildered rabbits.

A tiny figure climbed out through the skylight of the burning house, and a cheer went out.

'A rat! A Spanish rat, by G—' bellowed the Admiral and aimed a lofted spoon shot at the old caddy. It was badly sliced however and sailed harmlessly off in the direction of the railway line.

'Gooo-ooo Rooo-ooo!' frantically now but faintly to the watchers. And Guru did appear—but from the Boggley Road not from within the house—followed by three attractively dishevelled and flower-bedecked Angell sisters. Quietly Guru padded up to the flamboyant Admiral and tapped him on the shoulder :

'Why this?' he asked. And, gasping, Genevieve made a dash for the conflagration that had been her home, for Bruin was in there, her lovely Bruin with the brown muzzle and cool, glass eyes. Tessa was after her at once and caught her just in time, for, with a sigh, almost of relief, the old building tumbled in on itself, the walls floating down, the door swinging crazily a moment on its hinges (everything strangely submarine) and a roar and scatter of sparks bursting from its entrails. Silhouetted in the smoke Old Porson seemed to see Guru, seemed to lean towards him, seemed to shout something, seemed to raise his arms, seemed almost (but no one could really see) to smile, before he vanished in the smoke.

As he tumbled through shreds of rafters and felt the hot panting breath of eternity on the seat of his trousers, Old Porson did smile, continued to smile, his smile unfolding into a grin (or was it a grimace) and felt such happiness, such happiness, happiness that he had thought was never reserved for an old soak like himself, but was the right of the young and the beautiful and the rich.

Then, shortly afterwards, he sizzled up.

'Oh Bruin, Bruin,' Genevieve sobbed, much overwrought for the loss of her lovely bear, but the naval contingent, suddenly sobered as the Spanish man o'war bowed its last bow, looked at their guilty toes and were silent.

People. In Soft Meadows Cross. In the South of England. In the British Isles. In Europe (soon). In the world. In the Universe. In the Constellation. In the Firmament. In Time itself, or out of it. People. Little people. Snored. And breathed. People. Oh people, people!

PART TWO

CHAPTER ONE

Rehousing

Autumn is a consoling season in Soft Meadows Cross. The trees, shy bachelors at a nurses' dance, are reluctant to make the first move. Then as one blushes, all blush. Red and gold and lime spreading down their necks. They bow and scrape the floor and wave their arms about and ... their hair falls out.

British Rail makes no concession to the seasons and the view from the window of the commuter's special is very much the same at any time of the year. Banks of wizened grass, like the laps of old, old ladies, iced car-parks, a trading estate which hides its generosity (shoes, sweets, sanitary towels, soap) coyly behind the tight-fistedness of grey walls and grey brick and grey concrete. Old tyres, coiled machinery, small houses with cataracts of tattered grey lace over their windows. Allotments, condescension in the very word, and soot and oily snow on the brave patch of runner beans.

It sometimes astonished Colonel Gilbert Tomlinson, for instance, that a world created by man for man's delight could contain so little that was beautiful. He would say as much to the driver of the 8.43, who would gob in reply. All the beauty in Tomlinson's life seemed to reside in the pink nails of his outrageous secretary, who ruled Cannon Street in a despotism so cruel that (as it sometimes seemed) gilt edged shed a point at the inclination of her eyebrow, and Lloyds ran the Lutine Bell at the flaring of her left nostril. And oh, the favours she might graciously consent to bestow on him!

While in Soft Meadows Cross Celia, happy in her ignorance and the esteem of the villagers, played patience and solitary Scrabble by the hour.

Autumn was a consoling season for Mrs Connolly, now that she had her 'word' and the memory of those brittle, brown hands on her knotty neck. Each morning and evening she

171

practised religiously what Guru had taught, and became a little less sour, less pinched, less unimportant. Ever limberer and even slenderer.

And Mrs Skullham? For whom had *she* sacrificed her afternoons of contract bridge? For one who lay ravaged by pneumonia on Albert's bed. One who, long before he was fully recovered, would be murmuring about Guru and Tessa and Abby and Genevieve and his duty and his post. Mrs Skullham told him nothing of the burning down of the House, but as soon as ever his temperature was sub normal she got the Farquhars to lend her Du Pont for the afternoon and took the Macfisheries Man out to see the ruins. In silence he unravelled one etiolated hand from the wispy tartan rug and wound the window down. In silence he looked at the fallen beams and charred rooftree. Where the bracken ended, the blackened ash began. He began to speak but Mrs Skullham laid a finger to his lips :

'No need,' she said, 'no need at all.'

'They were so—' And the finger was replaced by thin but kindly lips, dry but comforting, which did not press his apart, nor even impose themselves upon his, but just softly brushed them, like the chalked tip of a billiard cue. The Macfisheries Man said no more. And Du Pont, who had been redundant since Rose-Marie's recovery, eased the big black car into gear and sidled off, taking his passengers on a scenic ride through Boggley, Whitebone, Cruxted Impervious, Maddocksford, Tingle Barnet and Corfe, returning via Tweetey, Juniper Hill, Kingston Salome, the deserted aerodrome at Mumsey, Whitehorn Abbas, Underbadger and Gruntham. They passed a funeral in Soft Meadows Cross Churchyard.

'Can that be . . . ?' asked the wretched Macfisheries Man. Once again a kindly (but misleading) finger on his lips.

It was Old Porson (a little hair and a little bone) who was being laid to rest under the consoling turf. The grave-diggers replaced their divot and the Vicar made some appropriate remarks about 'the fairway of life'. Now at last Old Porson was drinking at the nineteenth, the ultimate privilege for a faithful, old caddy.

Hardly bigger than a headstone and scarcely any warmer, Little Jasper stood still as a plinth, his half-moon face so pale, and the wind blowing through his muddy breeches. He was Dedicating his Life.

After the simple ceremony the Vicar raced indoors and tore his cassock off with trembling, nicotined hands. These days he was always in a hurry. For Jack Rubin in his well-meaning way had influenced the Vicar more than he would have deemed possible.

The last furlong ... that last half furlong when that splendid young animal, Tongue of Flame, had got up to beat that disappointing old jade, Doubting Thomas, well that thrilling half furlong had been the climacteric of the Vicar's life. For a few days Jack Rubin, under siege, it seemed, from the Vicar whose telephone buzzed like an electric saw, had reluctantly passed on tips, uninspired guesses, gossip from impoverished associates in the trade, anything which Jack had been able to call, with a conscience only slightly cloudy, a 'good thing'. And, unaccountably, the 'good things' had won. One after another at prices from 5/2 to 20/1 they rolled merrily in, a bonne bouche of goodies. And with an increasingly, as the days passed, sour smile, Jack Rubin paid up. For the clerical gentleman did have an irritating habit of gradually increasing his stakes.

Finally Jack Rubin had told the Vicar that things could not go on as they had been doing. He was delighted, of course, to have made his contribution to the upkeep of the Church, but he would not care to take the responsibility (as he put it) of pulling it down again—which was his colourful way of saying that the Vicar had had his lot. Who could blame Jack? He had to balance his books. From now on the Vicar was on his own, and, if he pleased, Jack Rubin would open an account for him at Ladbroke's.

The Vicar had pleased. In ten days racing he had made £720, not far off a year's salary. Another £280 and he would have been able to start his exorcism of the death watch beetle and re-roof the whole building and install the oil-fired central heating without which no faith can long survive. Furthermore, though the bookmaker's information *was* good, the Vicar had come to have faith in his own (well, not *entirely* his own; of course, he acknowledged a nudge here and there from divine providence) skill. And that had been the beginning of the end.

Sitting on his desk was a note from Ladbroke's—'we refer to your account and would point out that the amount outstanding is now in excess of the agreed credit limit'. Briefly, it seems that either the Vicar's skill had been suspect, or divine providence had become skittish, nudging the horses, tripping them up even, because the Vicar had lost not just the year's salary he had originally won, but six months salary on top of that. He could almost hear the death watch beetles cackling in the woodwork.

And so once again he had telephoned Jack Rubin, and confessed all. What could he do now? How to crawl back into the Garden of Eden (and out of the red)?

'On your stomach shall ye go,' said Jack, but kindly.

'Oh, I know, I know, don't think I don't.'

Jack was not happy about it, but the Vicar worked on him to such effect that Jack admitted that he *had* heard of this system, he *did* know of people who would vouch for it, but, of course, there *was* (as with all systems) some element of risk . . .

'What system? What—'

'Nothing to do with horses.'

'Horses Schmorses,' muttered the Vicar uncharacteristically. And Jack, not without forebodings, had passed on his friends' system. He argued to himself that the odds were so very slightly against the player that it only needed a very little faith, a very minor God, a gentle puff of luck, any one of the three, and the Church would be militant once again. Rabbi Keitelmann might not approve, but a friend in need . . .

And so, having buried Old Porson, the Vicar tore off his cassock, wrenched off his dog-collar, telephoned his bank manager, and sprinted up to London. But he had not been able to raise enough money, not really enough. His system (a modified martingale) was one of those which required an increasing roulette stake.

He played with £1 chips at a Soho club, entry to which was swiftly gained by murmuring: 'Jack Rubin sent me', which induced deference and an invitation to come in 'as a guest of the Committee'. He won for an hour, a matter of some forty pounds, until he encountered the inevitable losing run, twelve losing bets in succession. His loss on the sequence was £298.

He had no more money. He would have won on the next spin of the wheel. Hypnotised and horrified he watched. Tinkle, plunk. He glided out of the club like a wax-work on wheels. He bumped into policemen and apologised to lamp-posts. A kindly off-duty traffic warden, concerned at his glassy eyes and wax complexion asked him, was he all right.

'I am a victim,' cried the Vicar, 'of the Permissive Society.'

'Aren't we all?' said the traffic warden, who was, in a way, not, taking him home for the night and letting him sleep (as if he could sleep!) on the sofa.

And what of Jack Rubin? Self-knowledge proved to be a painful tutor. He gave up playing poker at the Golf Club and on Hannah's ninth birthday came unexpectedly home to tea (racing was abandoned because of fog). They never noticed his doomy face, and Miriam's pleasure and the children's delight almost renewed a right spirit within him.

'I *knew* he'd come,' said Hannah, 'I just *knew* he would.'

'I brought you a present.'

'Oh Jack,' said Miriam.

'What've you brought?' asked Ruthie, although it wasn't her birthday, I'll bet it's something *useful*.'

'Now, Ruthie.'

'Here you are, Hannah. First a kiss,' she leapt into his arms and hugged him, 'and then a present.' And he held out his arms, although there was nothing in them.

'Oh Daddy,' said Hannah, 'it's the most marvellous present I ever did have.' The other children were mystified. 'What is it?' they asked, 'what *is* it?' except for David, who had always shown early signs of being a pragmatist and he said: 'There's nothing there.'

'Oh yes, there is, isn't there, Hannah.'

'Yes, of course, Daddy.'

'It's a magic button. It can do magic.'

'I'm a leopard,' yelled Rachel, leaping up and down on the spot and smearing her face with coal. The others ignored her.

'William sent me a conker, a forty-twoer,' said Hannah. 'He says it's been baked.'

'Half-baked, knowing William'—and David laughed unnecessarily loudly.

'Now, David, it's not that funny, you know it isn't.' Jack and Hannah were dancing round the room followed by Little Jo, who was hopping. Ruthie, feeling left out, said:

'There's no music, is there, Mummy?'

Miriam joined in the dancing: 'Of course there's music. Magic button music.' Soon they were all dancing and dancing as though they could all hear the music.

Maybe they could. In any case they danced. And danced, and danced. Until Little Jo fell over the coffee table, and cried. Which made Rachel cry. And all that that involved. There was birthday cake for tea with marzipan and pink icing. Ruthie had a sugar sandwich and no one said a word. It was that sort of afternoon.

'I'm glad you came home,' whispered Miriam into a kissed ear.

But then Jack, who had almost forgotten, took her sadly aside and tried to explain.

'One thing I must know,' said Miriam (a remarkable woman in many ways), 'is it your choice, or is it that Indian's?'

'Mine. He was instrumental, but . . . no, it *was* mine.'

Miriam sang poignantly a snatch of a song they had shared once in Leeds.

> 'I've packed my bags and sacked my valet,
> I've said farewell to Sunshine Alley,
> I'm leaving town, you see . . .'

'It does seem a waste after all these years,' said Jack, but his voice betrayed the sentiment.

'Is it anyone in particular, or just the idea of it?'

Jack wouldn't answer. He beamed nicely, and went and helped Hannah to cut the cake.

But he had been changed, touched and changed. Everything touches, everything changes. We carry the mould with us. Jack knew this. He could only now have played at happy families. Play is something. But Jack had other ideas.

The person who took the Admiral's golfing humiliation most hardly was the Admiral. He was seen no longer at the Golf Club where Solly assumed power. The Admiral was not much seen in Soft Meadows Cross at all. He would sometimes drive his battered old Bentley, gripping the wheel as fiercely as the helm in a Force Ten storm, down to the river—not far from where —University had their boathouses. And there he would sit, glowering at the fragile craft as they sliced against the stream, shouting imprecations at the silver-plated young oars-men, honking his horn to encourage them, snorting through his chagrined purple nose. On other days he would lie slug-a-bed, trying to dream of the Great Days, days of Polo and jig-a-jig, of smuggled opium and rum, of the Casbah and the Dogger Bank, of San Francisco and the Great Barrier Reef, while, in the neighbouring bedroom . . .

The Electricity Board had given up answering Jessica's letters. The pylon was ten points of the law. There it was and there they intended it to stay. It was not the sort of thing you could dig up with a trowel or deface with obscene graffiti. It was itself obscene. And so, the Admiral's wife, frustrated by officialdom and its symbol and ignored by her husband, had gone hunting and returned with—his wrists and ankles tethered to a pole, his belly slit and his fur hot with fresh blood—the Farquhar chauffeur.

Du Pont had not been unimpressed by his daily trips with Mrs Skullham and the Macfisheries Man. His work was with machines, but he had a machine of its own, and it was some-thing more than lymph and tissue. Or rather, the lymph and the tissue seemed not entirely mechanical : they began to behave, at times, and uncharacteristically, eccentrically.

Du Pont became a victim of Jessica's blood-letting instincts.

'Oh, won't you drive me? Oh, be my chauffeur!' she would murmur to him, and slip him into gear. He looked so *dicky* in his hat, she couldn't help herself, but Du Pont she could certainly help.

'Oh, be my chauffeur!'

Rehearsals for *Hamlet* became regular features of Soft Meadows Cross evenings. Snatches of Shakespeare blew across the misty pastures like torn scraps of paper and many was the golfer thrown out of the rhythm of his swing by a ghost or a murder or a smattering of incest.

Daily were the discoveries relating to the character of Hamlet,

M

and his affections and disaffections with his friends and family.

HAMLET   (Act 5, Scene 2): Laertes, you but dally,
          I pray you pass with your best violence,
          I am afear'd you make a wanton of me.

LAERTES : Say you so? Come on (they play).

OSRIC : Nothing neither way.

LAERTES : Have at you now.

(In scuffling they catch one another's rapiers and both are wounded.)

KING : Part them, they are incens'd.

HAMLET : Nay come, again.

Cecil Sparks's gloss on the above: 'How is it possible for professional commentators, their ears pricked and tuned to the slightest hint or suggestion of double-meanings in the writings of the bland old man, to have missed the obvious sexual connotations in the above which suggest so powerfully the illicit relationship between Hamlet and Laertes. Why, the whole vocabulary of fencing is a metaphor for making love, and that is the way *we* must fence, Caedmon, you and I.'

But as with any corporate, artistic endeavour worthy of the name, Hamlet was not always calm waters and a cool breeze. Could be little doubt, for example that there was trouble brewing on the Fortinbras front. Rusty Motorcade did not take at all kindly to Cecil Sparks's interpretation of the Hamlet/Laertes syndrome. Or it would be more accurate to say that it wasn't so much the interpretation that bothered him as the rehearsal techniques adopted by the actor/manager. In his rehearsal tights with a gross codpiece that he had got from God knows where, Sparky made a grotesque enough figure, but both fencing and scuffling in Ophelia's grave, he imposed an intimacy upon young Caedmon Tomlinson that Rusty thought abominable. But what can a mere Fortinbras do? Certainly the strain under which he was rehearsing gave Fortinbras a life and vigour that was most refreshing.

But what Rusty, with jealous Keble eyes, failed to appreciate was that, since his evening with Candida, Cecil's assaults on Caedmon's virtue had the force only of habit. Indeed there were times when Cecil began to wonder whether Hamlet was a homosexual at all.

And it happened that Caedmon possessed a not inconsiderable talent of his own. Once when she heard him speaking the speech :

'Laertes :   How now? What noise is that?
            O heat dry up my brains, tears seven times salt,
            Burn out the sense and virtue of mine eye.
            By Heaven, thy madness shall be paid by weight
            Till our scale turns the beam. O Rose of May!
            Dear maid, kind sister, sweet Ophelia :
            O Heavens, is't possible a young maid's wits
            Should be as mortal as an old man's life?
            Nature is fine in love, and where 'tis fine,
            It sends some precious instance of itself
            After the thing it loves.'

Auntie Clockwise was heard to remark that for all his inexperience Caedmon had a power, a quality of pathos that was rare enough amongst professionals. It was the young Lewis Waller (she claimed) of whom she was peculiarly reminded.

Perhaps the greatest disappointment so far was Rose-Marie's Ophelia. One could have expected her to be all the things she was in her life, that is attractive, intelligent and serious, and so she was. But she was also inconsolably sane. One could travel for a week on a Red Rover ticket and never meet a saner Ophelia.

As for Hamlet, Cecil had at least the figure for the part. In his tight costume his stomach rose and fell away in a gentle curve like a penguin's and the silver cross which dangled round his neck slap-slapped against his sinking chest as he came and went. But he did posture so! And mince so! And contort his face so! And speak the lines in such a fanciful, laboured way. One example should suffice :

'Ghost :   Adieu, adieu, Hamlet : remember me.
Hamlet :   Oh all you host of Heaven! (and stretched his chin
           up to heaven) Oh Earth : (creasing his brow and
           pointing his nose at his toes) what else? (looking
           from side to side like a frightened doe).
           And shall I couple Hell? (in a sibilant aside)
           Oh fie : hold my heart; (which he did, clutching
           a fistful of breast-flesh and kneading it like dough)
           And you my sinews grow not instant cold; (where-

upon he dropped like an old man with palsy).
But bear me stiffly up (suddenly strutting like a
marionette): remember thee? (long, long pause,
almost as if he had forgotten thee, although that
was not what he intended to convey)...' and so
on.

Apart from *Hamlet*, preparations for the Arts Festival were
backward. The Vicar's bell-ringing, well, nothing had been done
about that; all the Vicar could ring was his hands. There were
to be no flower arrangements from Thelma, en route for South
Africa. And who in any case could think of flowers in such terrible times as these? Flower-arrangements! Prettily blew the
flowers on Old Porson's grave! And prettily the wild flowers
would come to rest in the charred ruins of The House. Scabius
and wind-flowers, convolvulus and cow-parsley. Perhaps Dr
Bushey tended the flowers in the place whither he had gone,
and what had become of the wreath Celia had sent poor Albert
Skullham? Withered! They did say (Mrs Connolly said, who
would say anything) that Mrs Skullham...but no, such things
were not to be believed. All the same, the Macfisheries Man had
not been well, that much was evident, and Macfisheries had
had to send for another man (a well-spoken one, and neatly
turned out in his spotless, white smock, but a stranger, and
resented).

What else remained festive in the Festival? It was doubtful
whether the Admiral would sing his shanties. And when Wendy
Pakenham submitted her new-style action paintings to Cecil
Sparks in his capacity of hanging committee for the Exhibition
of local artists' work, he rejected them out of hand.

'But I don't understand it! You always said you despised
the figurative.'

'A lot of things have changed, ducky.'

'But what about loyalty? Does that mean nothing?'

'Art means more.'

'Art! A fat lot you know about art. Oh *please*, Sparky.
Berger may be coming. Imagine!'

'How pleasant for him.'

'Why are you so cruel to me?'

'Trash! An exploitation of the senses, and a prostitution of the emotions. I refuse to turn your affections into an industry, thank you very much.'

'There speaks the great novelist!'

'Well, at least I haven't compromised myself.'

'You seem to forget that it is I who has to make the beds. And it's easy to talk of integrity when you're still on Chapter One.'

And then one afternoon a Scotsman and a Jew ... that is to say, one afternoon Throggie popped into Jack Rubin's to have a dollar on a horse called Harry Lauder. Jack, startled, looked up from his *Sporting Life* and rapped his head on the corner of the ante-post blackboard.

'Aie!' wailed Jack in pain.

'Aye, we mun tak' ye hame,' crooned Throggie. And having taken him to his home, had put him to bed. Poor Jack had scarcely been conscious, but had kept keening about Miriam and the children and how he loved them really and how he had decided to leave them, stuff like that. Throggie had understood 'Wummen!'—and in his voice disapproval ... and disgust. *Disgust!* Even concussed Jack had not been prepared for that.

> 'There's muckle a lass wi' troosers
> And there's muckle a lass wi'oot
> But there's niver a lass in Gallowglass
> Who'll no deserve the boot.'

That, unexpectedly, had been Throggie too. Long after Jack was snoring in Throggie's pyjamas Throggie stayed. And Throggie was still there in the morning. Dissenting adults; a Scotsman and a Jew. Throggie stayed. A week. Ten days.

They had golf in common; something else too. One morning when Jack was in the bath Miriam had telephoned. She was understanding and generous and apologetic to Throggie, before Throggie had had a chance to do more than grunt. Nor did he. Never a word to Jack's wife, nor never a word about her to Jack. Put the treacherous receiver back on its hypocritical rest.

'Did I hear the phone?' Jack had asked, glistening and soap-scented from the bath. Throggie had explained that it was a wrong number, that someone had wanted to buy a dog.

That night over whisky Throggie had talked about his terrible mother and her tarse; Jack about his restless marriage. In the morning they had woken up to find themselves in the same bed. It became a habit.

Accommodation for Guru and the Angell sisters had not posed a problem. They simply hadn't been offered any. Public opinion held that the best thing to do with those degenerate girls was nothing, and so nothing was done. As for the abominable Indian; all else had failed, total non-commitment might succeed. A wordless pact was made, and even those who secretly black-legged (including Rose-Marie, who really would have helped if she had not lived at home, Victoria, who now had a spare bedroom, and Miriam, who had a spare bed) were rebuffed by whichever of the sisters they approached. Separately and severally the three girls had linked arms and declared that by Guru's side was where they belonged, and by Guru's side was where they would stay. That was that.

It was Little Jasper who took it upon himself to do something for Guru and the sisters. He collected rugs and blankets and pillows, house to house, claiming that it was on behalf of Oxfam, and how could they withhold their bedding what with the starving millions in Asia and Africa and . . . He was such a wrench to the conscience with his torn trousers and grubby knees that soon enough he had more blankets than he could conveniently carry and dumped them down at the feet of the war memorial—the marble widow who dominated the high street with such soulful arrogance—and it was there at those marble feet that Guru and the Angell sisters made their new nest. Fortunately the weather had improved but the outspread wings of the marble widow provided shelter from wind and dew and birds. With a smug, well-how-about-that look on his face and precocious selflessness, Little Jasper took pains to see his friends comfortably bestowed. A brazier and some tins of food . . . it all looked most welcoming.

However, it was hard for the locals to ignore Guru and the girls in their new settlement. Ladies slipped away from their shopping for a brisk consultation, while Abby and Genevieve whom the fresh air particularly improved, wrote symbolic poetry and Tessa gave change—she had decided that Guru should charge for his services. Local tradesmen noticed a wonderful quickening in their turnover, and stifled their protests, while the police had no complaint so long as the traffic kept moving and public decency was not outraged. Of course there were complaints, but Mrs Connolly was raucous in her new policy of live and let live, and everyone else was busily employed preparing for the festival. And Little Jasper was having the time of his life.

When he had dedicated himself at Old Porson's funeral to Guru, it had all seemed so simple. Exposed within a brief week of his life to two angels (the Angel of Death and the Indian one) Little Jasper had grown suddenly up. He had stopped sneezing for one thing; and he had started thinking. He grew distant and unapproachable. At school in his English compositions ('Taking Exercise', 'The Village Street', 'Why I should like to go into Politics') a weird streak of poesy became evident. He looked inordinately old, like a weather-beaten jockey (F. Durr or J. Sime) and would join Guru and the girls immediately after school with the windows of his eyes wide open and his adoration flapping in the breeze.

All this Guru appeared to take for granted. It was left to Tessa to smile nicely down at him and offer him tangerine slices, which he refused.

Apostles were in fashion.

But after a few days of their new life tensions began to increase amongst the three sisters. Genevieve, who had been deprived by the loss of her Bruin, began to mope somewhat and cling sentimentally to Guru. Tessa pretended to be above all that sort of thing but was unable totally to keep jealousy out of her inquisitive eyes. She rattled the shillings ferociously and as for Abigail, she seemed to grow more and more etiolated, almost fading away entirely, like Tinkerbell, until revived by a command from Guru or an offhand caress from Guru, or a thought suggested by Guru, or even an uninterrupted stare at Guru.

At night there was scarcely room for the four of them under the marble widow, and on those occasions when Abigail played the odd girl out (Guru kept to a strict rota) Tessa and Genevieve found it hard to enjoy the privilege of Guru's company for worrying about Abby's gasps for breath and flutterings of hands and morbid signs of a chronic lung condition. Abby didn't stint herself when it came to symptoms.

However Abigail it was who made the greatest progress in the techniques of Kama Sutra when Guru took the girls off to the security of the Soft Meadows. The 'pressing position', the 'twining position', and the 'splitting of a bamboo' had been quickly mastered by all the sisters, but only Abby learned the 'position of Indrani', and was well on the way to the secret of the 'fixing of a nail'. It might be thought that such accomplishments would endear Abigail especially to Guru; such, however, was not Guru's way.

As the days passed the girls strove in vain in a rivalry that was not entirely frivolous to get from Guru some hint or clue that such and such a girl in such and such a mood was pleasant to him, such and such a girl in such and such a mood displeasing. But Guru was bland, and in his blandness lay the true cause of the girls' growing discontent. An unpalatable truth, the choice of a favourite, even a whimsical switching of affections, all this they could have faced and accepted; but blandness made them rude to one another, and blandness it seemed possible might even lead to their eventual dispersal.

'Oh,' Genevieve would sigh, 'my soul is like the lotus, opening its petals at noon when the master walks by the Ganges.'

'You've never seen a lotus and you've never been near the Ganges,' was Tessa's comment. And Abby would chip in with: 'She hasn't, but I have. In my dreams I have. One night I shall become the lotus. Think of me sometimes, sisters, when I am a lotus.'

'Honestly!' Tessa would say. And then add wistfully: 'but I have seen things ... and I know things, too ... such things.'

One could not reasonably expect such a state of affairs to continue indefinitely.

CHAPTER TWO

Rejoicing

Monday dawned inauspiciously. Ragged clouds hung heavily over the Gruntham housing estate, like clumsy old daddy about to sit on a pile of children's bricks. But the air was too clear. It pierced into the naughty crannies of yards and illuminated the scars and blemishes of pitted brick and concrete. A pitiless damp morning indeed. Disgruntled fish snapped at the stagnant surface of ponds and, hoop-la! there were rings round their gills. A cocker spaniel went for his matutinal dip; was attacked by starving crows. A baby woke, chafed by a nappie, and bawled. A jet from Singapore or Saudi Arabia circled the sky while its turbo-prop passengers snored, and the stewardess snatched a quick drag in the pilot's cabin.

'Take down your knickers, love,' the pilot drawled perfunctorily.

'Switch over to automatic then.'

'Can't we for once . . . ?'

'No we can't!'

There were flags dripping above the main street of Soft Meadows Cross, and flags depended from the service stations on the motorway approach road. None of the flags fluttered; all dangled.

Melody Rosewort and 'Curtain-Rod' Huskisson took the nine fifty-three from London. 'Curtain-Rod' Huskisson and Melody Rosewort had been carefully selected to open the festival. Huskisson was the specialist on the Arts Council for opening festivals. He opened them with distinction. He opened them like clams. And an Arts Council representative was a sine qua *pro proximo anno* non. Melody Rosewort was a personality, hence her long barley-coloured hair, her long corn-coloured legs, her long speaking, melting, slow-burning glances and her big boobies.

Tickets had been reserved for the two of them and they shared a compartment, sitting opposite one another blithely unaware for the whole of the journey of their common destiny. From time to time the Arts Council man looked up the skirts of the Celebrity and from time to time the Celebrity, contentedly aware of these surreptitious glances, crossed her fillies' legs with a thunder of silk and fish-net. Huskisson, dipping his head again into his notes, would draw faces in all the 'Os', while Melody closed her lavish eyes and thought of the Spanish Armada.

The suburbs flew past the window on wings of soot and grime . . . Poddersley Hill, Shagfield Cross, Ripplemartin, Kleptobailey, Tamtam Junction, Fergus Bar and Bury St Herbert. At Fishook Melody sneezed and at Flintsnapper Halt 'Curtain-Rod' dozed, and at Soft Meadows Cross a damp reception committee was waiting on the platform.

Cecil Sparks had a Michaelmas Daisy in his button-hole, and his Auntie stood upstage of him, legs wide apart in case the express came through. Mrs Connolly was in Lupin blue and Colonel Tomlinson (reluctantly taking the day off work) escorted his wife. The Admiral was too pump-full of bile and alcohol to have made it (to the bilges!), but Jessica was there; also the Vicar and the Farquhars.

'La la,' murmured Cecil, 'la creme de la creme, no less.' A photographer, Hugo Feldstein of the —shire Hammer, asked Huskisson to go close up to Melody, and Huskisson smiled in a green sort of way, while Melody tossed her mane to keep it sleek and licked her lips to make them shine. After this Cecil made a pretty little speech of welcome full of obsequious phrases and everyone clapped politely.

Then off they all trooped to the School Hall.

They had taken the children's drawings from the walls. In place of them they had brought out the loyal, old flags whose faded and battered appearance represented only too eloquently the patriotism of those who had hung them up. Flags which had done duty for V.E. Day and V.J. Day and the dawn of the new Elizabethan Age (June 6th and raining, remember?). Flags which had fluttered at gymkhanas till ponies bolted and coconuts shied. Flags, which had streamed out nobly on St George's Day, now bedecked Elsinore, and flopped in front of the large desk which had been set up to accommodate the guests on the castle battlements. Whimsically a tape had been stretched across the front of the stage and a large pair of gold-sellotaped scissors were laid splayed and ready for action.

Curtain-Rod Huskisson made an extremely long and insupportable tedious speech on behalf of his 'ministress' as he fancifully called her. How encouraging it was that a small rural community, burble, burble . . . How dangerous it would be if the metropolitans had the monopoly of, chunder, chunder . . . How impressive it was to see the . . . well, impressive, arrangements which had been made for, peep, peep. But the 'peep, peep' was wow on the microphone, and not Huskisson. (Although as a representative of the Arts Council he did, from time to time 'peep, peep'.)

Melody Rosewort made a more successful speech. 'I came down on the train with this fellow,' she said in her vermilion voice, 'only I had no idea he was from the Arts Council on account of he looked up my skirt like anyone else.' People chuckled uneasily. Said the Colonel : 'She has a nice figure, that girl, you know'—but Celia refused to concede the point. Melody concluded : 'So now I suppose you all expect me to cut this bloody thing, and then we can all go off and have a gin at the boozer.' With which she snipped the tape delicately, like an umbilicum.

The damp crocodile that Huskisson and Rosewort led down the High Street slithered to a stop outside the War Memorial where Guru was advising a bewildered housewife that numbers are pre-existent to consciousness and that counting to a million would bring peace of mind, 'a purposeful purposelessness'.

Melody, mistaking Guru for a fortune-teller, wanted to see his crystal ball, but was hastily bustled into the Police Station, where, in the charge-room, were displayed fifty-seven paintings, and everyone of them a gem.

Sergeant Cabinet-Kyke had kindly made the room available, but had stipulated that 'nothing must be moved, or there'll be the devil to pay'. The idea of a Police Sergeant in the pay of the devil had amused Cecil Sparks but posters depicting the Colorado Beetle and persuasive broadsheets about a virile career in the force ('Call yourself a man? Do a man's job !') had posed aesthetic problems to the hanging committee that he had found at times to be almost insurmountable.

But there they all were.

There was 'Moonlight over the Old Canal', and 'Despair' and 'Apple-Blossom at Dawlish' and 'Josephine at her toilet'. There were five girls' heads and three boys' heads and five nude studies, two of gentlemen with blurred parts, two of ladies with wisps in their laps, and one entire man painted by the Admiral's wife in a fit of nostalgia. It was Number Twenty-four in the catalogue. People paused in front of Numbers Twenty-three and Twenty-five and looked askance; pursed their lips; or licked them. Another picture to attract attention was an unusual design by the Macfisheries Man, helpfully entitled: 'Badgers attacking Macfisheries Man'. Some wit had defaced the title to read 'Budgens attacking Macfisheries Man'. Thus the picture excited much mystification and some small reputation as 'a satirical work'.

Wendy Pakenham's action pictures had, after a few critical hours, been accepted by the Hanging Committee, which was being (there is no other word for it) blackmailed. The artist had threatened to write to the mother of the Hanging Committee with full details of Candida's association with the Hanging Committee.

In the end Berger was unable to come from London, but Kartoffeln came in his place. Kartoffeln knew his onions. Kartoffeln sniffed his way from exhibit to exhibit snorting disparagingly, until sticking one rosette (thoughtfully provided by the gymkhana committee) on the Colorado Beetle poster, one on the police recruitment advertisement.

He adjudged no entry worthy the third prize, and returned to London.

And off everyone went to hear the bell-ringing.

Victoria led her children, each waving his Union Jack, to the Church where they were to display their skills in campanology. If each child rang each bell at the right moment, 'The Happy Wanderer' chimed out loud and clear. It was an 'if' formidable enough to sink a second Titanic. But the children, assured of a triumphant outcome by their omniscient teacher, gabbled excitedly and happily.

Full of dread and hating all the youth and innocence that he knew would upbraid him (millstones, oh he understood about millstones!) the Vicar wandered the borders of his demesne and then returned to his church to find carved deep into the stone :

'How punishment? When Day of Judgement? Watch this space !' It must have taken *hours*.

Oh Christ, but he was broke; and dishonoured. And here were all the children now. Their eyes accused him.

'Find your own way to the belfry !' he yelled at them. 'I don't give a bugger what you do.'

There was quite a crowd up there. Friends and smirking relations. The children rang their hand-bells any old how. The Vicar's anger had upset them, no knowing how much. 'The Happy Wanderer' sounded horrible. Everyone clapped when it was over. Of course the children knew that they had been bad and despised those who clapped. With such venom did they then peal those church bells that over God's fertile country-side the clangour sounded a note far removed from the sentimental reassurances that church bells are supposed to supply. Horses whinnied and reared in surprise. A visiting bishop fell off his bicycle.

But it would be misleading to suggest that the Festival was entirely a fiasco, even at the start. For example, whatever the snorting Kartoffeln said, the art exhibition obviously pleased a great many people. To see a vulgarisation of what is already familiar by somebody with whom you are comparatively intimate, why, that is a large and satisfying part of our local culture. Much the same might be said of Jocelyn Pedal's piano recital at Gin House. A kind of margarine man, but one who knew which side his bread was buttered, Pedal concentrated on the best loved items from his BBC series 'That strain again'. This included the Moonlight Sonata and souped up selections from 'The Sound of Music' which he played with a roguish twinkle in his watery eye and a breath-taking cascade of black notes. Celia Tomlinson had herself wiped the ivories with gold-top milk for the occasion and had placed upon the hips of the Bechstein a selection of silver-framed family photographs. As your eye fluttered from one to another you could watch Ethie turn from a laughing baby to a pouting schoolgirl to a petulant deb, and Caedmon in a similar progression. Grannies and granpas were there too to complete the cycle, and since, if every girl grows like her mother it follows that she grows like her grannie too, in those sprightly old miseries you could see Ethie and Caedmon grow old. So it was wiser perhaps *not* to allow your eye to linger too long on the photographs (how the eyes sink, the cheeks waste, the jaws thicken, well they *do,* there's no denying it), but to rest upon Jocelyn Pedal himself, which was a much more rewarding experience. *He* was eternal spring. When he played the Tritsch-Tratsch Polka his long aesthetic head with its floppy blond locks and swan-nose nodded and shook in time to the beat; its expression winsome and humorous. When he played Chopin's 9th Nocturne (Opus 32, No. 1) ('We are carried into darkened threatening pianissimo from which burst petulant explosions until again a mystic bell rings out and carries us to the end') he became rock-still, his eyebrows pent-house high, his mouth twisted in the anguish of the dark night of the soul. But when he played Strauss waltzes he became debonair, with a suggestion of cruelty and rape around the nostrils. All in all a splendid performance; the piano shuddered on its casters, and many of the notes were correct.

As the day sped by Huskisson took cold from standing so long in the rain and Melody became melancholic. They even grew quite fond of one another and exchanged mournful glances of complicity. By the time they were ushered into the school hall for *Hamlet*, they were touching fingers.

CHAPTER THREE

Reproaching

'Honestly, Auntie, what do you expect me to *do*? I can't give you it all to yourself and have the others all muck in together. I mean we must observe the decencies.'

'You should have thought of that before, Sparks. Always were a thoughtless child. Late with thank-you letters.'

'Oh, Auntie, no.'

There were only two dressing-rooms. A compromise was called for. Eventually a corner of the smaller dressing-room was curtained off for Gertrude and the other ladies of the cast had to make do as best they could in the little space that remained. A waiting-lady stuck a star on her curtain in a spirit of irony which Auntie Clockwise, with dignity, chose to ignore.

Within her bower the illusion of professionalism was maintained. Telegrams, by God! Stuck to the mirror. Remarquable! And on her mirror, in lipstick: 'Good luck, darling, I shall be thinking of you. John'. John? John *who*? Her husband was called Jasper and her son had been called to serve his country, and was now called her tragedy.

In the other dressing-room was a kind of Dantesque scene. The good burghers of Soft Meadows Cross in socks and suspenders, in doublet and hose. The costumes, hired in a set from Berman's, had been designed for younger, slimmer actors. The dressing-room had been designed for children. The smell was abominable. Consequently Cecil Sparks had shut himself in the lavatory in order that he might be alone. As he applied his Leichner Nos. 5 and 9, he needed to think princely, Danish thoughts, and he did, he managed it. In an instant it became clear to him what Hamlet was, *really* was, or at least what his would be, *really* would be, and that *that* was how he had to do it, *his* way.

He and Hamlet, torn between dreaming and doing, both. He and Hamlet, torn between men and women, both. Nothing absolute, nothing coarse.

191

'In every man's life there comes a time' (thought Sparky on the lavatory with a shaving mirror perched on his knee) 'when a man must act in the way which he knows to be right.' This thought seemed so basic to his very existence that he spoke it, spake it even, aloud.

From outside the door a gruff voice replied:

'Well get on and bloody do it, then! There's others waiting, you know.'

Cecil applied a pale lipstick and a false beard, went over his first few speeches ('A little more than kin, and less than kind,' 'Not so, my Lord, I am too much i' th' sun', 'Ay, Madam, it is common') and then got off the pan and came out, Hamlet.

The hall was well-filled and almost everyone had a family interest. Doris Skullham had clearly taken trouble with her appearance. Although she was still in mourning her hair had been tinted and swept impressively and expensively back. And we know whom that was for. The Farquhars had come to cheer Rose-Marie; they didn't know what they liked but they knew about Art, and Shakespeare was Art, so *that* was all right.

Celia Tomlinson, who had helped with the costumes—at least her 'little woman' had—was there in a positive glow of possessiveness; her husband and both her children were to perform.

Victoria tinkled ineffectually at the piano while Candida, in a white trouser suit (her going away costume) sat surrounded by Envy and Contempt who pointed and whispered but failed to say good evening. She held her head high, and clutched in the palm of her damp, white hand was a ticket to London—one way.

The Admiral, thighs like felled oaks, glowered at his programme in which local motor traders wished the production every success and the Star Of India, Gruntham, curried favour with a specimen menu and prices, mild to very hot. The Admiral broke wind and eructated and spluttered and growled and his hands shook. His wife squeezed the knee of Du Pont, sitting on her leeward side, and ignored her disintegrating husband. And Du Pont looked so splendid in his chauffeur's cap. Didn't the German ones wear boots? Surely they did. She would join the émigrés. (for Dr Bushey had been taken away, and Dick and Thelma had gone to South Africa, and

Candida—they said—was leaving and dear old Albert Skullham
was dead. The village would be full of drapers—or worse.)
She would go to Germany for the chauffeurs. The Admiral
would be better off without her.

Then a flicker of the lights indicated that it was time for
God to Save the Queen, and everybody stood up, the gentlemen pressing their genitals against the backs of the chairs in
front, the ladies, of course, doing no such thing. 'In this age
of atheism and disillusion,' Rusty muttered tiresomely as usual,
'one might expect the Queen, as head of the Established
Church, to be called upon to save God.'

The lights dimmed. A susurration of anticipation breezed
through the hall. Elsinore! Midnight apparently, and the
weather conditions stormy.

'Who's there?' cried Colonel Gilbert Tomlinson matter-of-
factly above the tempest.

'Nay answer me,' Wilfred, the organist, insisted in his unlikely deep voice. 'Stand and unfold yourself.'

It was generally considered, when Cecil Sparks's production
of *Hamlet* came to be spoken of, that the device of doubling
Hamlet with the ghost, that, at least, had been a fine
imaginative stroke. In effect, Hamlet knew all along what
had happened to his father in the orchard, and what the ghost
tells him is what he had already *worked out for himself*. And
so in Act One Scene One when the watch see the ghost, there
the ghost was, not perhaps too clearly defined as was proper
on such a stormy night, but a recognisable ghost none the less.
And in *that* scene 'the ghost' was Hamlet himself camping
about under a grey army blanket. Act One Scene Four posed
a different problem, allowed of a different solution, for there,
and in the other ghost scenes, Hamlet himself sees the Ghost.
Well, since even Hamlet could devise no way of being in two
places at once (to be or not to be, not both), in those scenes
the ghost was represented by 'a friend of Hamlet'. The scenes
in which the ghost appears to the other courtiers are merely
play-acting (and we know how Hamlet loved that) to justify
in front of witnesses by an apparently supernatural command
what Hamlet knew perfectly well he was going to have to do
to Claudius. And who is the friend of Hamlet who per-

N

sonifies the ghost for the benefit of Horatio and the others? Why, Ophelia of course, who would do almost anything for Hamlet. We know that. No wonder she goes mad, because in this interpretation *she finds herself indirectly responsible for her father's death.* 'You see, we are all to some extent mad,' Sparky claimed, 'because we all to that extent killed our fathers.' 'But what about Hamlet?' someone had objected, becoming a little confused, 'surely he killed his step-father?' 'Well yes, so he did in default.' 'In default?' 'Don't be stupid, darling, his own father was killed before *he* got a chance to have a go at him. But he would have killed him in the end. Claudius could safely have waited till Hamlet was king and *then* killed him.' 'How?' 'Why, through Laertes, as he does anyhow.' 'But if Laertes *loves* Hamlet . . .' 'I've explained all that already. Let's get on with our rehearsal, darlings, shall we?'

If there was a criticism of the early part of the production, it had to be that there were too many actors wringing too much emotion from too few lines. There was a competitive element in many of the performances that was not in the best traditions of the theatre. Sammy Green, for instance, who had taken over the part of Claudius at short notice from Dick Worsley, was inclined to rant a bit and to elbow other actors out of his way. Some of them resented this and took no trouble to hide their resentment. Auntie Clockwise was magnificent of course, and her entrance, resplendent in an Aladdin's cave of costume jewellery, elicited spontaneous applause, which she acknowledged with a royal salute, so to speak, raising and lowering her chunky forearm in a majestic Bensonian gesture.

Ethie, prompting for the first act, during which she had no lines to speak, grew impatient with some of the actors and showed perhaps a touch too much initiative; was sharply rebuked once or twice; shed tears in her dark little corner.

But Cecil was wonderful. He made a ridiculous Hamlet. He made an ugly, and a foolish and a witless Hamlet. He made a bombastic and a craven and at times almost an insupportable Hamlet. He knew the lines that had to be spoken, but misunderstood entirely what they portended. He had latched onto the notion that Hamlet was a solitary, yet played him sometimes like an auctioneer. He neither craved pity nor respect. He was not funny, as Hamlet should be, nor consumed inside, as

Hamlet should be, nor quick-tempered, nor fleet-footed, nor fast-minded. He had none of the attributes of a princely Hamlet, nor none of the simplicity of a common Hamlet. At times he was only a Hamlet because the programme said he was.

And yet, all this being allowed for, all his grossness and misreadings, all his clumsiness and superficiality, admitting that he had no more grasp of the complexities of Hamlet's character than a sleepy child his conscious sensibilities, could no more call up the Hamlet within him than an Archbishop the joy of his first curacy, and yet... Cecil Spark's Hamlet had his moment of sublimity. The passage was in Act Three Scene Two, as follows:

'Hamlet: Will you play upon this pipe?

Guildenstern: My Lord, I cannot.

Hamlet: I pray you.

Guildenstern: Believe me, I cannot.

Hamlet: I do beseech you.

Guildenstern: I know no touch of it, my Lord.

Hamlet: 'Tis as easy as lying: govern these ventages with your finger and thumb, give it breath with your mouth, and it will discourse most eloquent music. Look you, these are the stops.

Guildenstern: But these cannot I command to any utterance of harmony, I have not the skill.

Hamlet: Why look you now, how unworthy a thing you make of me: you would play upon me; you would seem to know my stops: you would pluck out the heart of my mystery; you would sound me from my lowest note to the top of my compass: and there is much music, excellent voice, in this little organ, yet cannot you make it speak. Why do you think that I am easier to be played on, than a pipe? Call me what instrument you will, though you can fret me, you cannot play upon me. God bless you sir.'

And for this brief moment Cecil Sparks's Hamlet seemed to speak for all misused people, all actors in the hands of unworthy scripts, all those in business to unworthy organisations, the sellers of detergents, the sellers of pulp magazines, the sellers of shoddy; for all the exploited, the instrument, who, through some misfortune of birth or circumstance or character defect find themselves played upon, their ventages arbitrarily blocked, fretted and untuned. For all the unpaid creditors of society, the crippled and alone, the sexually and the mentally sick, those whose instruments are played upon ham-fistedly, are crooked, but are still played, played upon. Even for all poorly created characters in tawdry books denied the reality they have a right to demand, fleshless phantasms of an author's whim.

And how did Cecil Sparks's Hamlet speak for these unfortunates? Because he himself was one of them, knew them, understood them, one of them, one of *us, one of us!*

'God bless you, sir.'

The play proceeded peaceably enough for several hours until the first scene of the fifth act and Ophelia's funeral. She had been a happy little Ophelia really, skipping and dancing about the stage, smiling and singing, a credit to her family. The news of her death had come as a shock to everyone. And now here they all were, an impressive line of mourners and Caedmon, marvellously deranged with grief, leaping into the grave and clasping to him his dead sister (secretly Rose-Marie, having remembered all her lines in the right order, was able to shut her eyes and thoroughly enjoy this part of the play. He was such a pretty young man, and the way his long mop of tawny hair whipped her cheeks was most agreeable. She wouldn't mind dying, if this was what it led to).

But then Cecil Sparks had to spoil it all.

'Hamlet: This is I, Hamlet the Dane. (Hamlet leaps in
   after Laertes.)
Laertes: The devil take thy soul.'

On the stage of the School Hall, Soft Meadows Cross, there was room in the grave for one, even two, not three. Poor Rose-Marie had to fend for herself as best she could; even so she could not avoid being somewhat trampled upon—as indeed Ophelia was.

The part of Fortinbras in Hamlet is rather typical of Shakespeare's after breakfast writing. Although spoken of, he doesn't make an appearance until Act 4, Scene 4, where after only nine lines of dialogue—eight of them his, it is true—he exits with his army, not to reappear until after all the fun and games at the very end of the play. Rusty Motorcade had remained in the stalls while Hamlet dillied and dallied. It might have been pleasant to watch all that was going on. All that was going on; pregnant phrase! All too well he knew, could see. Hamlet indeed and his love for Laertes! That was one way of looking at it, but not Rusty's way. In his opinion Hamlet was not in love with anyone, in his opinion Hamlet was out of love with God; that was Rusty's professional opinion, and in his opinion God must be out of love with Cecil Sparks or He would not have permitted him, *would not have permitted* ... It was plain enough what Cecil Sparks (unbeloved of God and Rusty Motorcade) was up to, and when eventually he leapt into that already crowded grave it must have been plain to the whole audience. In the stalls Fortinbras simmered.

'Hamlet: Thou pray'st not well:
    I prithee take thy fingers from my throat;
    Sir, though I am not splenetive, and rash,
    Yet have I something in me dangerous,
    Which let thy wiseness fear. Away thy hand.'

No well, it was too bad altogether. In the name of the theatre, in the name of art, in the name of Shakespeare (what the hell *were* they doing in that bloody grave? There was a lot of bumping and boring certainly. Rusty stood up to see better. 'Sit downs' peppered his back like grapeshot), it was too bad.

'King: Pluck them asunder.'

'Yes!' cried Fortinbras.

'Ssssssssh!'

Rusty had had enough. What did this outrageous, *old* man with the paunch and the tired, hanging face and the *dirty* habits (you could tell just by looking at him), what did he know of cricket in the Parks and strawberries on the boat-houses, and the *gold* of Caedmon, and his innocence? None of them could understand that. On the back of his hand he noticed a dead ladybird, squashed with shell split, one black spot on each half; which he shook furiously off. And in the autumn what did they know of Caedmon's curiosity, his questing for a truth which Rusty could not supply, but he could supply honour and decency and faith and what did this appalling old man know of these fine toys? The play must not be allowed to continue.

'Hamlet: Come show me what thou'lt do.
  Woo't weep? Woo't fight? Woo't fast? Woo't tear thyself?
  Woo't drink up eisel, eat crocodile?

I'll do't.'

'Fortinbras: (from the stalls) Take up the body; such a sight
as this

Becomes the field, but here shows much amiss.

Ophelia: (faintly) Air!

Hamlet: Sssssh.'

There was a stir of unease throughout the auditorium; a
breeze that bore locusts on its back. Hamlet faltered in his
stride; amateurs, amateurs, the world was full of amateurs!
Rusty barked in triumph. 'Give up, Sparky, come up outa that
grave, leave the kid alone, you can't win.'

'Sit down and belt up!' shouted Candida.

Ophelia: 'I can't breathe.'

'Sssssssssh . . .' Locusts' wings.

There was one, at least, professional in the world. Stepping
stage centre, she folded her arms across her magnificent frowning
bust, and, directly to the front row of the stalls:

'Queen: This is mere madness:

And thus awhile the fit will work on him:

Anon as patient as the female dove,

When that her golden couplets are disclosed,

His silence will sit drooping.'

Hamlet made a final despairing grab at Laertes, as he saw
his production tottering around him. *His* Hamlet. His *Hamlet.*

'Hamlet: Hear you sir:

What is the reason that you use me thus?

I lov'd you ever.'

Whereupon Fortinbras leapt onto the stage, threw off his
overcoat, toppled into the grave.

'Never! *You* never loved him.'

'I did,' said Hamlet, '*once* I did. Why do you have to interfere?'

'Nobody,' muttered Rusty, 'nobody in this dump of a place
knows the first thing about love.'

'Hey, steady on,' said Caedmon. He disapproved of such
insupportable generalities, and besides the Gravediggers' spade
was piercing his spine. But Rusty was not to be denied:

'I love. I'm not ashamed to admit it.'—whipping off his
breastplate, gauntlets and greaves—'*I love Caedmon in-
tellectually.*' And drew his sword. Backstage Guildenstern

gasped. 'Oh my Gawd,' said Cornelius (prompting). In the stalls Celia Tomlinson leapt to her feet, pink with disbelief and russet with rage. On stage Hamlet threw himself upon Fortinbras, and hit him several times with Yorick.

'Oh well,' murmured Laertes, 'it's nice to be popular.'

A while later, the production having been abandoned and order being partially restored, the Vicar was called upon to say a few words in the cause of his Church Restoration Fund, to which the evening's profits were dedicated.

He stumbled and failed to negotiate the steps onto the stage; was helped up. He was shabby and had nothing prepared. Mysterious ciphers, additions and subtractions were scrawled around his dog-collar in green Pentel. His hands trembled and the scrawn of his neck hung loose. He looked at the black under his fingernails and then at the faces of his flock. Moutonneux. The lights confused him. His brain was afloat with jetsam of cards and dice. Drowning horses whinnied pitifully. He splashed around. Scraps of words floated into his mind . . . drifted out . . .

'The Church . . . so to speak . . . Restoration Fund, yes.' He scratched his nose. 'Well, we all know what the Church is, and I, well, I am the restoration, and, of course, the life. Yes. And it is incumbent upon me . . . I am well aware . . . to say . . . and . . . a few . . . excuse me.' He hid his head in his hands; some small security was still to be found in those warm palms.

A breeze of unease buzzed through the audience. Heads turned on their stalks.

And heads turned back and then shook in weary resignation as Guru, followed at a discreetly servile yard by Little Jasper, pattered up the aisle again.

The Vicar peeped between his fingers. Guru looked infuriatingly compassionate and calm.

'You're always interrupting me,' whined the Vicar. 'I've had enough of it.'

'How punishment? When Day of Judgement?'

'Not that again.' Anger gave the Vicar eloquence. 'Well as it happens this time you've come straight to the Professor of that particular subject. I've been doing some research since we last spoke and I'm happy to tell you there *is* punishment all right. Don't worry, I know. We inflict it upon ourselves. And as for the day of judgement, well, that's here and now, that's yesterday, today and tomorrow. There, that's your bloody encyclical!'

But Guru was in no way non-plussed by this new-style Vicar. 'Ah,' he said, 'good. Statement of faith is good. Nonsense, of course. Now *I* tell you. Now I tell you everything. Now I tell you secrets of all the universe. And see'—he held up his arms— 'nothing up my sleeves.'

As a general rule the British public are potentially very hot on secrets of the universe. If secrets of the universe could be frozen, attractively packaged and backed by a mass advertising campaign, they'ld rival fish and chips. Thus the audience in the School Hall at Soft Meadows Cross did not grow impatient. The Angell sisters' eyes brimmed over with love and receptiveness, while Victoria took out a biro and prepared to make notes on the back of a gas bill.

'I say, look here, I didn't anticipate this, did you?' murmured Huskisson to Melody Rosewort.

'I tell you truth!' cried Guru.

'Allelluyah!' cried little Jasper.

'I tell you wisdom!' cried Guru.

'Oh wise Guru!' cried little Jasper.

'I tell you ...'

He told them of The Path and of The Way, and of the many Pilgrims along the Way. He told them The Song Celestial and of Gautama the Buddha, its hero. He told them of Enlightenment and of the Universal Mind. Of Ultimate Reality he said but little ('The Tathagata has no theories') but he discoursed at some length on the Three Signs of Being, on the impermanence and mutability of all life, and (placing a warm hand on the Vicar's ungracious arm) on the Omnipresence of Dukkha (Suffering). He argued with some fervour against the concept of the Individual Immortal Soul, but offered consolation in the Four Noble Truths, and the Noble Eightfold Path to Nirvana. He quoted the last recorded words of the Buddha— 'Be ye as those who have the self as their light ... betake yourselves to no external refuge—work out your own salvation.' Oh, and then he told them the secrets of the universe.

When he had finished there was a long silence in the hall, but the wind rattled the windows in appreciation.

Lamely Rusty Motorcade said at last: 'Yes that's all very well as far as it goes.'—but Guru interrupted him in an irresistible voice 'It goes to Nirvana. Foolish young man!' (and spreading his arms wide) 'You blind children of Britain, what is there so great in your imaginations, so fixed in your souls, so true, so good, that you believe, that you know to be true? Tell me, show me. How do you occupy yourselves that is so uplifting, so spiritual that I should learn from you? Is your bridge, your golf, your cocktail, is this *your* Nirvana? Do you thus see beyond the stars? And you would teach Guru what? To pray? To plead? or to beg? Is this the way mankind shall seek out his salvation? On his knees? No, you should not pray. Your God is dispersed with your empire. He gave beads to cannibals and they ate Him. What is your God? Where is your God? Does he believe in you? And what do you think, you British, when you come to die? To whom do you cry as you stand on the precipice of dissolution? *Work out your own salvation.* You wish that I lead you, that I show you the Path? I could. My blood is warm as yours. You wish to see it? You may. Your God, he showed his blood, and the sky darkened for two thousand years, as he died. Now you are tired and I feel it, and unhappy, and I sense it, and lost, and I can understand it. And your weariness and sorrow and confusion is mine, I promise you. See, I too have grey hairs. See, my eyes too are red with dust and weeping. You wish for a prophet, you wish to be told, yet shut your ears with gossip, your mouths with other men's words. I love you. *Work out your own salvation.* I cannot help you further. *Work out your own salvation.* I told you the secrets of the universe. You do not love me, I know that, yet I love you, as Siddhartha loved you, who saw life plain. I point the way, that is all. There is no salvation through the grace of another, though there is love. Work out your own salvation. I am leaving you.'

(Everyone went home). Poor Hamlet, denied his revenge, went home to the yapping of his dogs, whom he had forgotten to feed, but was consoled by the promise of occasional visits to London and the novel enticement of Candida's generous legs.

Poor Fortinbras, exposed for what he was, no soldier, no saint after all, packed up his things and drove straight back to Keble, where there is no shortage of saints, determined to become a scientist instead. Poor Ophelia, battered and trampled, and paralysed (temporarily) in the legs, was driven home by her love-sick chauffeur to a night of soul-searching; she was *determined* to work out her own salvation. Tried all night; never really succeeded.

Genevieve and Abigail were wringing their hands by the war memorial, and even Tessa's eyes were filmy. Guru had not even said good-bye.

'What shall I do?' cried Genevieve, 'his neck was like alabaster, and the veins on his marble arms—'

'Who cares what you do?' cried Abby, jealous of her sister's eloquent despair. 'I loved him, *I* did! And I ... I shall light a charcoal fire and all the winter waste sorrowfully away. Oh!' and her hands fluttered like pinioned butterflies.

'I shall say nothing,' said Tessa, but sniffed.

And all the others, Throggie and Jack, Solly and Sammy, the Admiral and Jessica, Victoria, Mrs Skullham and the Macfisheries Man, all of them, all those people, went up the High Street, over the Meadows, along beside the golf course, through the rain, placid and irritable ... For tragedy cannot touch with its bear's paw the even tenor of life in Soft Meadows Cross.

It may be significant that Hamlet never died, no more did Laertes, no more did the King, no more did the Queen, in the village's one and only production of Hamlet. Polonius died but he was an old man and a rather foolish one, and old and foolish men may die freely in Soft Meadows Cross.

They all went home.

It is not sensible to walk along motorways at night. The authorities have not made allowances for such behaviour. They have provided no refuge, nor shelter, no warm shed in which to meditate while the rest of the world goes by. A motorway is no place for nocturnal pedestrians. Bats and foxes and owls are there in abundance, attracted by the light and the noise. Small mammals are doomed, like the car, to be killed by curiosity. But late one night two pedestrians did walk along the M Something-Or-Other. They walked arrogantly along the tarmac, eschewing the grass verge and the central divide. Articulated lorries and caterpillar trucks thundered past and blew grit into their eyes. They staunchly continued, undeterred by such discouragements.

After a while the two pedestrians, a small brown man with bare feet and a little, disreputable-looking boy stopped and conferred on the verge; then the boy turned back and retraced his steps, whistling softly to keep his spirits up, for he felt suddenly lonely. The brown, barefoot man continued, but a porcupine paid the penalty of indiscretion and rolled over, yelling shrilly.

In a mental institute nearby, Dr Bushey, soon to be treated electrically, yelled also.

EPILOGUE

Perhaps it ought to be mentioned that some eight months after the events recorded on the preceding pages the triple accouchement of Tessa, Abigail and Genevieve Angell ended between the hours of one and three in the morning with the simultaneous birth of three sets of triplets, some dusky, some less so. Three threes are nine and nine screams tore aside the thick rep curtains of the night—the coincidence was strange, but it would be rash to call it mystical.

Little Jasper consented to act as godfather to all the babies. How sturdy he had grown in eight short months! And what a lot he had to teach his nine brown charges. Even he, sometimes, in some lights, looked a little brownish. Mysterious.